Praise for *BLACKOUT*

"Easily the best yet. Beautifully written and elegantly paced with a plot that only gradually becomes visible, as if the reader had been staring into the freezing fog waiting for shapes to emerge."
—*The Guardian* (UK)

"Ragnar Jónasson does claustrophobia beautifully."
—Ann Cleeves

"Jónasson's writing is a masterful reinvention of the golden-age classic style, both contemporary and timeless . . . enclosed by the poetic beauty of the location."
—*Crime Review*

Praise for *NIGHTBLIND*

"Story's got me gripped but even more satisfying is how the characters are never just there as pawns in the plot."
—Ian Rankin, author of the Inspector Rebus series

"Excellent . . . Jónasson plants clues fairly before a devastatingly unexpected reveal, without sublimating characterization to plot."
—*Publishers Weekly*, starred review

"The final surprise carries a real shock; and of course the advent of the Icelandic winter is likely to chill hearts even below the Arctic Circle."
—*Kirkus Reviews*

"A unique Nordic noir of the first order."
—*BookPage*

"Jónasson delights in playing with the expectations of his audience, pulling the carpet out from under us on more than one occasion. Pure entertainment."
—*Mystery Scene*

"British aficionados of Nordic noir are familiar with two excellent Icelandic writers, Arnaldur Indridason and Yrsa Sigurdardóttir. Here's a third: Ragnar Jónasson . . . the darkness and cold are almost palpable."

—*The Times* (London)

"There will be no better way to start the year than by reading *Nightblind* by Ragnar Jónasson . . . Jónasson's books have breathed new life into Nordic noir." —*Sunday Express* (UK)

"*Nightblind* . . . certainly lives up to the promise of its predecessor. . . . This is an atmospheric portrayal of a claustrophobic place where everyone is connected . . . economical and evocative prose, as well as some masterful prestidigitation." —*The Guardian* (UK)

Praise for *SNOWBLIND*

"Jónasson skillfully alternates points of view and shifts of time . . . The action builds to a shattering climax."

—*Publishers Weekly*, boxed and starred review

"A classic crime story . . . first-rate and highly recommended."

—Lee Child, author of the Jack Reacher thrillers

"A modern Icelandic take on an Agatha Christie–style mystery, as twisty as any slalom."

—Ian Rankin, author of the Inspector Rebus series

"This classically crafted whodunit holds up nicely, but Jónasson's true gift is for describing the daunting beauty of the fierce setting, lashed by blinding snowstorms that smother the village in 'a thick, white darkness' that is strangely comforting."

—*The New York Times Book Review*

"A chiller of a thriller whose style and pace are influenced by Jónasson's admiration for Agatha Christie. It's good enough to share shelf space with the works of Yrsa Sigurdardóttir and Arnaldur Indridason, Iceland's crime novel royalty." —*The Washington Post,* Best Mysteries and Thrillers to Read in January

"Jónasson's whodunit puts a lively, sophisticated spin on the Agatha Christie model, taking it down intriguing dark alleys."

—*Kirkus Reviews*

"In this debut novel, Jónasson has taken the locked-room mystery and transformed it into a dark tale of isolation and intrigue that will keep readers guessing until the final page." —*Library Journal Xpress*

"Jónasson spins an involving tale of small-town police work that vividly captures the snowy setting that so affects the rookie cop. Iceland noir at its moodiest." —*Booklist*

"Required reading." —*New York Post*

"What sets *Snowblind* apart is the deep melancholy pervading the characters. Most of them, including Ari, have suffered a tragic loss. That's bad for them, but along with the twenty-four-hour darkness closing in, it makes for the best sort of gloomy storytelling."

—*Chicago Tribune*

"Perfectly capturing the pressures of rural life and the freezing, deadly Icelandic winter, *Snowblind* will keep readers on the edge of their seats—preferably snuggled beneath a warm blanket."

—*Shelf Awareness*

"A real find. I loved it. The turns of the plot are clever and unexpected, and Ari is a wonderful character to spend time with."

—*Mystery Scene*

"*Snowblind* has the classic red herrings, plot twists, and surprises that characterize the best of Christie's work. Jónasson's latest is nicely done and simply begs for a sequel." —*BookPage*

"Seductive . . . an old-fashioned murder mystery with a strong central character and the fascinating background of a small Icelandic town cut off by snow. Ragnar does claustrophobia beautifully."

—Ann Cleeves, author of the Vera Stanhope and Shetland Island series

"A dazzling novel . . . Thór is a welcome addition to the pantheon of Scandinavian detectives. I can't wait until the sequel!"

—William Ryan, author of the Captain Alexei Korolev series

"A classic whodunit with a vividly drawn protagonist and an intriguing, claustrophobic setting, *Snowblind* dazzles like sunlight on snow, chills like ice, and confirms the growing influence of Scandinavian crime fiction." —*Richmond Times-Dispatch*

"A satisfying mystery where all the pieces, in the end, fall together."

—*Dallas Morning News*

"[Ragnar] definitely shows a knack for the whodunit business."

—*Star Tribune* (Minneapolis)

"A chilling, thrilling slice of Icelandic noir."

—Thomas Enger, author of the Henning Juul series

"An isolated community, subtle clueing, clever misdirection, and more than a few surprises combine to give a modern-day, golden age whodunit. Well done! I look forward to the next in the series."

—Dr. John Curran, author of *Agatha Christie's Secret Notebooks*

"An intricately plotted crime novel, *Snowblind* is a remarkable debut. Ragnar Jónasson has delivered an intelligent whodunit that updates, stretches, and redefines the locked-room mystery format. A tense and thrilling book that paints a vivid portrait of a remote town in long-term decline, facing the chilling aftershocks of the global financial meltdown. The author's cool, clean prose constructs atmospheric word pictures that recreate the harshness of an Icelandic winter in the reader's mind. Destined to be an instant classic." —*EuroDrama*

"Jónasson has produced a tense and convincing thriller; he is a welcome addition to the roster of Scandi authors, and I really look forward to his next offering." —*Mystery People*

"*Snowblind* is a dark, claustrophobic read, and Jónasson evokes perfectly the twenty-four-hour darkness, the biting cold, the relentless snow and fear of a killer on the loose in a village suddenly cut off by an avalanche. His crisp, bleak prose is an exemplary lesson in how to create atmosphere without producing overinflated books that would cause their own avalanche if dropped." —*Crime Review*

"Ragnar Jónasson is a new name in the crime-writing genre and I urge anyone who is a fan of Nordic crime noir to rush out and get yourself a copy of *Snowblind*; this you will want to add to your collection. It is really that good." —*The Last Word Book Review*

"If Arnaldur is the King and Yrsa the Queen of Icelandic crime fiction, then Ragnar is surely the Crown Prince . . . more please!"
—*EuroCrime*

"A delight." —*ELLE* (France)

BLACKOUT

Also by Ragnar Jónasson

Nightblind
Snowblind

Blackout

RAGNAR JÓNASSON

translated by Quentin Bates

Minotaur Books
New York

This is a work of fiction. All of the characters, organizations, and events portrayed in this novel are either products of the author's imagination or are used fictitiously.

www.minotaurbooks.com

Library of Congress Cataloging-in-Publication Data

Names: Ragnar Jónasson, 1976– author. | Bates, Quentin, translator.
Title: Blackout / Ragnar Jónasson ; translated by Quentin Bates.
Other titles: Myrknætti. English
Description: First U.S. edition. | New York : Minotaur Books, August 2018. | Series: Dark Iceland | "First published in Iceland under the title Myrknætti by Veröld."
Identifiers: LCCN 2018003910 | ISBN 9781250171054 (hardcover) | ISBN 9781250171061 (trade paperback) | ISBN 9781250171078 (ebook)
Subjects: LCSH: Police—Iceland—Fiction. | Violent crimes—Iceland—Fiction. | Suspense fiction. | Mystery fiction.
Classification: LCC PT7511.R285 M9713 2018 | DDC 839/.6934—dc23
LC record available at https://lccn.loc.gov/2018003910

Our books may be purchased in bulk for promotional, educational, or business use. Please contact your local bookseller or the Macmillan Corporate and Premium Sales Department at 1-800-221-7945, extension 5442, or by email at MacmillanSpecialMarkets@macmillan.com.

First published in Iceland under the title *Myrknætti* by Veröld

Previously published in Great Britain by Orenda Books in association with Goldsboro Books

First U.S. Edition: August 2018

10 9 8 7 6 5 4 3 2 1

For my mother and father

Author's note

Special thanks are due to Detective Eiríkur Rafn Rafnsson, Prosecutor Hulda María Stefánsdóttir, Dr Helgi Ellert Jóhannsson and Dr Jón Gunnlaugur Jónasson. Any mistakes in the final version of this book are the author's responsibility.

The extract from the poem by Jón Guðmundsson the Learned is taken from *Fjölmóður – ævidrápa Jóns lærða Guðmundssonar*, with an introduction and notes by Páll Eggert Ólason.

Information about the historic effect in Siglufjörður of volcanic eruptions in Iceland are taken from the book *Siglfirskur annáll*, written by my grandfather, Þ. Ragnar Jónasson, and published in 1998.

One must allow the
black of night to elapse,
with the passing of the ages
once lots are drawn,
endure in silence
hardship's burden,
this is God's gift to
which he bears witness.

Jón Guðmundsson the Learned (1574–1658)
From his poem *Fjölmóður*

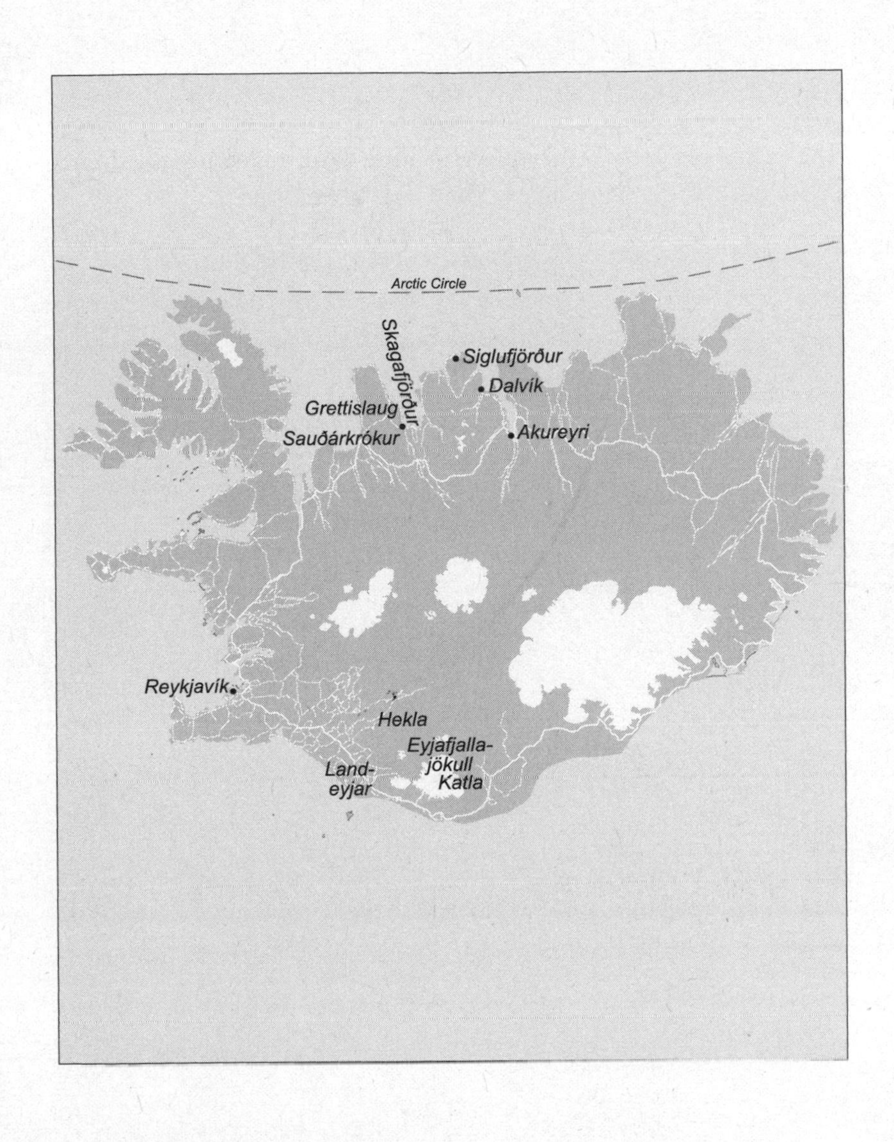
Arctic Circle
Skagafjörður
Siglufjörður
Dalvík
Grettislaug
Sauðárkrókur
Akureyri
Reykjavík
Hekla
Eyjafjalla-
jökull
Land-
eyjar
Katla

The events of *Blackout* take place in June 2010, following the events of *Snowblind*, the first book in the Dark Iceland series.

PART I: DAY 1
SUMMER

1

How do you like Iceland?

If for nothing else, he had come to Iceland to avoid that kind of question.

The day began well, as the fine June morning dawned. Not that there was any clear difference between morning and evening at this time of year, when the sun stayed bright around the clock, casting blinding light wherever he looked.

Evan Fein had long anticipated visiting this island at the edge of the habitable world. And now here this Ohio art history student was, on his first visit to Iceland. Nature had pooled its energies, as if to add to the woes of the financial crash, by presenting Icelanders with two volcanic eruptions, one right after the other. The volcanic activity appeared to have subsided for the moment though, and Evan had just missed the events.

He had already spent a few days in Iceland, starting by taking in the sights of Reykjavík and the tourist spots around the city. Then he hired a car and set off for the north. After a night at a campsite at Blönduós, he had made an early start, setting out for Skagafjörður. He had purchased a CD of old-fashioned Icelandic ballads and now slotted it into the car's player, enjoying the music without understanding a word of the lyrics, proud to be something of a travel nerd, immersing himself in the culture of the countries he visited.

He took the winding Thverárfjall road, turning off before he got as far as the town of Sauðarkrókur on the far side of the peninsula. He wanted to take a look at Grettir's Pool, the ancient stone-flagged hot bath that he knew had to be somewhere nearby, not far from the shore.

It was a slow drive along the rutted track to the pool, and he wondered if trying to find it was a waste of time. But the thought of relaxing for a while in the steaming water and taking in both the beauty of his surroundings and the tranquillity of the morning was a tempting one. He drove at a snail's pace, lambs scattering from the sides of the road as he passed, but the pool stubbornly refused to be found. Evan started to wonder if he had missed the turning, and slowed down at every farm gate, trying to work out if the entrance to the pool might be hidden away – across a farmer's land, or down a side turning, a country lane. Had he driven too far?

Finally he saw a handsome house, which, on closer inspection, looked to be half built. It stood not far from the road with a small grey van parked in front of it. Evan pulled his car to the side of the road and stopped. And then started with surprise.

The van driver, the house's owner, perhaps, was lying on the ground near the house. Unmoving. Unconscious? Evan unbuckled his seatbelt and opened his door without even turning off the engine. The age-old ballads continued to crackle from the car's tinny speakers, making the scene seem almost surreal.

Evan started to run, but then slowed as the whole scene came into view.

The man was dead. There was no doubt about that. It had to be a man lying there, judging by the build and the cropped hair. There was no chance of identifying the face, though. It was erased by a spatter of blood.

Where there had once been an eye, there was now an empty socket.

Evan gasped for air and stared numbly at the corpse in front of him, fumbling for his phone, the incongruous sound of his Icelandic ballads in the background.

He turned quickly, checking that the man's assailant wasn't behind him.

Nothing. Apart from the dead man, Evan was alone.

Next to the body was a length of timber, smeared with blood. The weapon?

Evan retched as he tried to stifle the thoughts that flooded his mind.

Think. Be calm.

He sat down in the pasture in front of the house, and punched out the emergency number on his phone, wishing fervently that he had picked another destination for his holiday.

Iceland is one of the safest places on earth, the travel guide had said.

Evan's eyes darted around, taking in the warm summer sun casting her glow across the verdant fields, the stunning mountains hovering in the distance, the glint of her rays on the bright-blue waters of the outlying fjord and its magnificent islands.

Not anymore, he thought, as the operator was connected.

Not anymore.

2

The buzzing of a fly that had strayed through the open bedroom window woke Ísrún, prompting her to check the time and then curse when she realised how early it still was. She yawned and stretched her arms. A little more sleep wouldn't have done any harm, and her shift on the news desk wasn't until nine-thirty. She lifted herself on her elbows and gazed out the window at the tall trees in the communal garden outside and the block of flats on the opposite side of the road. It looked like an uneventful day ahead. The eruption had subsided for the moment, and now that summer was here, the city was quiet. And so was work. She'd been to a summer festival with a cameraman the day before, and her only task was to put together some lightweight filler material to bring the evening news bulletin to a close on a light-hearted note. Chances were that they wouldn't run it anyway, as something meatier usually came long to take the place of the frothier material.

She'd been with the same news team for ten years now, albeit with a few breaks, joining straight from college on a freelance basis, and continuing throughout her psychology degree. Although she'd made a respectable attempt to work in the health sector, she found herself missing the newsroom buzz, and had dipped in and out over the years – while completing her master's degree in Denmark, and even after taking up a hospital post in Akureyri for a while. But eighteen months ago, Ísrún had resigned from the hospital and returned to Reykjavík, searching out her old job in the newsroom.

Many of her old colleagues had moved on, replaced by new faces, but some of the stalwarts were still there. When she had first applied for the TV newsroom all those years ago, she had not seriously expected to get the job. She had thought that the scar on her face would undoubtedly preclude on-screen work, but she flew through the selection process and it hadn't turned out to be a hindrance to her career. She stroked her cheek now, her scar as familiar to her as any other feature, the legacy of a childhood accident – an elderly relative had spilled hot coffee over her when she was just a few months old. One cheek was permanently disfigured, and although she had learned to apply makeup to make it less obvious, it couldn't be ignored. But perhaps her scar was the reason why she had been so determined to apply for a TV job; it was an opportunity to show the world – or at least audiences in Iceland – that she wasn't going to let it stop her.

Ísrún sat up in bed and looked around the airy, understated room with satisfaction. Living alone suited her. She'd been single for the last two years – the longest time she'd been without a significant relationship. Relocating to Denmark to study for a few years had ended things with her last boyfriend. They'd been together for five years, but it hadn't been enough to make him want to join her there – or, indeed, wait for her to come home. *Oh well,* she had thought. *That's his problem.*

To her surprise, television work turned out to be more rewarding than psychology, but what she had learned certainly helped with her work as a journalist. Her job gave her the opportunity to see something different every day – talk to interesting characters and hope that a decent scoop would come her way. Those were the best days. A little pressure could become addictive, but she didn't enjoy the stress of the constant deadlines. Shifts were frequently short-staffed and it was often a struggle to delivery by the end of the day. Spending time on a story was a rare luxury, as was researching things in any depth.

Ísrún closed her eyes again, willing herself to fall back into slumber. The fly continued to buzz somewhere in the room, and her eyes snapped open with frustration.

Out of bed and on the street in her running gear just a few minutes later, determined to make the most of her unexpectedly early start, Ísrún took a deep breath of the morning air, missing its usual freshness. It tasted sour, tainted with the volcanic residue from the eruption in Eyjafjallajokull glacier, in the southern part of Iceland, which had spewed ash earlier in the spring, interrupting air traffic across half the world. No wonder the fly had sought shelter indoors. During and after the volcanic eruption, ash had frequently been carried over the city, even though the volcano was quite a distance away. It affected everyone, irritating eyes and hampering breathing. On the worst days it was recommended that people suffering from asthma and similar conditions should stay indoors. The eruption had now ended, with only this residual ash remaining, but there was some fear that this seismic activity could trigger an eruption of another ferocious volcano, Katla, with far more devastating consequences.

Ísrún lived in a small two-room apartment, in a block near the University of Iceland, and she made a habit of running along the seashore whenever she had the opportunity, preferably in the mornings before changing into her work clothes and leaving for the TV station's offices. She was determined not to let the volcanic pollution stop her. During her run she thought ahead to what would undoubtedly be another routine day awaiting her.

Her old red banger, a car that had been in the family for years and was given to her by her father when she was twenty, still got her to work on time. Strictly speaking, the car was practically an antique, but it served its purpose. The traffic was quiet today – one of the advantages of the news desk job was the nine-thirty start, well after the morning rush hour had tailed off. Less popular were the frequent late shifts that took her past the evening bulletin and into an inevitable meeting afterwards. Working on the later bulletin was often a better option, however; she lost an evening, but gained the following morning off in lieu, and that time could be precious.

Hell! She had forgotten that Ívar was running the shifts today and tomorrow. There was a tension between them that was bordering on hostility. He had been appointed two years before, while she was still trying to forge a career in psychology. He considered himself some kind of big shot, having been poached from a competing station, and despite the fact that she'd more than proved herself over the past eighteen months, he still looked on her as a beginner. He didn't seem capable of trusting her with anything serious, and she knew she didn't have what it would take to hammer the table with her fist and fight her corner. Maybe she would have done a few years ago, but that time had passed.

⌖

She took a seat in the meeting room. Ívar sat at the end with his notebook, from which he was never far away, and a sheaf of papers – press releases that would find their way to one of the journalists or to the bin.

'Ísrún, did you come up with any material from the summer festival?'

Did she detect a note of condescension there? Did the easy stuff always come her way? Or was she just being unnecessarily suspicious?

'Not yet. I'll have it done today and it'll be ready for this evening. Two minutes?'

'Ninety seconds, tops.'

Her colleagues had slowly gathered at the table and the morning news meeting had formally begun.

'Did anyone notice the air pollution this morning?' Kormákur asked, leaning back in his chair and gnawing at his pencil. He was known as Kommi, mainly because everyone was aware how much he disliked the nickname.

'Yeah. It's ash from the eruption blowing this way, stuff that built up during the eruption itself, or so I'm told,' Ívar said.

'I thought the eruption was all over,' Kormákur said, and then grinned. 'We can probably squeeze one more story out of it.'

'Ísrún, can you check it out? Do something with a bit of menace to it, maybe. The eruption returns to Reykjavík – that sort of thing?' Ívar smiled.

Condescending fool, she thought, glaring at her notebook.

'But let's have a look at the serious stuff,' he said.

Exactly, Ísrún thought, raising her eyebrows with irritation.

'I hear someone found a body up north, not far from Sauðárkrókur, next to a building site. Nothing's confirmed yet. That's definitely our lead, unless there's another eruption.'

Kormákur nodded. 'I'll get onto it right away.'

It didn't look like it was going to be a slow news day after all … for some.

3

It was still a surprise to Ari Thór Arason that he had stayed with the Siglufjörður police as long as he had. Almost two years had passed since he had moved north after graduating from police college, having already abandoned a theology degree.

That first winter in the north had been hell and the weight of snow had been relentless and suffocating. But when the warm, bright days emerged from the frozen darkness, his spirits had lifted and he saw his new home with fresh eyes. And he now had a second winter behind him. Although he still found the isolation of the winter darkness oppressive, he was getting used to it, even enjoying the sight of a fresh fall of snow on the colourful buildings that hugged the coast, and the icy grandeur of the mountains that enveloped the village. Yet it was a relief when the sun finally showed up after its winter sojourn behind the mountains. As they edged their way into June, there had already been a few warm days – a little later than down south, but that was only to be expected. Even the sun appeared to forget the northernmost village in Iceland from time to time.

Tómas, Siglufjörður's police inspector, had called that morning and asked Ari Thór to come in earlier than scheduled. Although his shift didn't start until midday, he was on his way to the station by nine. Tómas hadn't said much on the phone, but Ari Thór had been sure he could hear real concern in his voice. The truth was that Tómas was never particularly cheerful these days. It had been a blow when his wife decided to Reykjavík to study. Nobody, except maybe Tómas, seriously expected that she would ever come back to Siglufjörður. They were still together, on paper, at least, which was more than could be said for Ari Thór and his former girlfriend Kristín.

Their relationship had unquestionably fizzled out, although Ari Thór harboured hopes that he'd be able to breathe new life into it again. Four years had passed since they had first met, back when he had been studying theology and Kristín was still a medical student. There had been an instant attraction and she had managed to coax him out of his shell – a damaged young man who had lost both parents at a young age and been raised by his grandmother in a way that had made him self-reliant, even as a youngster, capable of fending for himself and reluctant to let anyone come too close.

Kristín had brought him a longed-for warmth and security, but things had started to come apart as soon as the new job had taken him to Siglufjörður. Kristín had been deeply upset by his decision and remained in Reykjavík, not even taking the time to come and stay with him over Christmas. He had been just as hurt by her reaction, and their relationship became increasingly distant, frosty. And then he took a wrong turn. The piano teacher in Siglufjörður, a young woman from the Westfjords, Ugla, had captivated him in much the same way that Kristín once had, providing him with a cosy escape from the chilly isolation of Siglufjörður. What began with a kiss had ended in her bedroom, and there was no way that he would ever be able to convince Kristín that he hadn't been unfaithful to her. The snow and the winter darkness had created a mirage; the isolation crushing his conscience and convincing him that he was in love. However, as spring dawned over the Siglufjörður mountains, he knew with unswerving certainty that Kristín was the only one for him.

But it was far too late. Rashly, he had called Kristín to let her know that he had begun seeing someone in Siglufjörður and to end their relationship, and there hadn't been much more to their conversation than that. He had heard a crash, and assumed that she had hurled her phone against the nearest wall. It wasn't until later that he found out she had given up a temporary appointment for the summer and an opportunity to finish her medical studies at a hospital in Reykjavík so that she could move north to Akureyri to be close to him.

How could he have been so stupid?

Of course, once he finally admitted that he'd had a girlfriend in Reykjavík all along, the relationship with Ugla didn't go any further either. If she had been holding a phone, it would have gone the same way as Kristín's, but hurled at him instead. The piano lessons stopped there and then.

He missed Kristín. After they had parted he had tried to call her several times, but without success, and there were no replies to his emails. Some months had now passed since his last attempt to contact her. He knew she had moved to Akureyri to finish the final year of her medical studies, and had heard from mutual friends that she had taken a job at the hospital there. It was painful to know she was so close, when another kind of distance yawned between them. He had immersed himself in work after that, pushing himself harder than he had ever done before. There was little else for him to do.

Ari Thór intended to buy himself something healthy for breakfast on his way to the station. A small cruise liner had docked that morning and the town hummed with activity, tourists snapping photos among the groups of local youngsters who were busy with rakes and other tools, doing summer work for the town council. The aroma of cinnamon and chocolate from the bakery was a temptation, but that hardly constituted a healthy breakfast. He paused for a moment as the scent washed over him. The quality of Siglufjörður's cinnamon buns, known as *hnútar*, left the Reykjavík version he was used to in the shade. A peek through the window, though, showed that a crowd of tourists had the same thoughts on their minds, so something from the bakery would have to wait until later. Instead, he stopped off at the little fish shop on the Town Hall Square and asked for some dried fish. It wasn't his usual breakfast, but it was certainly a healthy option.

'Catfish, as usual?' the fishmonger asked.

'Yes, please.'

'There you go, Reverend.'

Ari Thór scowled to himself, paid for his bag of dried catfish chunks and said a curt goodbye as he left. The 'Reverend' nickname continued to surface occasionally, having appeared when people had found out about his curtailed theological studies. He still hadn't got used to it, and sometimes the taunts stung.

Tómas immediately sniffed the air when Ari Thór sat at the table in the station's coffee corner and unwrapped his unusual breakfast.

'Not that stuff again, Ari Thór! And now for breakfast? Don't you ever get tired of it?'

'Even city boys like me can enjoy a traditional breakfast,' Ari Thór answered, continuing to pick his way through his fish.

'Jokes aside, Ari Thór, there's something we need to deal with. Hlynur's on his way and he can take today's shift,' Tómas said.

Tómas had changed after his wife had moved south, he seemed to have aged ten years. His zest for life had faded, and although there hadn't been much there before, the hair on his head looked even thinner.

There was no doubt that Tómas was a lonely man. Ari Thór knew that his youngest son had also left home and now lived in the student hall of residence at the college in Akureyri during term time. He had found himself summer work with the local authority there and had rented a place to live with two of his classmates. He visited his father occasionally at weekends, but that was it, so Tómas was pretty much alone in the house in Siglufjörður.

'A body's been found,' Tómas announced, when Ari Thór had taken a seat.

'A body?'

'That's right. In Skagafjörður, on Reykjaströnd, next to a summer house that's being built there, not far from Grettir's Pool.'

'Is this any business of Siglufjörður's?' Ari Thór asked, and immediately regretted the abrupt question. He was tired after staying up long into the night, having expected to be able to sleep in that morning. He rubbed his eyes.

'Some tourist from America found the body. He drove past it on his way to the pool,' Tómas continued, ignoring Ari Thór's interruption. 'It looks nasty. They've sent me some pictures of the scene.'

'A murder?'

'No doubt about that, Ari Thór, and a brutal one, too. The victim's practically unrecognisable. He was smashed in the face with a length of timber. It seems there was a nail in it that went right through one eye. The reason we've been asked to help with the investigation is because the victim had his "legal residence" here.' Tómas's tone indicated that the man hadn't been born in Siglufjörður.

'An out-of-towner?'

'Exactly. Elías Freysson. I don't remember ever meeting the man. He was a contractor working on the new tunnel. I said we'd find out what we can about him here, and I want you to manage that.' His voice was decisive, firm. 'Of course I'll work on it with you, but it's time you took on more responsibility, Ari Thór.'

Ari Thór nodded his agreement. He liked the idea. His weariness fell away and he was instantly more alert. It occurred to him, and not for the first time, that Tómas was looking at the possibility of moving south to be with his wife, and wanted to leave the Siglufjörður station in safe hands.

'You said Hlynur would be taking the shift today. So he won't be involved in this investigation?'

'That's right, my boy,' Tómas said.

Ari Thór breathed easier and hoped that his satisfaction at Tómas's answer wasn't too obvious. He couldn't work with Hlynur. They didn't get on, on top of which, for some unknown reason, Hlynur had been almost useless for the last few months. He always arrived at work tired, often still half asleep and was increasingly absent-minded.

'All right. I'll get on with it right away,' Ari Thór said. 'Who was Elías's boss at the new tunnel?'

'I know that Hákon is the foreman there, Hákon Halldórsson,' Tómas said. 'He's a Siglufjörður boy,' he added, and Ari Thór understood from his voice that this was a key item of information.

4

When Hlynur Ísaksson arrived at the Siglufjörður police station for his shift, he saw Ari Thór and Tómas there, chatting amiably. He had an instant hunch that there was some secret to which he wasn't supposed to be party and, to an extent, he was right.

'Ari Thór and I need today for interviews,' Tómas said in an offhand way. 'A body has turned up not far from Sauðárkrókur, and it seems the deceased had some connection with Siglufjörður.'

Hlynur nodded, doing his best to pretend that he didn't mind not being involved.

'Can you take charge of the shift here today?' Tómas asked, probably not expecting a reply. 'Later on you'll need to go over to the primary school for me. It's the last day of term and we've been asked to present some awards. I was going to do it, but it's unlikely I'll be able to fit it in.'

Hlynur felt his heart begin to pound. Cold sweat appeared on his forehead. This was something he wouldn't be able to do.

'Couldn't Ari Thór sort that out?' he mumbled.

'What? What d'you mean? I need Ari Thór with me today, as I just told you,' Tómas said, with a sharper-than-usual edge to his voice.

Hlynur was about to answer back, but found his tongue tripping over the words.

'Well,' he said at last. 'I won't make much of a job of it. We'd better not bother with it.'

'We will bother with it, damn it. You're going. No arguments,' Tómas said, and was gone.

Hlynur nodded and looked down at his hands. He longed to go

home, retreat under the bedclothes and rest. There was an uncomfortable unease in the pit of his stomach. He had worked with Tómas at the Siglufjörður station for six years and had considerably more experience of police work than Ari Thór, but he felt as if the balance of power had shifted over the last few months. For whatever reason, Tómas seemed to have more trust in Ari Thór these days, Hlynur brooded, less than pleased by his instructions for the day. It was certainly true that Ari Thór had made a great effort recently and seemed to be highly capable, even if there was little variety in the unchallenging cases they dealt with.

Hlynur, however, had been a shadow of himself since those damned emails had started arriving.

'You're losing your edge,' Tómas had told Hlynur, just after New Year.

The two of them had been on duty, taking a break in the station's coffee corner. Hlynur knew from experience that Tómas would occasionally come out with something unexpected, and without any kind of preamble. But Hlynur had been taken completely by surprise, aware of his jaw dropping. Moments before they had been discussing mundane matters. It had been a bleak day in Siglufjörður, with low clouds and a cold wind off the mountains. The corner of the station where they habitually took coffee breaks was equally cheerless. There were a few mugs in the sink that nobody had found time to wash up and two opened packets of chocolate biscuits by the thermos. An old calendar from a bank down south, and dating back to the boom years, lay on the worktop. No one had the heart to throw away this memento of a past time when Iceland's economy had been buzzing.

Hlynur had stared at Tómas. 'Losing my edge? What d'you mean?' he had asked finally, all too aware that Tómas was right, and equally aware of the reasons for his poor concentration.

'Are you losing interest in the job? Sometimes you seem to be miles away, preoccupied. And you're not as conscientious as you used to be,' Tómas said, devastatingly straightforward; as always, the shrewd observer.

'I'll get my act together,' Hlynur muttered.

'Is anything wrong?'

'No,' he replied tersely, hoping that Tómas wouldn't see through the lie. To his relief, Tómas didn't pursue it.

The first email had arrived a year ago. Hlynur had been sitting in bed with his laptop when it dropped into his inbox like a bolt of lightning from a clear sky. He found himself shivering uncontrollably as he realised that his past was about to catch up with him and there was nothing he could do to avoid it.

He lived in a newish apartment. It was a bare place, with blank walls and no more furniture than was necessary. But that suited him. Never keen on cluttered old houses with creaking floorboards, he was pleased with the place he had found. It was bigger than he needed and one room had become a storeroom for the things he had brought with him from down south when he had decided to take the job in Siglufjörður. There were boxes of books that he never opened, DVDs he never watched and clothes he never wore.

The youngest of three brothers, he had been brought up in Kópavogur, a town in the Reykjavík area, by his mother, who worked from morning to night with a day job at the council offices, and then took whatever cleaning or other work came her way outside office hours. He had never seen much of her and, when he did, she was usually grey with exhaustion, seated with her three boys at the dinner table in their apartment. Hlynur clearly remembered eating haddock every Monday, their meals always home-cooked in a household that had no spare cash for junk food. The family was rarely able to allow itself even a little luxury.

Hlynur later discovered that his father had been a man with a weakness for the bottle. He had often disappeared for short and then longer periods, eventually disappearing for good when the third boy, Hlynur, had been born. By then he had taken up with a woman somewhere in the Westfjords and, when he could stay sober, found what work he could at sea or on shore, seldom paying a visit to Reykjavík. As such, the boys grew up without a father. A few years after his departure to the Westfjords, he lapsed into a drunken stupor and didn't wake up, worn out after a short, harsh life. Hlynur's mother waited for almost a year before she told the three boys about their father's death; none of them had been present at his funeral.

Hlynur had hazy memories of the day she told them. His older brothers took the news badly, having a clearer understanding of the seriousness of it all and memories of their father before he had left them. And, although Hlynur was the only one who had no recollection of their father, little by little, the blame for his death was laid at his door.,

'Dad left when you were born,' was something he had heard more often than he liked.

Perhaps it was for this reason he had never formed a relationship with his brothers; the older two formed an alliance against him, and their mother was too busy to see what was happening. He never dared to fight back against his brothers, and instead he vented his anger and hatred at school – on children who were easy targets. He became an expert in bullying and violence, taking all his frustrations out on those weaker than himself.

But now these emails had started to arrive. It was clear that this dark past had come back to haunt him.

Once his college years started, his behaviour had changed for the better, as he shook off his anger and began to sympathise with those he had hounded, realising that he had been responsible for inflicting misery on innocent people. But at first, he made no attempt to atone for his misdeeds. That was to come later as the guilt began to gnaw at his conscience.

He left home right after leaving college and enrolled in the police college, serving in various places around the country, including in Reykjavík. That job went with cuts to the police force, however, and he ended up in Siglufjörður, where he was offered a permanent post. He had little contact with his family anymore. His mother still worked for the council in Kópavogur, albeit part-time now, another victim of public-sector cuts. He encountered his brothers only when their mother invited them all for dinner on the rare occasions that he was in the Reykjavík area – a couple of times a year at most. He was happy to keep it that way; he had little in common with his family.

Hlynur had made a few good friends in Siglufjörður, but he preferred to spend his evenings in front of the television, saving his spare cash to travel. The last trip had been to a gig in Britain with his friends from Siglufjörður; before that, a football match. There had been a few turbulent relationships with women over the years, most of them when he had been younger and still living in Reykjavík. Now there was someone special in Sauðárkrókur, and, while he wasn't quite ready to think of her as a permanent girlfriend, there was time for that to change. Although her family was from the south, she taught at the primary school in Sauðárkrókur. Every now and then they'd meet and spend a night together – usually at her place, as she rarely came to Siglufjörður. When he had an evening off duty, he'd sometimes drive over to Sauðárkrókur –around the magnificent mountains that guarded the winding road to Skagafjörður, sometimes in the cold winter darkness and always too fast for safety. Now that summer was here he made the trip in the magical evening light, which gave him the opportunity to admire the fjord's islands and the lonely rock of the Old Woman next to the island of Drangey, still standing long after the Old Man had toppled beneath the waves. He wondered whose fate was worse: that of the Old Man claimed by the sea or the Old Woman left standing there alone.

But these days he had little time to think about a future with his girlfriend. These relentless emails were eating him up inside. They glued his uncomfortable past to his present. Consumed by guilt, he slept badly, and sometimes not at all.

He had deleted the first of the emails long ago, without replying, trying without success to ignore it. The return address gave no indication who the sender might be, its provenance a free email account set up overseas – purely to plague him no doubt.

He was aware that he should have made an effort to trace the sender, perhaps to report the content of the email, but at the same time he was reluctant to pursue the issue. He knew well enough, or thought he did, why the message had been sent, and he had no desire to share those reasons with his colleagues. He had hoped that the matter would end there, with just a single message designed to disturb his peace of mind.

But that hadn't happened. The first message landed in his inbox on the tenth of May the previous year, one Sunday lunchtime, as he enjoyed a lazy day off. The next arrived two months later, from the same sender. There was no signature, but the wording was the same.

This time he didn't delete it. With a certain perversity, he would open it when the mood took him, both at home and when he was on duty, reminding himself of the vile things he had done in the past.

Hlynur never ceased to hate his old self for those ancient sins. He had done his best to atone, to the point of leaking information about a police investigation to one of his former victims. But he knew that sooner or later there would come a day of reckoning, and it nagged at him constantly.

The emails continued to arrive, and now he kept them all, consumed by self-loathing. He read them over and over, fixated by their contents, but aware of the toll they were taking on his health, his fragile state of mind.

He had still not replied though. He had nothing to say; no defence to offer. He felt like a criminal on trial, one who had declined a defence and decided not to comment, simply waiting for a verdict to be handed down.

Hlynur was in no doubt about the context of the emails, and he remembered the boy clearly. They had been in the same class from the age of six onwards. He had been a tubby boy called Gauti, who wore thick glasses. Shy, he said little, but that was enough to make him the target of all of Hlynur's pent-up anger and frustration. Hlynur's assault on him had begun on the very first day and after that Hlynur had ensured the boy did not experience even one good day at school. Ignored at home by the elder brothers who clearly resented him, Hlynur victimised other children at school as well, but

Gauti was easily his favourite. He never answered back and appeared to shrink further into his shell as the attacks on him intensified. For the first few years the bullying was only verbal: jokes at Gauti's expense during and outside class, teasing that seemed so innocent on the surface that the teachers paid no attention. In fact, it was systematic psychological torture, and Hlynur had relished it, becoming addicted to the feeling of power that came with it – so different from the weakness he felt when he was at home with his brothers. And he discovered that he found it easy to beat people down, in the same way that he later, in his role as a police officer, developed a particular aptitude for persuading suspects to confess their misdeeds.

As his school years progressed, Hlynur's intensified his bullying of Gauti and his other unfortunate classmates, becoming coarser and more blatant, even escalating into physical abuse on occasions. The youngest of the family at home, Hlynur was nevertheless strong for his age and he took advantage of this. Gauti bore the brunt of physical rage, particularly during swimming lessons, when Hlynur began to hold his victim under the water while the teacher was looking the other way. He held him captive in the water for longer and longer periods as the year advanced, the boy's eyes bulging with fear. Letting him up for air, he'd whisper into Gauti's ear, *Next time I'll teach you how to die*.

He couldn't understand why Gauti didn't just give up, why he didn't stop coming to school. It was as if he had been brought up not to cheat or play truant, and this frustrated Hlynur, somehow diminishing his sense of power. Gauti was absent occasionally, maybe more often than was normal; but then he was a sickly child.

Hlynur could hardly bring himself to think back to those days. His conscience had become an increasingly heavy burden as he grew up. He did what he could to make up for the misery he had caused, and bitterly regretted what he had done; but sometimes the memory of those school years would overwhelm him, stinging like a thousand needles. He had been the strong one, and he was now being tortured by his own past. He couldn't help but wonder what memories the others had, those he had hounded, teased and punched, day after day.

There was no doubt about the reason behind these painful emails. He knew exactly what sins he was being called on to account for: the bullying to which he had subjected Gauti. There was no shred of doubt about that. The wording of every email had been precisely the same; just a single sentence.

Next time I'll teach you how to die.

5

Kristín was at the eighteenth hole of the Akureyri golf course. She had arrived early, alone, but now the place was busy with golfers. There was something relaxing about golf that gave her an opportunity to put aside the stress of work and get some much-needed fresh air. It also allowed her to forget about Ari Thór and the whole mess their relationship had become.

The golf course had become a friend in the desert, an oasis where she could recharge her batteries before the rigours of the day.

The extent to which she found herself enjoying the game had been unexpected. She had taken a short golf course the previous summer and found that the skills she had learned years ago playing with her parents quickly returned. As the weather brightened, out came the clubs, and she soon became a regular on the golf course, usually early in the morning, before her shifts began.

She had rarely looked up from her books during her years as a medical student, but these days she had an increasingly urgent need for exercise, and found herself determined to keep in shape. The pressure of work had taken her by surprise; in comparison, studying had been child's play. It was probably the increased stress of her job that was behind this interest in sport, although she suspected that it could also be because golf was one sport that Ari Thór abhorred. He had frequently made plain his opinion of their friends who played; in his eyes, the TV test card was more entertaining than a golf tournament.

All in all golf gave her the opportunity to kill two birds with one stone: doing something healthy and relaxing, while spending time somewhere there was absolutely no likelihood of encountering Ari Thór.

They hadn't spoken for a year and a half, ever since the day he had told her, or at least hinted, that he had been unfaithful to her with some woman in Siglufjörður. She hadn't asked for the details, but that was the last time that particular mobile phone was ever used, shattered to pieces as she hurled it to the floor. The depth of her own fury had astonished her; she was known for her even temper.

Their relationship had already been put under pressure when he had taken the decision to move north to Siglufjörður without bothering to consult her. But the admission of infidelity had come like a slap in the face; it was a total breach of trust. Although she'd never actually expressed it, she had always cherished the dream that they would spend their lives together in a comfortable house in one of the Reykjavík suburbs, with a couple of children and maybe a dog.

Kristín tried to convince herself that she had recovered from the shock, that she was over him and their relationship, but she knew that wasn't the case. It would take time. Ari Thór had tried to contact her, but his dozens of phone calls and emails had gone unanswered. He didn't deserve a reply.

It was the travesty of trust that had forced her to see how much she loved Ari Thór, and even now she struggled with the pain of their parting. She was almost relieved that she hadn't asked for the details of his relationship with the woman in Siglufjörður, consoling herself with the fact that it was better not to know. But on the other hand, her imagination tended to take over when her thoughts drifted in that direction and she found herself brooding over a virulent hatred of a woman she had never seen and whose name she didn't even know.

Apart from that, life was routine; work, work and then more work.

She finished her round at par. There had been better days.

Kristín was getting used to living in Akureyri. After that last conversation with Ari Thór, as she was trying to regain her bearings, she had called the National Hospital in Reykjavík, hoping to reclaim her summer placement, but it had by then been allocated to her friend, so she knew that there was no job to go to there. There was nothing for it but Akureyri; a city girl stranded in a small coastal town. She found a small apartment that she was able to furnish simply with colourful prints on the walls and the stacks of medical textbooks she had accumulated during her years of study piled on the floor, waiting for the bookcases she intended to get round to buying.

She knew nobody in Akureyri, apart from one young man, Natan, a student at the university there and a mutual friend of hers and Ari Thór's. Occasionally they'd meet and chat over a coffee and while she suspected him of leaking news of her to Ari Thór, she decided against saying anything; it was just as well that Ari Thór was aware that she was doing fine on her own, that she had got over him easily. Perhaps that wasn't quite true, but she was working on it and hoped that a man she had met on the golf course would help with the process.

She had made his acquaintance three weeks ago at the first hole, early one morning, a time when she had expected to have the course to herself. But he had been there at the same early hour, and with a warm smile, he'd asked if she was alone or if she'd like to play a round with him.

'It's so dull going round on your own,' he had added cheerfully.

She nodded in agreement, but she didn't share his sentiment. There was nothing like a solo round, with no interruptions. Just her, alone in the crisp morning air. But Kristín agreed; his good looks piquing her interest.

He told her he was self-employed, working in computers. He was a good few years older than she was, not that an age difference was a problem if they were to get along. Maybe Ari Thór had been too young for her? She preferred men who were slightly older, with a respectable touch of grey in their hair.

He suggested they meet again to play another nine holes.

After that, their first proper date was at a coffee house on a Thursday evening. She was punctual, but he was already seated at a corner table and had ordered hot chocolate and apple pie and cream for them both. Was this her perfect man?

Kristín told him that she was still trying to regain her equilibrium after ending a long relationship. He told her that he was in much the same position, although he later clarified this by telling her that his wife had actually passed away.

The following week, they met again for a lunch date at a fish restaurant in town, but this turned out to be less successful, as neither of them was comfortable trying to talk over the background clatter of cutlery and glasses. He wanted to take her out to dinner, but her rota at the hospital ruled out that possibility for the time being. The following week didn't look any more promising.

She climbed into in her cheap old Japanese rust bucket – the luxury four-by-four would have to wait until her many years of study were further in the past – and thought about what the day might bring. The summer weather was beautiful, with the particular deep inland warmth Akureyri enjoyed, standing as it did at the head of a winding fjord. The summers were warmer here than anywhere else in Iceland, with hot, still days under cobalt blue skies, while the winters were usually gentler than anywhere else on the north coast, courtesy of the sheltered location between high mountains.

But she would be confined to the hospital wards – each day the same as the next. Medicine had failed to excite her enthusiasm, and she worried that she had spent too many years studying something that didn't suit her after all. She shook her head as if to clear it and banish her unhelpful thoughts. Everything takes time, she told herself and these first years were always going to be the toughest. A doctor had once told her that medicine was a calling rather than a job, and that each day brought tiny miracles. That wasn't something she had experienced so far, and she was never excited by at the prospect of work. Maybe Ari Thór had done the right thing in heading in a new direction, giving up his theology studies when he saw that he wasn't suited to them. She smiled to herself, surprised at the direction her thoughts had taken: to Ari Thór, yet again. She reminded herself that wasn't the way her life was going. She had chosen her path, and rarely went back on a decision once it had been made. She was just tired after those long shifts; it was nothing more than that.

It was proving difficult, however, to dislodge that man from her mind.

6

One year earlier

It had been a long day and I was exhausted. I had done my best to make a career out of psychology, but now I was back at work on the news desk and had been dropped in at the deep end. It was easier when I was a few years younger. Now I was approaching thirty, the decade in which 'anything seems possible' almost behind me and it looked like it was time to start growing up.

I sat over my laptop, letting the minutes meander past, and tried to put my thoughts in order. Then I lay back on the old blue sofa and closed my eyes. The sofa had come from a junk sale. While it was a handsome piece of furniture, it wasn't particularly comfortable. All the same, I stretched out on it. The day at work had been so challenging, I lacked the energy even to make my way to the bedroom.

I'd have to get used to this new routine. I was more than aware that I hadn't been myself recently: my blood pressure too high, my throat was sore, and feelings of stress threatened to overwhelm me. There was no such thing as a quiet day on the news desk. No matter what was going on in the world or in the personal lives of the people behind the scenes, the news was broadcast at exactly the same times every night and there was no room for error – or excuses. It had to be ready on time. Considering the pressure and the pace, it was an unbelievably poorly paid job. At the hospital there would be down time – mornings, sometimes even whole days without anyone chasing me for anything, days when it was possible to relax and recharge. The thought of having even a short break at the news desk was just laughable. Life was in the moment, the buzz of rolling news and covering events as they happened. One, two, three jobs allocated, a few phone calls, on the spot with the cameraman, interview done and edited, commentary written and recorded – all at high speed, keeping pace with breaking news. That was the pattern for every single day. But, despite the pressure, I really enjoyed it.

I was about to leave for a week's holiday, intending to use the time to write an article about the grandmother I had never met. It would be published after the summer by a magazine – an account of a housewife in the years after the war. It was really more of a tragedy, and there were good reasons why I wanted to write the story.

I let my thoughts wander back in time.

I was a little girl, eight or nine, sitting on a chair behind my grandfather's house in the countryside, in Landeyjar, by the shore, a couple of hours east of Reykjavík. The garden was an enchanting place in the golden summer sunshine, a playground full of old stuff that nobody had got rid of, even one ancient, rusty car with no engine. Grandad's wooden shed with its little windows was home to folded-up garden furniture and toys, an old saddle, racquets and balls that had seen better days. It was warm, with something of a breeze. The fence that guarded the edges of the garden cried out to be fixed. The roses had seen no attention since Grandad Lárus had lost his wife, Ísbjörg, my grandmother.

It was a week-long visit to the old man. My parents had come as well, but had taken themselves off for a drive. I was alone in the garden when Grandad appeared with a large box.

'There's all kinds of stuff in here … your grandmother's things,' he said, looking at me quizzically. 'I was stuff clearing out and found it. Your father or his sister must have packed it all away after she died. I suppose it's best to throw it away, though. It's probably not good to go hold on to someone's private things.'

I was named after my two grandmothers: my paternal grandmother Ísbjörg, and my Faroese maternal grandmother, whose name was Heidrún. Ísrún was a combination of the two names and I'd always taken a secret pleasure at its pretty originality. Ísbjörg had passed away young, at not quite fifty.

'Your grandmother smoked far too much,' my father would remind me regularly. 'It was cancer that took her.'

I have never smoked.

I had never had the opportunity to meet Ísbjörg. She died several years before I was born. And it was rare that I saw my Faroese grandparents. But Grandad Lárus in Landeyjar had always featured in my life. We often went to see him, and in the winter he'd come and stay with us or with one of my father's sisters in Reykjavík.

I always felt an inexplicably close link to my grandmother Ísbjörg. People were always saying how alike we were, both in our looks and mannerisms. She was like a distant image, a vision I could see but barely make out, the woman I shared so much with but had never met. I often thought how wonderful it would have been to know her, and cursed the cancer that had taken her away from me.

My heart beat faster when Grandad appeared with the box. Ísbjörg's things!

He had also brought a rubbish bag with him, and he opened it as he started to root through the box. A few bills went into the bag, and then there was an old exercise book.

'Her recipes,' he said. 'Do you want them?'

I nodded eagerly, honoured to be given this little book of memories. I clutched it to my chest as if it was something rare and precious. Even now, having left home long before, that recipe book still had pride of place in my kitchen, and it had also come in useful.

A diary came out of the box next. It was beautifully bound, but worn and secured with an old-fashioned lock. There was no key attached, but that wouldn't prove to be much of an obstacle.

'Your grandmother kept a diary when she was young, and again after the illness took hold, right up until she no longer had the strength to hold a pen,' Grandad Lárus said quietly, turning over the book in his hands.

'May I have it?' I asked. I wanted to snatch it from his hands and snap open the lock.

'She never showed me what she had written,' he said, his eyes still fixed on the diary.

'May I have it?' I asked again.

'Have it? No. It's going straight into the rubbish. She wrote it for herself alone, not for anyone else.'

Grandad dropped the diary into the rubbish bag. I quietly decided to steal it as soon as there was a chance.

'I'll take the bag to the incinerator,' he said, when he finished examining the contents of the box.

I went with him, hoping he'd change his mind.

I had to have that diary. It was the only thing that could give me any insight into the thoughts of my grandmother, Ísbjörg.

The seconds crawled past, like a slow-motion replay, as Grandad took the bag and hurled it into the flames.

It was so final and so brutal. The opportunity to lay my hands on the diary was gone.

I saw it happen again and again in my mind in the following years, as I tried to work out for myself what might have been in that diary, which was now gone for good. That moment has never left me and neither have I stopped wondering what was in the diary, what details there were of my grandmother's life, and what she might have written that could have brought us closer together.

7

News of the corpse's discovery spread rapidly as one news site after another picked up the story, but none had reported that the victim's legal address was in Siglufjörður, where life continued as usual.

It was going to be a sunny day, as if the weather had decided that the brutal killing of one of the townspeople was no reason for dropping a few grey clouds into the otherwise perfectly blue summer sky, untroubled by a breath of wind. The news from down south was all about the ash clouds from the eruption that were slowly poisoning Reykjavík, the tainted air brought to the capital by the easterly breeze. No ash from the volcano had reached Siglufjörður as it was too far north. But during the eruption, Ari Thór had heard from a friend of his in town that there were times when ash from volcanoes in the south had fallen over Siglufjörður: once in the nineteenth century and again in the big Katla eruption of 1918, and now people were afraid that the recent eruption of Eyjafjallajökull might wake old and powerful Katla from her century-long sleep.

Ari Thór had arranged to meet Hákon Halldórsson at a coffee house by the small marina. He knew that he was a foreman on the new tunnel that was being constructed between Siglufjörður and neighbouring Héðinsfjörður, as part of the new road link to Akureyri, the nearest large town. Once the construction was finished, the two places, Siglufjörður and Akureyri, would be little more than an hour apart.

The coffee house overlooked the fjord, its deep-blue waters stirring gently in the warm summer breeze, as the brightly painted local boats nodded at their moorings. According to the information Ari

Thór had been able to prise from Tómas, who had an encyclopaedic knowledge of the town's inhabitants, Hákon was best known for having been the singer of a band called the Herring Lads. Their heyday had taken place long after the herring had departed, but they had been quite popular nonetheless, playing at dances around the country and producing three albums. Hákon was no longer a young man, but seemed never to have quite left his pop career behind. When the weather allowed, he drove around in an antique MG sports car that Ari Thór had noticed on more than one occasion, speculating that its owner might be clinging on to his youth.

Hákon rose to his feet as Ari Thór approached. The MG's owner was a thickset gentleman with a protruding belly, dressed in jeans and a leather jacket over a knitted sweater, not quite ready to take summer on trust and careful to keep any chill wind at bay. He was short, with grey hair and an unkempt, full grey beard. He shook Ari Thór's hand firmly.

'Aren't you the Reverend?' he asked cheerfully.

'No,' Ari Thór replied with a sigh. 'My name's Ari Thór.'

Hákon dropped back into his chair outside the coffee house and waved Ari Thór to sit next to him.

'Ah, sorry. I was told you'd studied theology. So what's this all about?'

When he'd called earlier, Ari Thór had only revealed that he needed to talk about one of Hákon's staff.

'A body has been found over at Reykjaströnd in Skagafjörður.'

Hákon made no reply, his countenance as rugged and stern as the mountains under which he had been brought up. It would need more than a death to knock him off balance.

'Haven't you heard about it?'

'Well, yes. It was on the news this morning. Was it murder? That's the impression I got.' Hákon remained calm. 'One of my boys?' he asked finally, and at last there was a tremor of uncertainty in his voice.

'That's right,' Ari Thór said. 'I have to ask you to keep this confidential. We're not releasing the name of the deceased right away.'

Hákon nodded, although both he and Ari Thór knew that it wouldn't be long before the name would become public knowledge, whether Hákon or someone else was the source.

'His name's Elías. Elías Freysson.'

'Elías? Well…' Hákon was surprised, or at least seemed to be. 'And I thought he was a good boy.'

'Good boys can be victims of murder, too.'

'If you say so,' Hákon mumbled, almost to himself.

'Had he been working for you long?'

'He wasn't working for me, not strictly speaking,' Hákon said, almost carelessly. 'Elías was a self-employed sub-contractor. He'd been working with us in the tunnel for about year and a half. There are … were … four of them: Elías and three boys who work for him. I say boys, but one of them is older than Elías and the others.'

Ari Thór had already dug up all the information he could find about the victim before meeting Hákon. Elías had been thirty-four, unmarried and childless, his legal residence registered as an address in Siglufjörður.

'I understand he lived here in the town, on Hvanneyrarbraut. Is that right?' Ari Thór asked, a formality creeping into his voice.

'Yes, that sounds about right. He rented a place there from Nóra, not far from the swimming pool. I've never been there.'

Hákon sipped his coffee.

'Did he live here most of the time?'

'Yes, as far as I know. He took on jobs here and there. The latest was some summer house he was working on … in Skagafjörður. Is that where his body was found? Poor bastard.'

There was a new note of sympathy in Hákon's voice, and for the first time it seemed to have dawned on him that his colleague was dead.

'I can't say too much at present,' Ari Thór said apologetically. 'Can you give me details of the men who worked with him?'

He tore a page from his notebook and passed it across to Hákon, who wrote down three names, consulted his phone and added three phone numbers.

'There you go. They're all decent men.'

Not killers, was the unspoken subtext.

About to stand up, Ari Thór saw that a few passersby had stopped, glancing over to where he sat with Hákon but pretending to admire the little boats at the pontoons or the gleaming cruise liner at the quay. There was no doubt they were wondering why the foreman of the tunnel was chatting to the police. The gossip would start to fly around soon enough.

'Listen, my friend,' Hákon added suddenly. 'That artist guy is the one you ought to be talking to. Those other boys wouldn't hurt a fly.'

Ari Thór sat up straight in his chair.

'*Listen, my friend*,' he said coolly, his tone measured. 'You don't tell me how to do my job…'

Hákon looked up in surprise and hurried to interrupt. 'Hey. Sorry…'

'I don't care if you used to be some kind of celebrity,' Ari Thór added. 'So who's this artist?'

'His name's Jói. I don't know his full name he's just called Jói. He's a performance artist, whatever the hell that is. He's … you know…'

'No, I don't know,' Ari Thór said and waited patiently for Hákon to stumble across the right word.

'He's one of those greens,' he said, with clear disdain in his voice.

'He and Elías knew each other?'

'Yeah, they were co-operating on some charity concert, in Akureyri. Elías was always doing charity stuff. He's … he was … setting up a concert for the charity that Nóra runs. Household Rescue, you know…'

This time Ari Thór knew exactly what he meant. Household Rescue had been set up in the wake of the financial crash to provide help for families and individuals who had suffered due to the economic situation, people who had seen their jobs disappear or who were simply struggling to make ends meet. The charity had been established as a grass-roots organisation by a group of locals, including a few people in Siglufjörður, and it had started well. Ari Thór himself had donated a few thousand krónur at the beginning, and the organisers were always looking for further support.

'What kind of co-operation was this? Was Jói planning to do some kind of performance as part of the concert? Was Elías working for Household Rescue?' Ari Thór immediately regretted asking quite so many questions all at once, a beginner's mistake in any interrogation.

But Hákon didn't seem concerned and answered carefully.

'Let's see … Elli … Elías, that is, he offered to organise a concert in the spring, with all the proceeds going to Household Rescue. He did all the preparation. Jói sings and plays the guitar as well. He was going to perform at the concert, but they fell out for some reason and that's all I know about it. So, to put it in a nutshell, Jói's the man you ought to be asking the questions, rather than Elías's workmates.' He smiled broadly.

'We'll see.' Ari Thór stood up. 'Thanks … my friend.'

He walked swiftly away.

8

After the morning meeting Ísrún visited the Meteorological Office to enquire about the ash that was continuing to settle on the city. She spoke to a young woman, who apologised, explaining that she had only recently graduated and hadn't worked there long, but seemed to have every fact and figure relating to the ash and to Reykjavík's air pollution at her fingertips. She would be perfect for an interview, thought Ísrún, but when she suggested it, the young lady's tone changed immediately. She flatly refused to be involved, and for the first time in their conversation, there was a long silence.

'Can't you just quote me?' she asked eventually.

'Unfortunately that never comes across well,' Ísrún said, and gave her the spiel she knew almost by heart. 'For a television audience it's vital that viewers can see who we're talking to. You won't even notice the camera,' she said, adding a white lie.

Ísrún had to be at her most persuasive to encourage the woman to agree to an on-camera interview, and eventually she succeeded. By then, however, Ísrún was beginning to have second thoughts. Nervous interviewees didn't perform well for the camera, and even the shortest piece could involve endless retakes – sentences re-shot again and again. Sometimes it was easiest to speak to politicians as most of them had no trouble holding forth in front of a camera. Ordinary people would frequently be able to speak at length but then dissolve into nervous wrecks once a camera was rolling in front of them. Ísrún had a sinking feeling as she recognised the young meteorologist as just one of those people.

'Won't people notice how nervous I am?' she asked.

'Don't worry about it. The camera hides that kind of thing,' Ísrún lied smoothly.

'If it looks bad, you won't show it, will you? Just quote me instead.'

'Of course we will,' Ísrún murmured. Her conscience was beginning to nag her, but she needed an expert, and this woman knew everything there was to know about the subject.

The details of the ash cloud itself weren't too interesting and would never make headlines. The ash had been polluting the air in Reykjavík for weeks, although this was a particularly bad day.

So, following general questions about the ash, Ísrún decided to focus on the danger ahead: the potential eruption of Katla.

'What about Katla?' she asked. 'Isn't there a chance that it will erupt now? It's way overdue, the last eruption was in 1918.'

'Well … well,' the young woman stammered, not quite prepared for this line of questioning. 'Of course there is a real risk, we indeed think it is overdue…'

'And the impact of a Katla eruption? Total air traffic chaos?'

'Yes, I think so…' And then she seemed to realise that she had fallen into Ísrún's trap and given her a great headline. 'I mean, no, there is no way of telling. It depends on the ash and the direction of the wind, so many variables.'

'Thanks, that was all. We'd better be going now,' Ísrún said. 'I'm sure I'll be able to use some of what you've said.'

'Please don't use that last bit – about Katla,' the woman replied, shaking Ísrún's hand. Her palm was damp with sweat.

'Maybe not, let's see,' Ísrún replied, fully intending to put a bit of fear into the audience's hearts by predicting a full-blown Katla eruption.

Some people just don't want their fifteen minutes of fame, she decided, shaking her head in frustration. Or even, as in this case, only sixty seconds.

'Things will get worse later in the day,' the woman added as they left, as if offering something in exchange for the Katla story. 'The wind's changing and it's going to bring a heavier ashfall this way.'

Good news, thought Ísrún, as it could mean that her piece would be placed closer to the opening of the news bulletin, even if the dead man up north would undoubtedly be their lead story.

⌖

The newsroom was buzzing with talk about the murder case when Ísrún returned.

'We have a name,' she heard Ívar call to Kormákur. 'Elías Freysson, address in Siglufjörður. Contractor. Involved in some charity event up north. That might be a smart angle to take. Philanthropist murdered! Something like that. Just find a good angle on it.'

'A good angle? Kormákur replied, looking uncomfortable. 'The man was murdered.'

Ívar smiled awkwardly and turned to Ísrún.

'How is your minor stuff going?' he asked loudly, as if to ensure that everyone could hear.

'Not bad,' she said, looking away. A few years ago she wouldn't have let anyone walk over her like this, being given only the most trivial material to work on and then ridiculed in front of her colleagues.

⌖

'Ívar.'

He looked up to see Ísrún standing by the newsroom manager's desk and wondered what she would be angling for now. Maybe she'd complain about his 'minor stuff' quip, twenty minutes after the event.

'Shouldn't you be finishing that volcanic ash piece?' he asked sharply. He never bothered to be polite at work, except when dealing with management, of course.

She hesitated.

'Come on ... what is it?' he asked with a sigh.

'I was wondering if I could work on the murder story with

Kormákur. Things are pretty quiet on my patch,' she said, flushing. She looked unhappy.

'Quiet? That doesn't sound good.'

'I'm scheduled for shifts over the next few days so it wouldn't be a problem to follow the murder as well as my usual stories,' Ísrún said, with an uncharacteristic determination that took him by surprise.

'I can hardly put two people on the story,' he said. 'Have you finished editing the summer news piece?'

'Not entirely, but it's nearly there. Couldn't one of the summer temps finish it?'

'We'll see. It'll probably go into the late bulletin.' Ívar's patience was wearing thin. 'And the ash pollution thing?'

'I did an interview with a meteorologist at the Met Office earlier and we should be able to use some of that,' she said awkwardly, looking unsure quite how to assert herself. 'I'd like to go up north,' she finally added firmly.

'North?' Ívar replied in amazement.

'Yeah, Skagafjörður. That's where the body was found. Maybe Siglufjörður as well.'

'Hell, Ísrún, we can't send you off around the country just like that. We have to watch every penny. End of story.'

'But…'

'End of story.'

'It's just that…' she dropped her voice and leant closer. 'I had a call just now and I think we should follow it up.'

'A call? Explain. Who called?'

'Sorry. I can't tell you that.'

'Why the hell not?' snapped Ívar, catching himself just before his fist hammered the desk.

'It was a friend of mine in Akureyri. He said he knew the victim, but I'm not sure how much I can tell you.'

'Out with it!' His voice gathered volume.

'You'll have to let me follow it up.'

'All right. Do what you like.' Ívar was struggling to maintain his composure, already turning over in his mind the possibility that she might be vying for the desk chief's job, a post he coveted.

'He told me that Elías had been involved in some kind of drugs ring up north,' Ísrún suddenly whispered, as if parting with a state secret.

'Drugs? Really?' His voice registered genuine surprise. 'See what you can dig up. I can't promise anything for fuel or accommodation expenses unless you come back with a scoop. And I can't let you have a cameraman. You'll have to deal with our stringer up north if you get something worth filming. And if you don't, just send Kormákur your notes and he'll use them in his reports.'

Ívar did his best to emphasise the *his*; if Ísrún was a rival, he judged it would be better for Kormákur to get the credit if anything came of all this.

'Fine.' Ísrún smiled.

It was rare to see her with a smile on her face, reflected Ívar.

'I'll be on my way this afternoon. Don't worry about accommodation. I can find a cheap place to stay in Akureyri. I know it well; I worked at the hospital there.'

'Well, you should never have left,' he muttered under his breath.

Ísrún left the room without offering a response to his rude remark. She didn't feel it deserved one. The real reason why she left Akureyri would have come as a shock to Ívar; it was possible that she would have seen him rendered speechless for once. But she was satisfied that she had managed to hold her own and that she would soon be on her way northwards.

Perhaps she had crossed a line by making up the story about Elías being involved with drugs, but it was a tiny lie, and something had to be done to get herself on the story.

9

Southern Iceland – one year earlier

My holiday had begun. I was hoping to have a week in the south of Iceland to get over the pressure and the overwhelming fatigue I was experiencing.

I was planning to work on the article about my grandmother, although I was maybe still searching for some sense of what my grandmother had written in her diary, something I had probably been seeking since the moment I watched my grandfather throw the book into the incinerator.

Of course I had always known that the diary was lost. In my heart of hearts I knew I'd never really know what she had written in it, yet I still found the fact hard to accept.

Maybe Grandad Lárus, who has been dead for many years now, was right. Ísbjörg had written the diary for herself, not for anyone else.

I drove eastwards in the rust bucket, on my way to Landeyjar, forced by the car's modest power to keep to the legal speed limit.

Finally, as I rounded the last bend of the rutted gravel road, Grandad's old house looked down at me. It stood on a low hill of its own, with a view over the green lowlands on the landward side, high mountains with snow still crowning their peaks in the far distance and, on the other side, the Westman Islands rising from the sea.

It had been a boundless playground for a small girl visiting her grandparents. There was always a brisk breeze blowing here, bringing the smell of the sea with it, even at the height of summer – or that's what my memories of the place told me.

I drove up the track to the house, opened the gate with its crown of barbed wire, forgetting for a moment that a couple with two small children had bought the house after Grandad died.

A newish pickup was parked in the yard and a cheerful dog greeted me as I got out of the car.

In terms of my article, it was unlikely that I would gain anything from this visit, but something drew me to this place.

A young woman came to the door and stood in silence as she looked me up and down, taking in the scar on my face and then averting her eyes, pretending not to have seen it. Her pause was long enough to remind me how much I stood out from the crowd.

People have suggested exploring plastic surgery, but it's not something I've ever contemplated. I suppose that deep inside I don't mind being different, taking on the world and swimming against the tide.

'Good morning,' the young woman said, at last, and with a smile.

'Hello. My name's Ísrún.'

'Yes. You're on the news, aren't you?' the woman asked, and looked over my shoulder. 'No cameraman?'

'What…? No, I'm not exactly at work. I'm working on an article about my grandmother,' I said. 'She lived here.'

'In this house?'

'That's right. Do you mind if I come in and look around?'

She invited me in. I guess it was difficult to say no to someone who was a regular visitor on her TV screen.

I did my best to enjoy the visit. Memories came flooding back, even though the new owners had made many changes to the place. There was a new kitchen, and the bathroom had been fixed up properly. And, to an extent, the house's charm had evaporated; this was no longer the familiar ramshackle old house where Grandad had lived, but a smarter, more modern version of it.

I'd have liked to have spent the night there, if that had been offered. But I had arranged to stay with a cousin who had a farm not far away. I could write my article there, relax and share memories of my family.

I had also set up some time to meet with two women who had known my grandmother Ísbjörg well. They had said they'd be glad to recall their memories of the old days for me.

I was buzzing with anticipation for any clues, any tiny details that could give me an insight into my grandmother's life.

10

Svavar Sindrason sat in the old wicker chair and gazed into the distance. This was where he sat most often to watch the weather. The view in itself was nothing special, consisting mostly of next door's wall. But that didn't matter. It was the sky he liked to observe.

Occasionally he went to church, more out of habit than devotion, although he had his own faith. He had a belief in a higher power, but as he never expected to get answers, he rarely went to God for advice.

He was in his forties now. He hadn't intended to be living in the old house in Dalvík by the time he reached forty. The plan had been to salt away some money and move somewhere else. He was born and had lived here all his life, with only a few breaks. He had rented an apartment and worked down south for a while, even though he owned the house in Dalvík outright, now that his parents were both dead. Svavar liked the town, but he dreamed of a little flat somewhere in southern Europe, preferably close to the beach, where he could take it easy, and enjoy the sunshine and many long drinks. There wasn't much he wouldn't do to have those dreams come true.

A little earlier, Svavar had watched the news.

Now he sat by the window and thought about the Almighty.

For once, he was slightly confused.

Questions about life and death plagued him.

His own life and the death of someone else.

He wondered how far he would be prepared to go to save his own skin.

Svavar wanted to live to the full the one life he was offered – he had no intention of doing so under lock and key.

But it wasn't just the prospect of prison that concerned him. Svavar knew that if he was to go to the police, it was death that he should fear. His own death.

If only he could know for certain how serious the consequences of going to the police might be, perhaps that would help his decision. He certainly had a clear enough idea of what could happen if he *didn't* go to them.

Over the years the expression that something was a 'matter of life or death' had often tripped off his tongue, but it was only now that he was able to appreciate the true meaning.

He continued to stare out of the window in the hope that he would somehow be presented with an answer to his dilemma: do the right thing, save a life but face the inevitable consequences; or keep everything to himself and live with his conscience for the rest of his days.

11

The coffee corner at the Siglufjörður police station was a popular spot whenever there was something out of the ordinary to investigate. The first of the day's visitors was Ómar, the retired skipper, who made an appearance not long after the news was made public that the body found was that of a man who had not only worked on the new tunnel but also lived in Siglufjörður.

Ómar was one of the station's regular visitors – although of his own free will, looking for a cup of coffee at the police station whenever he felt like company. Nobody was quite sure what ship he had commanded, but the name 'Skipper' stuck to him as firmly as the Reverend nickname had attached itself to Ari Thór, who had never had a congregation.

'How are you, Ómar?' Tómas asked as they both took their places at the table.

'Not so bad, my boy. And you?'

Tómas wasn't prepared to chat about his own feelings. He knew exactly what Ómar was fishing for – probably some gossip about Tómas's wife, who had 'temporarily' moved south to Reykjavík. Tómas suspected that his communication with his wife or, rather, the lack of it, had become a popular topic for the gossips around the town.

'I'm fine,' Tómas said, with more enthusiasm than he felt. *In fact*, he thought, *sometimes I* am *fine,* but that was only when he wasn't thinking of his wife. He longed to move to Reykjavík to be with her, but that was easier said than done. He'd considered a short career break, maybe a year's sabbatical, to go and live in the south. He'd been pleased and reassured to see that there was a resilience about Ari Thór, and Tómas considered the possibility that he might be able to run things on a temporary basis if Tómas were to take a break.

'Keeping busy today?'

'Well, as busy as usual,' Tómas replied, keeping his answer deliberately short.

'Dreadful to hear about that fellow who was … *murdered*,' Ómar said with a dramatic emphasis on the last word.

'Yes. You knew him?'

'No. Good Lord, no. He was just a contractor here, wasn't he? Making some money out of the tunnel? Everyone seems hell-bent on making something out of it. I hear he lived at Nóra's place.'

'That's right, he rented it from her,' Tómas confirmed, taking care not to give the old man too much information. The investigation was being handled by CID in Akureyri, assisted by the local force in Sauðárkrókur, and, in a more minor way, the Siglufjörður police.

Ari Thór had already been busy working on the case, and had interviewed Hákon, or 'Hákon the Herring Lad', as Tómas habitually referred to him. Hákon had given him the names and contact details of Elías's three closest colleagues. One of them, Páll Reynisson, had been a police officer in Siglufjörður at one point. Then there was Svavar Sindrason, resident in Dalvík, and a third man, Logi Jökulsson.

Tómas and Ari Thór had then taken part in a conference call and had been told that Svavar Sindrason had already been interviewed. He had known Elías for a long time but had not been able to provide much information. He had been aware that Elías had a job on the side, working on the house in Skagafjörður; Elías certainly hadn't kept it a secret.

The likelihood was that the murder had taken place at night, but with little traffic surveillance in the district at that time and no traffic cameras, it would be close to impossible to work out who had been travelling through the area.

As for Svavar himself, he said that he had been asleep all night. As he lived alone, that would be difficult to confirm.

It hadn't been ruled out that the killer could have been a woman. Comparatively little force had been behind the blow, and the length of timber hadn't been particularly large. The real damage had been caused by the nail that had protruded from it.

Nóra Pálsdóttir's life could be divided into three distinct sections: a disastrous marriage; foreign travel, and peering into other people's mouths. She had studied dentistry because her father had been a dentist and no other career path had even been mooted in the household in which she had grown up. In reality she had no interest in her work and organised things so that she could spend as much time as possible travelling. After ten years of marriage, her husband had realised that she loved her travels more than she loved him, promptly divorced her and took an unnecessarily generous proportion of her wealth with him in the process. The divorce was perhaps due, not so much to her love of holidays, as to her habit of being not entirely faithful to her husband.

She downsized, selling the detached house in downtown Reykjavík and moving away from the city centre, buying instead an apartment in the suburbs and channelling the resulting cash into her travel fund.

The journeys had begun during her university years, globe-trotting with a minimum of luggage, and preferring to be alone.

Living on a remote island in the north Atlantic was never going to satisfy her and she had always had a deep inner urge to explore the world, to experience distant and unfamiliar cultures and the natural world. So she took every opportunity to visit somewhere new, to leave Iceland far behind.

First it had been Europe, but as her earnings increased, more exciting destinations were added, in Asia, Africa and South America. She found her own favourite places in each hemisphere and made sure to visit them more than once. Her itinerary was relentless. With every new paradise she discovered, a return journey was planned, until it became clear, as the years passed, that time was a finite resource, and so were her funds. By the time she reached the age of sixty, she decided that enough was enough. One by one, her friends and acquaintances were retiring and began talking about travelling the world, taking cruises or walking holidays to foreign lands. But Nóra was exhausted, jaded by the constant trips.

Around the time that she retired, Nóra sold the apartment in Grafarvogur. She'd never really felt comfortable there, and one of the main reasons for this was that she had borrowed heavily against the equity to invest in the stock market. When the financial crash unfolded, she rapidly discovered that she'd lost almost everything.

There was nothing for it but to move away from the Reykjavík area and back north to her hometown, Siglufjörður, with just enough retrieved from the financial mess to buy a pretty house with a sea view, on Hvanneyrarbraut. She was able to defray her living costs by renting out the upper floor. In fact, having company upstairs turned out to be something she enjoyed.

Her intention was to relax in Siglufjörður, to enjoy life. And Nóra was able to achieve that, taking an active part in the town's social scene, experimenting with a few new lovers, and spending much of her time reading by the living-room window with its view over the sea and the mountains that ringed the town.

She was at home when the young police officer knocked at her door. Ever since the news that her tenant upstairs had been found dead, she had been expecting this visit. Rather than receive the police dressed in her usual tracksuit bottoms and flip-flops, she had smartened herself up. It was the least she could do.

She had hoped that Tómas would come in person, but instead it was the one they called the Reverend, a good-looking young man. He was much too young for her, of course, although she refused to rule anything out. He was a serious character, with dead eyes, she decided, as if he had lost something precious.

⌖

'Come in.'

The woman in the doorway gave him a smile that was almost fawning as she looked him up and down. 'You must be Ari Thór.'

It was still disconcerting that unfamiliar people knew his name, but he conceded that in a small community everyone knew who the police were.

'Thank you. I need to take a look at Elías's apartment. I understand he was your tenant.'

'Quite right. What's happened is dreadful. The poor man … he was so lovely.'

Her words didn't sound entirely genuine. *So lovely.* He wondered if that would be Elías Freysson's epitaph. Would it be carved on his gravestone?

'What on earth am I supposed to do with all his things?' she mused.

'We'll find out for you. There may be a relative to inherit his belongings, but first I need to look around. It's best if you don't touch anything for the moment,' Ari Thór said in a tight voice, avoiding unnecessary chat.

The walls of the hall were painted a dark shade of yellow and decorated with small graphic prints. A staircase on the right led upstairs, the passage painted the same shade of yellow.

Opening the door, Nóra showed Ari Thór into the living room. A small fireplace was filled with oddments and potted plants. The walls were hung with paintings from far-flung parts of the world: one from Africa, another of an Asian scene and a watercolour of Rio de Janeiro. This was clearly a traveller's home, a repository of memories.

'When did you last see him?' Ari Thór asked, when he had made himself comfortable on an embossed white sofa. She sat next to him, uncomfortably close.

'Yesterday,' she said. 'I ran into him in the hall early yesterday morning. As you just saw, he couldn't go upstairs without walking through my hall. I had the place modified when I bought it, so I could have separate apartments upstairs and down,' she said. Again, her smile was intense, discomfiting Ari Thór. He averted his eyes.

'Did he seem to be concerned about anything? Did you notice anything unusual about him?' he asked.

Nóra thought for a moment. 'Well, there's a question. Not concerned. More like *excited* about something.'

'About what, do you think?'

'I really have no idea, I'm afraid.'

'When did he move in?'

'A few months ago. I got to know him through Household Rescue. Have you heard about that?' she asked, her voice softening.

'Yes, and I contributed to it,' Ari Thór replied stiffly, preferring to keep the woman at a distance.

She brightened immediately. 'I'm delighted to hear it! Elías offered to help. He said he had plenty of free time and wanted to give something back to the community.' She paused for a moment. 'At the beginning of this year he told me he had to move out of the place he was living in, and needed somewhere to stay for a few months, until the tunnel was finished. I'd mentioned at a Household Rescue meeting that I had had the house altered in order to rent or sell the apartment upstairs. He was a perfect tenant,' she said, lowering her voice as if it were a mark of respect for the deceased man. 'There was never a sound from upstairs. And he had been away quite a lot recently.'

'You have access to his apartment?'

'Access? Of course. But I never went up there. It's important to respect someone else's privacy.'

Ari Thór felt there was a hint of guilt in her voice.

'In short, he was an angel. I love people who are prepared to sacrifice their time for good works. It didn't do any harm that he was drop-dead gorgeous as well, a real charmer, just like you.'

Her eyelashes fluttered. Ari Thór tried to ignore her gaze, but he felt his cheeks flush, and trying to stop them doing so was making it worse.

'Don't be bashful. There's no point being shy about your appearance,' she said, and the ingratiating smile made a reappearance as she leaned closer to him. 'Would you like anything to drink? Coffee? I have red and white wine as well.'

He rose swiftly to his feet. 'Let's keep things professional,' he said coolly. 'Would you be so kind as to let me into his apartment?'

It was an instruction rather than a request.

'Of course,' Nóra said, apparently taking his rejection in her stride.

She followed him up the stairs, unlocked the door and was about to go with him into the apartment. But he held up his hand and asked her, firmly, to remain outside.

The upper floor had clearly not been envisaged as a separate apartment. There were two rooms, with a small bathroom leading off one of them. Both had presumably been bedrooms at one time, before one had been transformed into an awkward combination of kitchenette and living room. A fridge took up space along one wall alongside a sink and a stove, and apart from that there was just enough furniture to fill the place rather than to decorate it.

The bedroom decor was bland, even colourless, with a double bed and a couple of monochrome pictures on the walls. There were few personal items – a jacket lying on the bed and shoes placed neatly together on the floor next to some weights.

Clothes had been thrown into the wardrobe and there was an open sports bag among the pile of garments. A white towel, folded and unused, could be seen hanging half out of the bag.

It was only when he had examined the bag's contents more carefully, though, that he decided he needed to call Tómas. Immediately.

12

It didn't take Ísrún long to track down Elías's ex-wife, uncovering both her name and her place of work.

She had an aptitude for gathering information about people on the internet, in an entirely legal way, of course. It amazed her sometimes just how careless people were about leaving all kinds of personal information on social media sites to be picked up by anyone who cared to look. This made background research so much easier, and now there were online newspaper archives as well, finding people's personal details was child's play.

The ash cloud over Reykjavík was becoming denser, the air felt gritty, as if filled with tiny particles of sand. The nervous girl from the Meteorological Office had been right. The heat was unusual for this time of year, but it was hardly possible to say that the weather was good, with the air so dry and dirty.

Leaving the TV station's offices and holding her breath for the short walk from the door, it was a relief to get into the car. In spite of the hot, stale air inside being almost overwhelming, Ísrún withstood the temptation to wind down the window as she drove down to the harbour where Idunn, Elías's ex-wife, ran a small café.

The port area was quiet, with only a few tourists braving the ash, as they waited to board a boat that would take them out to watch whales or puffins. Occasionally Ísrún would go down to the harbour at weekends to buy fresh fish at the market, halibut if it was available. More often than not, however, she had a weekend shift. And then there were the weekends when she could hardly trust herself to get out of bed.

The café had a homely feel to it, comforting music playing quietly in the background, wooden fittings giving the place a rustic warmth, and a thick aroma of freshly brewed coffee. The door was closed and all of the windows were fastened to keep out the sour air, although the lingering metallic stench of the ash cloud was evident even inside. A couple with a pram sat at one table, the woman sipping coffee while the man nursed a glass of water and hid behind his open laptop. An older gentleman stood at the counter, chatting to one of the café staff, a large dog at his side. Then Ísrún spied her: Idunn.

This was the same woman whose pictures Ísrún had dug up in an old newspaper archive, including one of Elías and Idunn at the fortieth birthday party of a popular politician. The only difference between now and then was that Idunn's hair had been coloured bright red.

Ísrún walked towards her and ordered a cappuccino.

As Idunn placed the cup in front of her, Ísrún took the opportunity to open a conversation. 'I'm sure I recognise you. Haven't we met somewhere?'

'I'm not sure. Could be, but I'm terrible with faces,' Idunn replied cheerfully.

'I never forget a face, it can be a curse sometimes. My name's Ísrún.'

Idunn gave her own name and all of a sudden seemed to recognise Ísrún, looking at her with sudden confusion.

'Well, I've a feeling I've seen you somewhere before. At a big four-O birthday party a couple of years ago?' Ísrún asked, pausing to provide an opportunity for a reply, and sipping her coffee. 'That's a fantastic cappuccino. Are you running this place?'

'Thanks. I am. Opened here not long ago. I had a café in the Kringlan shopping centre but wanted to move closer to the middle of town,' Idunn said with a smile.

Ísrún decided to let fly with both barrels.

'Oh God, aren't you Elías's wife? Isn't he the one who was found dead up north somewhere?'

The smile vanished suddenly from Idunn's face, replaced by a pained smirk.

'You can quit the play-acting. I've seen you on TV. News, isn't it? Whatever, you're no actress.'

Ísrún nodded and flushed with embarrassment, surprised and disappointed to find she wasn't as shameless as she had thought herself to be.

'But you're right,' Idunn continued. 'I was married to Elías. That's a long time ago now. What do you want to know about the miserable bastard?' she asked in an emotionless voice. 'Good riddance to him.'

Ísrún was left dumbstruck by this reaction. All her journalist's skill, built up over the years, left her for a moment and she felt as if the breath had gone from her lungs.

'The police contacted me this morning to say that Elías was dead,' Idunn said tersely, breaking the silence. 'I can't say I'll shed any tears over him.'

'Was he … Did he play away while you were married?' Ísrún finally asked in a quiet voice.

'Hell, yes. He was a complete shitbag. I still can't understand why I ever married him,' she said, and then seemed to regret her choice of words. 'Oh, for heaven's sake, don't quote me on the news, will you?' She paused for a moment, and leant towards Ísrún. 'All the same, you'd be wise not to make too much of a saint of him.'

'There's no chance of that,' Ísrún said, half to herself. 'But you must have got something out of the divorce?'

Idunn laughed, a bitter, tired laugh.

'If only. The bastard never had two pennies to rub together, not that I knew of anyway. I was the one who was the wage earner. He did very nicely out of the divorce and he even got my apartment in Akureyri. It's nothing special, just a cubbyhole of a place, but it'll be worth something. I managed to keep hold of the café. He's … was … such a tightwad that I don't think he even got round to registering the Akureyri apartment under his own name. On paper my company still owns it. I suppose because he didn't want to pay the insurance and council tax on it,' she said and smiled, brightening as this positive aspect of his death dawned on her. 'Hey, maybe I get to keep my apartment after all! It might be worth selling.'

'Sometimes there's good luck to be found in the unlikeliest of places,' Ísrún said, unconvincingly.

She thanked Idunn for her time, and gathered her courage to set off into the tainted air outside.

The sky was unusually dark, the sun hidden behind the thick mineral haze, even though there wasn't a cloud in the sky. Ísrún felt the ash settle on her tongue, as she breathed, as if she had had a mouthful of sand. She shuddered at the thought, hurrying to her car and setting off immediately; she felt like she was in a polluted foreign city in the middle of a heatwave, rather than a summer's day in Reykjavík.

She could hardly have chosen a better day to be leaving town. This would be the first time she had been back to Akureyri after leaving the place so suddenly a year and a half ago to return to Reykjavík. She gritted her teeth at the thought of the old wounds a return to Akureyri might open up, but told herself that she needed to do it.

Things were beginning to crystallise, and Ísrún felt she was on to something. She could reveal the real Elías Freysson.

'Kormákur! A word!'

Ívar sat in the desk editor's chair and yelled across the newsroom, as he usually did, a king overseeing his subjects.

Kormákur hurried over.

'How's it going with the murder story?'

'Nothing new,' Kormákur said.

'Nothing new? A man's been murdered. Don't tell me you're just going to sit here and wait for the police to get round to holding a press conference?'

Ívar's voice was stern, cut with sharp sarcasm.

'What? No, of course not ... but it's all just kicking off,' Kormákur stammered.

'It's going to be our lead tonight. For crying out loud, try and work a bit of tension into it, will you?' Ívar muttered something under his breath, and then leant in to whisper into Kormákur's ear. 'Listen, someone called Ísrún with a lead; some friend of hers, whose name she wouldn't give, said Elías had been involved in drugs.'

'Dope? A user?' Kormákur asked in surprise.

'No, smuggling.'

'Hell! That would be a proper scoop.'

'Wouldn't it just? She put her foot down and wanted to have a go at it, so if she sends anything in, I'll let you have it. But I still want you to look into this. I don't really trust her with something so big. Can you do that?'

'Of course I can.'

Kormákur hurried back to his workstation and called the police in Akureyri to see if there had been any connection between the murder victim and a drug-smuggling ring.

But the police were tight-lipped: they weren't providing any information until the press conference, and Kormákur put down the phone without having learned anything new. He wondered what exactly it was that Ísrún knew. He couldn't help hoping that she came back south with nothing and this would open the way to getting her sacked from the news team.

13

Kristín hurried along the corridor of the Akureyri Hospital. The years had left the yellow lino on the floor scratched and stained and the white tiles on the walls had long ago lost their sheen. It was a cold and unwelcoming environment.

The wards were already a hive of activity as her shift started. Kristín liked that; she was quickly bored when things were quiet, giving her too much time to think about the future. Like every doctor qualifying in Iceland, she would soon have to think about going abroad to specialise, but she pushed that thought to the recesses of her mind. She was in no frame of mind to make decisions that would dictate the course of her career. With years at the University of Iceland behind her, she was still facing another long period of study overseas. Sometimes she regretted choosing medicine, uncomfortable with the idea of spending years studying and then being limited to a particular field. Once the investment in this extensive process was taken into account, along with the pressure that the work brought with it, the money she'd earn was nothing special. She suspected that, with the economy stagnating in the wake of the financial crash a few years earlier and the cuts to the health service, she'd have to work abroad to make all that investment pay for itself. And that would entail even more decisions.

She felt her mobile, set on silent, vibrate in her pocket. She paused, plucked the phone from her pocket and saw that it was her friend from the golf course. They had planned to meet during the week.

She answered.

'Kristín?'

'That's me. Hi.'

His friendly voice gave her warm feeling inside.

'Am I interrupting anything?'

Kristín had always made work and study her priorities when she and Ari Thór had been together. Maybe that was one of the reasons they had parted?

'No, it's all right.'

'I was wondering if we could meet up tonight? Find a place to have a meal?'

'I'm sorry, but I'm already promised tonight.' She was disappointed. She needed to meet him, have a chance to relax and think of something else. 'Tomorrow evening?'

'Perfect.'

'We can meet at my place,' she said. 'My shift finishes at seven.'

She gave him the address.

'That's great. See you tomorrow,' he said.

She thought she heard real pleasure in his voice as he put down the phone. And she couldn't help feeling a keen anticipation – she was already looking forward to their date. Red wine, a few good cheeses to choose from – maybe he'd help her finally shake off Ari Thór.

14

He hadn't noticed her go downstairs, but Nóra was standing in the hall when Ari Thór came down, the sports bag in his hands.

'Are you taking that with you?' she asked.

'Yes,' he replied.

'What for?'

Her eyes widened with excitement.

'I need your key to the upstairs apartment,' said Ari Thór, artfully avoiding her questioning gaze. 'Do you have spare keys?'

This took her by surprise.

'What? Yes. Of course,' she said, going into her own apartment and returning with the key. 'I don't have any other ones,' she added, her eyes firmly on the sports bag.

'How did he pay his rent?'

She looked up with a smile. 'What do you mean?'

'Did he pay in cash, or did he transfer the money to your account?' he asked.

'Always cash. Why?'

'I'll be in touch later if there are any questions,' he said, allowing authority to permeate his voice in the hope that she would back down. 'I'd appreciate it if you didn't share anything about this visit with anyone. And please don't mention the bag to anyone,' he said, trying to make it plain by his tone that this was more than a polite request.

Ari Thór said his goodbyes to Nóra and got into the police four-by-four.

It was still bright over Siglufjörður. The sun gleamed in a clear blue sky, making the waters of the fjord sparkle. There were still a few patches of snow to be seen high on the slopes above the town, picked out in clear white by the bright sunshine. What he had heard on the news of the ash cloud hanging over Reykjavík could just as well have been news from the other side of the world.

His thoughts turned to more personal concerns. Kristín had long since moved out of his little apartment on Öldugata in Reykjavík, but he had delayed renting it out. Months passed before he finally summoned up the courage to advertise for a tenant. Last Christmas he had been able to take off plenty of time for which he had no need. He had travelled to Reykjavík the day before Christmas Eve, cleared everything personal from the apartment and put it into storage before meeting his prospective tenant. They agreed a one-year rental starting from the first of January, and Ari Thór felt relieved that he had finally dealt with the apartment, even though this brought to an end the time that he and Kristín had spent there together. That Christmas Eve he had spent alone in his car, driving up north, listening to the Christmas mass on the radio, whenever there was a signal to be found.

Ari Thór paused before driving away from Nóra's home, his memories tugging at his concentration. He shook his head and wiped his brow with the back of his hand. He needed to focus on the case.

Taking a deep breath, he set off towards the police station to collect Tómas. He had arranged to meet Logi Jökulsson, the third member of Elías's team at the tunnel site. They had set up a meeting in Skútudalur, at the mouth of the tunnel, and Tómas had offered to come along.

'How much do you reckon is there?' Tómas asked, once he was in the four-by-four.

'In the bag? A few million in foreign currency, I'd guess,' Ari Thór replied, raising his eyebrow at his colleague. 'And a stack of Icelandic krónur, probably several million. It's difficult to say. We'll need to count it.'

Tómas furrowed his brow. 'Do you think she knew about it? Maybe she'd had a look in the bag before you turned up.'

'Nóra?' Ari Thór thought. 'It's hard to be sure, to be honest.'

'I wouldn't put it past her,' Tómas replied, clearly suspicious. 'She's always been a devious one.'

'This kind of money doesn't just appear out of nowhere,' Ari Thór said. 'Elías may have been doing some cash jobs on the side, but that would never account for this much money.'

'I agree,' Tómas said. 'I think we need to reconsider what line of business Elías was actually in.'

⌖

Tómas and Ari Thór waited for Logi at the entrance to the new tunnel. A man who looked to be in his thirties emerged from the dark mouth of the tunnel. It was clear that he hadn't shaved for some time. His helmet was thick with dust and his boiler suit had not seen a washing machine for quite some time.

'G'day,' he offered curtly. 'Don't have much time, loads to be done.'

'We'll take as much time as we need,' Ari Thór said, unintentionally raising his voice. Then launched straight into his questions. 'How long had you known Elías?'

Tómas stood to one side and listened intently.

'Three years,' Logi said shortly, meeting the eyes of neither man.

'I understand there were three of you working with him: you, Svavar Sindrason and Páll Reynisson.'

'That sounds about right.'

'Was he a good foreman?'

'Not bad.'

'He paid on time?'

'Always,' Logi replied.

'Do you know of anyone who might have wanted to do him harm?'

'Wanted to do him harm? You're formal, aren't you?' he grinned and then was silent for a moment. 'How would I know if the man had any enemies?' he continued, as if irritated by Ari Thór's questions.

'How did you four get on?' Ari Thór persisted, keeping his gaze fixed on Logi, determined not to miss the slightest change in his expression.

'Pretty good. Svavar knew him best. You ought to have a word with him.' Logi yawned.

'We found a pile of money at Elías's place, including some foreign currency,' Ari Thór said firmly, and saw a look of surprise flash across Logi's face. 'You knew about this?'

'That the guy had some cash? That's no business of mine,' Logi said quickly, his composure clearly rattled. He hesitated for a moment, and added, 'But the answer's no, I didn't know about any money.'

Ari Thór paused, waiting until the silence had become unbearable before asking another question.

'You're sure about that?'

'Absolutely sure.' Logi's response was emphatic.

'You knew that Elías was working on a house over in Skagafjörður, though?'

Logi took a moment to think. 'Well, yes. He talked about it a lot. He was getting a cracking good rate for the job, so he said. Some doctor down south building himself a summer house.'

'When did you last see him?'

'The end of yesterday's shift,' Logi said irritably, not bothering to hide the fact that he was becoming annoyed by the questioning. 'Nine o'clock. He said he was going over to Skagafjörður right away and was going to work on the summer house.'

'What were your movements yesterday? Last evening and night?' Ari Thór asked, trying to keep his gaze steely.

'Eh? What the hell's that about? You don't think I bumped him off, do you?' Logi asked angrily. 'I went straight home after my shift, went to sleep and was there until this morning.'

'And can anyone confirm that?'

'Well … You can ask my brother, Jökull – and his wife, Móna.

They live on the floor below me. I can't leave the house without going through their place,' he said. 'We live in our parents' old house. The old man's dead and the old lady's in a home, so we share the house between us. Not separate flats, but a floor each, if you see what I mean?'

'Fair enough. But I expect you'd have been able to leave the house in the middle of the night without anyone noticing,' Ari Thór said, trying to provoke Logi, an approach he found often brought results.

'Yeah, maybe any other time, but not last night. My sister-in-law's pregnant. She wasn't well last night and she's having a tough time of it. She sleeps badly. They kept me awake, watching some video for half the night. I went down to see what was going on around three when I couldn't sleep.'

'What was the film?' Ari Thór asked.

'A thriller. *Seven*. Seen it?'

'We'll talk to them,' he said, leaving Logi's question unanswered.

'Please do. Can I get back to work now?' Logi asked abruptly.

'Of course. But don't go far. We might need to talk to you again tonight or tomorrow.'

'I'm not going anywhere until this fucking tunnel is finished,' he said, and strode away without a backward glance.

Ari Thór and Tómas returned to the car silently.

'I'll talk to his brother later to confirm his movements,' said Ari Thór, glancing in Tómas's direction.

'Perhaps you can be a little more gentle with them?' Tómas said amiably. 'Móna, Logi's sister-in-law, is a relative of mine. Not a close relative, you understand, but we know each other pretty well. They've been trying for a baby for a long time, so they're a little tense and excited now that she's pregnant, bless her.' He smiled.

Ari Thór sighed, irritated at being told what to do. Tómas had given him the investigation to run and he was going to do it his own way.

15

Ríkhardur Lindgren's one mistake had cost him dear.

In front of the mirror in his apartment in Reykjavík's exclusive harbour district, he saw clear evidence of how the years had treated him, and how they had started to turn him grey. In fact, he now saw that he was grey all over. There were wrinkles on his face and black circles under his eyes. His hands weren't as steady as they had once been, either. But that could just be the booze.

He couldn't always recall exactly how old he was, regularly having to subtract numbers to get the answer – not that he was remotely interested in knowing the outcome. To his mind he was a young man who was old before his time.

He turned around and inspected the apartment that he had just advertised for sale. It was a new place, tastefully if blandly furnished, with items purchased from the same shop without too much thought. The walls were white and mostly blank, as the murderously expensive paintings his parents had owned were in storage or with his sister. The only thing on his walls was the clock, its flat batteries ensuring that the time was always one minute past ten. His shelves were stacked with books, not a single family album among them, and there were no photographs to be seen.

Visitors had stopped coming. He wasn't in the phone book and his legal residence was registered elsewhere. The phone had been disconnected and he had acquired an unregistered mobile. Nobody ever rang, and that was just fine. At least he was free of night-time phone calls from overwrought people whose relatives had died.

Things were simpler, even good, now, despite the fact that his wife had left him and they were childless.

His parents – his father a Swedish chemist and his mother an Icelandic doctor – were both dead. His upbringing, first in Sweden and then in Iceland, had been almost idyllic. He was encouraged to follow his dreams, to embark upon his medical studies, which eventually led to a hospital post. Life had treated him well, and would have continued to do so if he hadn't allowed his fondness for a drink to spill over into his working life. There were a few near misses, and then there was that error.

The one that took a patient's life.

The subsequent investigation showed that others, too, had been harmed by his inattention, and two had subsequently died. All due to mistakes that could be traced to the doctor's love affair with the bottle.

Inevitably, there had been a scandal. The newspapers wouldn't leave him in peace. For longer than he chose to remember, he had been public enemy number one, with furious night-time phone calls that only ceased when he had the phone disconnected.

But that was all in the past – a few years ago, now – and the media had forgotten about him. Struck off, he was the subject of several private prosecutions and was ordered by the courts to pay damages. Not that he had been affected in any serious way. His parents had been very wealthy. But it all meant things had changed. He no longer had any desire to live in Reykjavík, rarely venturing outside and failing even to enjoy the exquisite sea view that stretched outside his windows. His curtains remained tightly drawn, and his life had become a moribund series of routines.

The radio alarm woke him every morning, but he habitually stayed in bed until midday. He'd have soup for lunch while listening to the news, put on a shirt and a pair of flannel trousers, browse through books in his living room and listen to a story on the radio before taking an afternoon nap with a couple of tablets to ensure he would sleep soundly for an hour or two. Then he would wake in time for the TV news as he made himself dinner; fish four days a week, beef mince on Fridays, chicken on Saturdays and lamb for Sunday.

Everything stayed that way, week after week, in endless repetition, both a comfort and a noose. He had stopped drinking, and that had turned out to be easier than he had expected, but there was always a threat lurking in the corners of his mind.

Unless there was something special – a visit to a doctor or a bank that demanded his presence in town – Ríkhardur left the house only once a week. First he'd go to the fish shop, then the supermarket and finally a bookshop.

He was accustomed to buying three books a week. Despite his virulent reading habits, he had never visited a library. He had no desire to read books that had been through dozens of other hands before his. *All those germs*, he thought, sickened at the thought.

Coming home from his weekly outing, he shut himself away in the tidy apartment that nobody else had entered for two years, and he felt safe, appropriately distanced. Secure.

He wasn't an easy man to find, and that was exactly what he wanted.

He was aware that he would be even more difficult to track down once he had moved to the north, but so much time had passed he knew that he was unlikely to provoke any real interest. Until today.

It had started just like any other. Newspapers, and then soup for lunch, listening to the midday news.

A man was found dead today on a building site at Reykjaströnd in Skagafjörður.

Ríkhardur had sat stock still, the soup spoon in his hand, staring at the radio as if he expected the newsreader to step out of it, to venture into his kitchen and confront him.

He placed the spoon carefully in bowl, his hands trembling slightly, and went to the office where there was a desktop computer, an old machine that he seldom used. Several months had passed since its last outing, but it finally whirred and rattled into life. After several failed attempts, he eventually found his way to a news website that showed him photographs of the murder site.

Over the years, his mood had rarely changed. He'd become devoid of emotion, and nothing touched or affected him.

But now he stood up so sharply that the chair toppled behind him onto the floor.

'What the hell?' he shouted, his heart pounding, every ounce of his being tense with affront.

16

The man who answered the door could only be Jökull, Logi's brother.

'Good morning,' he drawled, taking stock of Ari Thór through the lenses of his round glasses. There was a frostiness about him, but the family resemblance was unmistakeable. Like fire and ice, Ari Thór thought. Jökull was smaller than Logi, more lithe, but there was no doubt that they were brothers.

'My name's Ari Thór. I need a few words with you concerning the death of Elías Freysson,' he said with as much authority as he could invest in his voice, waiting to be asked to come inside.

But Jökull apparently had no desire to receive guests. 'Well … yes,' he said lazily. 'What do you want to know?'

'Where was your brother last night?' Ari Thór asked, deciding to get straight to the point.

'What? You don't think Logi did the man in, do you?' Jökull asked, in a slow, deep voice.

It had occurred to Ari Thór to soften the blow, reassuring Jökull that his brother wasn't under suspicion. But they did need to be sure of the deceased's workmates' whereabouts, so as to eliminate them from the investigation. And this cold, laconic man was giving him no reason to handle him with any delicacy.

'Who knows? Perhaps he's under suspicion…'

This elicited an immediate response from Jökull, who looked animated for the first time.

'Yeah, well. He was here at home all night,' he answered quickly.

'How can you be sure?'

'We, that's me and Móna, my wife, we were awake pretty much

all night. She's pregnant and hasn't been having a great time of it,' he said, re-arranging his glasses on his nose.

'Could he have left the house without you noticing?' Ari Thór asked, his voice brusque.

'Well, not unless he jumped out of an upstairs window,' he said. 'Look, I know he was home all night. He came downstairs and watched half a movie with us, *Seven*. Shift work does that to you, makes you end up sleeping at all kinds of strange times.'

'You do shift work as well?'

He seemed surprised at the question. 'No. I'm not one for heavy lifting. I'm better off in front of a computer screen. I work at the Savings Bank.' It was as if he expected Ari Thór to know who worked for the town's main service companies.

'I need a word with your wife as well,' Ari Thór said.

'What? My wife? I think she's asleep.'

Ari Thór stood on the steps, unsmiling, waiting for time to do its work for him.

'I'll fetch her,' Jökull said at last, with a sigh, and vanished into the house.

Ari Thór took a few steps back, and looked the yellow-painted house up and down while he waited. A small spider clambered up the wall. He guessed the house dated back to the sixties or seventies, and it looked like it had been recently painted.

'Hello?' The voice was tired. Ari Thór looked around and saw a heavily pregnant woman in the doorway. 'I'm Móna. You wanted to talk to me about something?' She leaned against the doorframe. 'You're Ari Thór, aren't you? Tómas is my cousin. He told me about you.'

'Hello. Just one quick question. Do you know where your brother-in-law, Logi, was last night?'

'Yes. He was here at home,' she said, clearly exhausted. 'We kept him awake.'

She patted her swelling belly and tried to squeeze out a smile.

'Thanks,' Ari Thór said. 'That tells me what I needed to know.'

Walking back to the squad car, his eyes were drawn to the mountains where there was still a bit of snow to be seen.

The shadow of winter and the heavy snow that would engulf the town as the long days turned into long nights was never far away in Siglufjörður.

17

When Ísrún heard on the radio news that Ríkhardur Lindgren was the owner of the house in which the murder had taken place, she drove straight to the office. She could still taste the polluted air in her mouth. The ash cloud over the city had grown thicker and heavier as the day passed. The sun was blotted out by the heavy haze, its presence behind the grey miasma hidden but still felt as the temperature continued to climb.

That damned volcano … Normally she delighted in hot summer days, but now she would have welcomed a cold northerly gale.

She remembered the Ríkhardur Lindgren case clearly. He had been in the news before she left to study for her master's degree, while she was still working on the news desk. Three people had lost their lives due to the doctor's drinking habit. But in the those days they'd had an unusually cautious news editor, who'd decided not to identify the doctor by name and played down the tragedy as it unfolded.

According to the national registry, Ríkhardur Lindgren's legal residence was now in Sweden. Ísrún had a friend, Elín, who had worked at a newspaper when the story was at its hottest and had written some pieces about it. She had since left journalism and moved to a job as a press secretary for a bank. Maybe she would remember something about Ríkhardur – some interesting angle on the story? This might be a chance to score a few points off Ívar, and still be able to leave town to travel to the north in good time.

'Hi,' she said when the phone was answered, 'it's Ísrún.'

'Ísrún! It's ages since I heard from you,' Elín replied pleasantly.

'Yes, I've been a bit busy.' That was an understatement. Life had been a roller coaster for the last two years, and with more downs than ups. 'How are things in the world of PR? I presume you're managing to spoon-feed your former colleagues with regular good-news stories?'

'It happens from time to time,' Elín laughed.

Ísrún decided to plunge straight in while she had Elín in a good mood: 'Do you mind if I pick your brains for a moment?'

'About what?'

'You remember Ríkhardur Lindgren?'

'Do I ever?' Elín replied, her tone sharp. 'That drunken arsehole.'

'Did you keep tabs on him?'

'Yes I did. After all, I wrote about him a few times, especially when the private prosecutions for damages were going on.'

'Does he live here or did he move to Sweden?'

'The last I heard he was living in a very high-end apartment his sister owns – in the harbour district, if I recall correctly,' Elín said with satisfaction in her voice; it was clear that she enjoyed helping out a colleague from her days in journalism.

Half an hour later Ísrún was standing in the entrance lobby of a newish apartment block on Vatnsstígur, a very expensive part of town.

The sister's name was nowhere to be seen. However, there was a single unmarked button; a flat on the sixth floor. It had to be the right one.

She pressed the button, but kept her face turned away from the camera lens next to it. No answer.

She buzzed a second time and waited.

The speaker crackled and a hoarse male voice said 'Hello?' in an abrupt tone.

'Ríkhardur? I'm from the city police… I need a word with you about your place on the north coast.'

He muttered something she couldn't understand and buzzed her into the building.

She took the lift to the sixth floor. A few years before she would have jogged up the stairs, but she didn't think she was fit enough for that anymore.

Finding the right door she pressed another buzzer.

As the man opened the door, she quickly put a foot inside, smiling as she squeezed herself through the narrow gap.

'Hang on,' he said in a confused voice. 'Don't I know you? That … that scar.' People didn't usually mention it, thought Ísrún. 'I've seen you on the television.' His voice was gaining volume now. 'You're no damned copper. You're a bloody reporter! Get out of here!'

'I'll make you a deal,' she said calmly. 'I have no interest in you and your wretched affairs. But I *am* interested in finding out about Elías Freysson. If you answer a few questions for me, I promise I won't mention you in my report. If, on the other hand, you decide to keep quiet…' she paused. She'd never been so coolly ruthless in the old days. The last two years had changed her. '… you can bank on the media being camped outside your door.'

He gulped.

'I have a cameraman waiting in the car,' she lied. 'I can give him a shout. There's no way you'll get out of the building without being filmed.'

He turned away and seemed to be thinking for a moment. 'What do you want to know about Elías?' he snarled as he faced her again.

'How well did you know him?'

'Not at all really. He was doing some work for me. I was told he was a skilled workman, and we agreed a fair price for a job.'

'Who put you in touch with him?' Ísrún persisted.

'A friend of mine in Dalvík. His name's Svavar. He and Elías were close friends; they'd worked together for years.'

'I want this Svavar's details – a phone number or an address.'

He nodded, seemingly defeated.

'Stay here,' he ordered and went into the next room. He returned a moment later with a piece of paper, with something scrawled on it in almost illegible handwriting.

'There you go,' he said in a harsh voice, handing her the note. 'And now be off with you.'

'What else do you know about Elías?' asked Ísrún, without moving. 'Anything that could be useful?'

'Hell and damnation; I didn't know the man at all,' Ríkhardur snapped. 'The bloody fool, getting himself murdered on my property.'

Ísrún stood her ground, watching Ríkhardur fume as he tried to think of a way to get rid of her.

'The only other thing I know is that he was involved in charity work, some concert in Akureyri. That's it. Now get out of here before I call the police.'

'Thanks for being so helpful,' she said with a smile and made her way out of the apartment. The door slammed shut at her heels.

She took the lift down and, getting into her car, headed for the road northwards.

Svavar's place in Dalvík was going to be her first port of call.

18

'Posh, aren't we?' Hlynur said, watching as Ari Thór opened a tin decorated with a Christmas tree motif, took a few tea leaves and put them in hot water to infuse.

'You don't know a good thing when you see it,' Ari Thór retorted. 'You just swill that muck you call coffee all day long.'

'So Christmas has come early for you, has it?'

Ari Thór smiled, declining to reply, then took his tea and left the room.

Hlynur stayed where he was, irritated by the superior smile he had seen on Ari Thór's face.

He could feel the jealousy growing inside him; outright anger even. Although perhaps that anger ought to be directed more at Tómas. After all, it was Tómas who had asked Ari Thór to handle the investigation, leaving Hlynur to deal with all the piddling little cases. Was he preparing Ari Thór to take on even bigger assignments? Or grooming him to be the next inspector at the Siglufjörður station? As the older man with more experience, Hlynur felt that he deserved priority.

Nothing ever went right for him. And he couldn't stop thinking about those emails – found it difficult to think of anything else. And now Tómas had put someone else on this big case, the most serious investigation of the last few years. That person being Ari Thór only served to magnify his misery.

He knew that he desperately needed to escape from this vicious circle of regret and self-pity, but it was easier said than done.

Would his career simply wither away? Would he be doomed to be a failure? Would he ever be able to haul himself back from the edge and make something of himself, putting the misery of his childhood and misdeeds behind him?

Once Hlynur had grown up and realised the pain he had caused all those years ago at school, he had been in touch with every one of those people whose lives he had made a misery and had asked for their forgiveness. Some took it well, others didn't. Gauti was the only one whom he hadn't been able to reach. He had finally tracked him down through the newspapers. But where he found him was on the obituary pages.

There was no doubt: Gauti had taken his own life. Hlynur was convinced that this could be traced back, directly or indirectly, to the bullying he had suffered at school. So in all likelihood it was Hlynur who was responsible for the suicide of one of his schoolmates – he'd bullied him to death. And he had left others deeply damaged, too.

Next time I'll teach you how to die.

Sometimes Hlynur was angry or bewildered when he read this spine-chilling message that appeared on his computer.

Who would dare send him this kind of thing? Someone he knew? Maybe someone in Siglufjörður? Was the sender out there watching him, following him to work and back? Some days he found himself consumed with the suspicion that he was being watched, that someone close at hand was following his every move. He constantly glanced over his shoulder to see if he was being followed.

Yet he still hadn't made any real effort to find out who could be sending him the emails. Could it be someone from Gauti's family, or one of his friends? Whoever it was, the messages continued to arrive, and they were undoubtedly real.

Maybe he did need to learn how to die.

His girlfriend in Sauðárkrókur had called that morning. He knew exactly what she wanted to talk about: the next step in their relationship. He definitely liked the girl, and under normal circumstances he would have been excited by the prospect – would have welcomed such a discussion.

But he didn't return her call.

⌖

Ari Thór sipped his Christmas tea. It tasted the same as any other tea, with no particular Christmas flavour to it. He wasn't even sure what flavour Christmas ought to have; had never even thought about it. He did recall that his late mother had occasionally mentioned that she associated the smell of apples with Christmas, probably because apples used to be difficult to come by in Iceland when his parents were growing up.

He turned instead to the case. He was pleased with his progress so far and was determined to do well.

After the news had been leaked that the owner of the house where the body had been found was none other than the notorious doctor Ríkhardur Lindgren, something had been nagging at the back of his mind. Could the killer have in fact set out to murder Lindgren?

Ari Thór had searched out information on the three people whose lives had been lost due to the doctor's mistakes. An elderly widow in a Reykjavík suburb had died during an operation, leaving behind a daughter, who lived in the same district, along with her children. A retired woman in Kópavogur had also died, but not before a painful struggle with the after-effects of Lindgren's errors. She had left a husband, who now lived in Akureyri, and several children. An elderly man in Hafnarfjörður had also died following an operation. This man had one son who now lived in Norway.

Ari Thór and Tómas were being kept up to date on the investigation's progress by the Akureyri police. But some journalist from down south had called the Siglufjörður station directly to ask if Elías had been involved in trafficking narcotics, declining to say, however, who the source of the tip-off might be. They had explored this new avenue of inquiry, but so far without any success. It was also apparent that Elías had recently spent a few days in Denmark, returning earlier that week. He hadn't booked any connecting flights with a local airline, but a search was in progress to find out if he had taken another flight on from Denmark with a foreign airline.

Ari Thór had been in touch with Elías's third colleague, Páll Reynisson, referred to by Tómas as 'Páll the Cop', since he had once been a summer relief officer at the Siglufjörður station. Páll was travelling north from Reykjavík and had promised to call in at the station as soon as he arrived.

Next, Ari Thór intended to track down the artist who called himself Jói. Hákon, the foreman at the tunnel, hadn't been impressed by him, and, if Hákon was to be believed, there had been some enmity between Jói and Elías in connection with Household Rescue, the charitable initiative to support those who had been left stranded by the far-reaching effects of the financial crash.

If it was true, this little fact could be promising.

19

The artist's house was on Hlíðarvegur. It was an old detached bungalow, painted white, its entire front festooned with climbing plants. A row of scarlet Russian dolls, picked out in yellow, occupied the sill of the window above the door, the largest on the left, descending in order to the smallest on the right.

There was no visible doorbell, so Ari Thór tapped on the glass, or rather the glass sculpture that occupied the centre of the front door.

A middle-aged man appeared around the corner of the building.

'Come round this way, will you? I'm working in the garden,' he said. He had a grey beard, full and thick, which reminded Ari Thór of Father Christmas. 'Tómas said I should expect a visit from you.'

Following the man behind the house, the first thing Ari Thór saw was a sheet of canvas, which occupied the middle of a lawn surrounded by currant bushes and shrubs. The canvas was decorated with footprints, and it was then that Ari Thór noticed that the man was barefoot, and that his feet were covered in paint.

While Ari Thór watched, the man dipped his right foot in a bucket, which appeared to be full of blue paint, and then hopped on one leg towards the canvas.

'You're painting?' Ari Thór asked, realising as he said it just how asinine the question was.

'You could say that,' Jói answered cheerfully.

'I hear you're a performance artist.'

'That's what I'm known as, but it's not easy to sell a performance, you know? So now I paint as well, just to keep myself afloat. And now and again I sing and play for money too. I've already sold this piece to a collector in Holland. I'm something of a name there, in fact. It's not bad, being able to sell overseas these days, now that you get a decent handful of krónur for every euro. And it's cheap enough to live here, especially as I don't need all that much.'

Wary of getting paint on his shoes, Ari Thór took care to move as little as possible.

'Have you lived here long?'

'When does anyone genuinely *live* anywhere?' Jói asked without looking up. 'I'm a citizen of the world, but I've stayed here in Siglufjörður more or less since birth. Others will have to decide whether or not that was a good thing.'

'What was?' Ari Thór asked, impatient.

'Birth,' Jói replied thoughtfully.

'Speaking of life and death,' Ari Thór said in a more formal tone, 'I understand you knew Elías Freysson, the man who was murdered the other night.'

Jói laughed mirthlessly.

'Yes. I knew him; a proper scoundrel, he was.' As if to match Ari Thór, his voice took on a harder, more serious tone.

'A real angel…' Ari Thór said, almost without thinking.

'What?'

'An angel of a man, or that's what people have told me.'

'He certainly knew how to make an impression, but I saw through him. I normally do. It's part of being an artist,' said Jói, hopping on the canvas on one foot.

'You had a disagreement?' Ari Thór asked bluntly. He was finding the artist's behaviour difficult to deal with.

'During the protests? No, I wouldn't say that,' Jói said, stepping off the canvas and dipping his left foot in yellow paint before continuing, now using both feet.

'What protests are you talking about?' Ari Thór asked, struggling to contain his bemusement.

'You didn't know about them?' Jói asked hesitatingly.

'I do hope I'm not interrupting your work,' Ari Thór said, irritated at not having the man's full attention.

'Don't worry about it,' Jói replied lightly. 'I like to work under pressure.'

'So tell me about these protests.'

'You could hardly call them protests. More a coffee-house movement. That's how we hold a protest out here in the country. We got together, maybe a dozen of us, and set up a protest camp at the new tunnel.'

'I thought people in Siglufjörður were in favour of the tunnel?'

'Not me. We wanted to protest at the environmental damage being done by cracking open the mountain with explosives. Then there's the fact that Héðinsfjörður, one of the most remote places in Iceland, will now be right on the main road. The place is a jewel of nature. It's a bloody scandal,' he grumbled.

'Was there any response?'

'You can see for yourself there wasn't,' he said shortly. 'The tunnel opens this winter, or so I'm told.'

'Were they all peaceful, the protests?'

'Pretty much,' he muttered.

'And what does that mean?' Ari Thór asked.

'Elías got uptight about it all. He had just moved up here. Started swearing at us. I was the only one who answered him back properly. We weren't far from a fight.' Jói paused. 'In fact, he knocked me over … Well, he gave me a push. I didn't respond. It was just in the heat of the moment. But I saw him differently after that, didn't like the man.'

He looked up and smiled awkwardly.

'Had you known each other before?'

'No, not at all. Although Elías had spent time in the country here, back when he was child – with a couple on a farm in Skagafjörður. For a few years it was a sort of summer camp for Reykjavík kids. But it's been abandoned since.'

'Maybe I ought to have a word with this couple,' Ari Thór said. 'Do you know where they live now?'

'You'd have to use some unconventional methods if you want to talk to them; they're both dead. But one of their children moved here after they died. That's Jónatan, lives next to the old churchyard.'

'I'll look him up when I get a chance,' Ari Thór said, deciding to try a new angle. 'Tell me about the charity concert you were organising. Weren't you supposed to appear there?'

'Yes, and I'm still planning to,' Jói said. 'It'll take place even though Elías is dead. In fact, there's a better chance of it going ahead now he's gone. I had been thinking of withdrawing from it completely, but there's no need for that anymore.'

'Why were you going to withdraw?'

'I was involved in organising the thing, along with Elías and Nóra, but she completely adored him. I guess she was the one who described him as an angel, right?' He grinned, but didn't wait for a reply. 'There was something fishy about the whole thing; Elías's part in it, I mean. He insisted on taking care of the financial side of things, and didn't want us involved in that at all. Nóra didn't mind, but I did. So I did my best to get a look at the paperwork – to get an idea of what was going on. Turns out I was right to be suspicious: there was a sky-high invoice from Elías and some company for costs that I didn't even recognise. My guess is that he was using the concert to get some kind of dirty cash into circulation.'

'Money laundering?'

'I guess that's the right expression. He must have been relying on nobody looking too closely, it being all for charity. But I just didn't trust the man, and that's the way it was.'

'I don't suppose you were in the area last night – when he was murdered?' Ari Thór asked, dropping the question in to make it sound like a casual aside.

'Good one,' Jói said with a smile. 'I was in Akureyri last night. Stayed on a campsite. I was drawing, not over in Skagafjörður doing someone in.'

'It's no great distance,' Ari Thór muttered.

'It's not that many kilometres, but there's a world of difference between drawing a landscape and murdering a man, isn't there?' Jói asked, looking up from the now colourful canvas.

'Could be,' Ari Thór said, as he turned to leave.

Ari Thór walked along Hlíðarvegur, down the steep slope of Brekkugata and towards the Town Hall Square, all the while lost in thought about the case.

As he entered the square he saw *her*.

Ugla. The girl who had destroyed his relationship with Kristín. No, that was wrong. She hadn't destroyed it – he had to bear his share of the blame.

It had been a few months since he'd last seen Ugla; and a year and a half had passed since they had last spoken.

She had entered the square from the opposite direction. So he could hardly turn around or step off the pavement and on to the grass without appearing to be avoiding her.

She looked up as their paths met but didn't return the smile he offered her.

He had once been captivated by this woman, but that emotion had gone.

Now he just missed Kristín.

20

It wasn't the first time that Páll Reynisson had driven through the Strákar tunnel, and it certainly wouldn't be the last. He was born and bred in Siglufjörður, and couldn't contemplate the idea of living anywhere else. As he emerged from the tunnel the fjord opened up and welcomed him with the familiar warm feeling it never failed to give him. *I'm home.*

Páll had spent two summers working under Tómas as a temporary police officer. Although he had enjoyed the work, it didn't grab his interest enough for him to want to make it a career. Instead he had trained as an electrician. His most recent job had been the Héðinsfjörður tunnel project, working as a contractor for Elías Freysson's small setup.

Altogether it was going to be odd to turn up at the police station where he had once worked and to be interviewed about what he did now.

⌖

Tómas had decided that he wouldn't take part in interviewing Páll. The fact that they already knew each other well would make it awkward, and in any case he was confident that Ari Thór would do a good job.

As he thought about Ari Thór, he wondered if it wouldn't be going too far to recommend him for the inspector post, not least as it would mean him leapfrogging Hlynur, who had considerably more experience. But Hlynur was far from being his usual self at the moment. In fact he was in a world of his own a lot of the time, somewhere far from the police station, his mind entirely on other things.

At first Tómas had wondered if it was something that would pass, fatigue or a temporary malaise. But the situation had become increasingly noticeable over recent months. Now it was so bad that he felt he couldn't trust Hlynur to deal with anything other than the most straightforward tasks.

He was no longer as punctual as he had been and every job he took on he dealt with almost unwillingly. His slipshod approach had resulted in a relatively straightforward drugs case being bungled; and worse was to follow when an elderly man suffered a heart attack at the swimming pool. Hlynur had been on duty and had attended the scene, but, according to those present, he had been as good as useless. He had said hardly a word to anyone, and had stared at what was unfolding as if he had been struck dumb. The man had fortunately survived, but it wasn't down to any effort on Hlynur's part.

If anything more serious than a traffic accident took place, Tómas had no choice but to deal with it himself or assign it to Ari Thór. Surely Hlynur had to be aware of this? They would have to find time to talk over the situation honestly, as soon as this murder case was out of the way.

Tómas was far from certain, however, that he would be moving south after all, so it could well be that he wouldn't need a successor, and wouldn't have to decide between the two men. The town had a strong hold over him. He struggled to put into words just why it clasped him so tightly; perhaps it was because the past was here, memories that he found impossible to let go. On top of all that, it was here that he had built up his successful career; here that he had dedicated himself so wholeheartedly to his work – more than likely he had been too dedicated. If he took a temporary leave of absence, might it turn too easily into a longer career break? The inspector's post wouldn't be kept open for him indefinitely. Was he prepared to take that risk?

⊕

'Take a seat,' Ari Thór said to Páll, determined not to let him get away with anything, even though he undoubtedly knew his way around the police station.

'It's nice to see the place again,' Páll said, appearing slightly unsure of his ground. 'I had a couple of good summers here,' he went on, as if keen to break the ice. 'People still call me Páll the Cop.'

'You don't lose a nickname easily in Siglufjörður,' Ari Thór said drily. 'What took you to Reykjavík?'

'Just a break. I had a day off yesterday and decided to run south to see what the big city has to offer. Just darkness and ash right now, it turns out.'

He leaned forward over the table and tried to smile.

'You stayed at a hotel?' Ari Thór asked.

'No. Stayed with a friend. You want his name and number?' he asked, now leaning back in his chair.

'Definitely.'

Páll gave him an address in Reykjavík and Ari Thór wrote down the information before continuing. 'When did you set off home?'

'This morning.'

'How was it working with Elías?' Ari Thór asked abruptly, hoping to catch Páll off-guard.

'It was a bit different,' said Páll, seeming to get into his stride now.

'How do you mean?'

'It wasn't easy to work with Elías and Svavar. They'd known each other for years and I had the feeling there was something they were cooking up between them, something I never got to hear anything about.'

'You mean another job?'

'Could have been. I just don't know,' Páll said and dropped his voice. 'Or else … something that was on the shady side, you understand?'

'Why didn't you inform us if that was the case?'

'It was just a gut feeling. I had nothing to back it up, otherwise I would have come straight here,' he said. 'But I do know that these last few days the two of them were tense – really nervous. It was as if something big was going on. But I never got to hear anything about it.' Páll shrugged as if to emphasise his point.

'How long had you worked together?'

'A year and a half, give or take. Elías took me on not long after he moved here.'

'What sort of character was he?'

Páll took a moment to think. 'It's hard to describe him. I just felt there was something sinister about him. He pretended to have this burning interest in charity work, for example. But that was clearly bullshit. The only person he had any interest in helping was himself. I think he wanted to make a pile of money and then move abroad. Svavar was always talking about moving somewhere warmer too.' He leaned forward again. 'I can tell you that was never going to happen, if he was on what I was earning. So either they were paying me a particularly lousy rate, or else they had some other shady job on the go that nobody else knew about.'

'What about Logi?' Ari Thór asked. 'Was he part of this … other job, do you think?'

'To tell you the truth, I couldn't be sure. I don't think so. They certainly trusted him more than they did me. Once a cop, always a cop, eh?' He grinned. 'I saw Elías talking to Logi the day before yesterday; they went quiet as soon as I turned up, so maybe he did have something to do with it. Or maybe they were going to let him join their secret society…' Páll spoke lightly, but there was an underlying bitterness that showed he resented having been left out in the cold.

Hlynur had watched as Ari Thór disappeared with Páll into the interview room.

He was all too aware that a year or so ago he would have been the one going in there, not Ari Thór. The old anger welled up inside him again.

He absolutely had to find out as soon as possible who was sending him these emails. Only then would he be able to get back some sort of equilibrium in his life.

Screwing up his courage, he looked again through Gauti's obituaries. It was a long time since he had last looked at them, but still he could not escape the same coincidence: Gauti had died on the tenth of May, and the first mysterious email had been sent to him on the same date, several years after Gauti's death.

According to the obituaries, Gauti had left a sister, younger by a few years. At the time of his death, Gauti's father was already dead but his mother was still living.

Hlynur jotted down the names and searched for them in the national registry.

Gauti's sister lived in the Reykjavík area. Their mother, however, had died just a year after her son. Hlynur easily found her obituary as well, and skimming through it the feeling crept up on him that she had died of sorrow, although there was no mention about whether or not she had taken her own life.

Hlynur felt sick. Wasn't the responsibility for Gauti's death a big enough cross to bear? Suddenly he had the deaths of two people on his conscience.

He felt a heaviness settle on his mind and a dark hopelessness engulfed him, however much he tried to shake it off.

Next he searched on the internet for pictures of Gauti's sister.

The sister's name was Oddrún. It was an unusual name, so Hlynur located a picture of her with very little difficulty. Gazing at the face looking out at him, he was sure he had never seen this woman before.

Tómas and Ari Thór had been asked to attend a status meeting in Akureyri that evening. Tómas suggested setting off late in the afternoon and finding a place for a meal on the way.

In fact, Tómas was pleased to have the chance to eat out and to enjoy some company over a meal. These days he was pretty much living on microwaved food. He had never got round to learning how to cook, so all he could really manage were ready meals; and occasionally he'd buy a frozen pizza and heat it up in the oven. He missed all the things his wife had cooked, from the everyday fare to the feasts she'd whip up on special occasions.

Most of all he missed the steak with béarnaise sauce and chips that would make an appearance on the menu once in a while; a slow but delicious way to hasten an early demise.

⌖

Akureyri was the last place Ari Thór wanted to visit. He wasn't ready to run into Kristín, at least not yet.

On the other hand, the visit would provide an opportunity to check out his theory about Ríkhardur Lindgren. Akureyri was the home of the widower of one of Ríkhardur's victims, a woman who had died due to the doctor's malpractice. He was hoping to be able to pay the man a visit without involving Tómas, and had laid plans to get Natan, an old schoolfriend who now lived in Akureyri, to drive him to the man's house. It was a shot in the dark, but it would be as well to check discreetly while the opportunity was there.

Ari Thór walked through Siglufjörður's town centre, crowded with tourists from a visiting cruise ship, milling about in the clear summer sunshine, a contrast to what he'd heard was happening in Reykjavík, where a thickening cloud of ash was gathering over the city.

He had been able contact Páll's friend in Reykjavík and confirm his story, as far as it went. Assuming this friend was telling the truth, Páll had been far from the murder scene. Now he wanted to call on the son of the couple who had owned the farm where, according to

Jói, Elías had stayed. Ari Thór still had a little time before he and Tómas had to leave for Akureyri, and hopefully something worthwhile would come of his short visit.

On the way he called Natan and arranged to meet him. Tómas had said something about getting a bite to eat in Akureyri; but Ari Thór decided he'd have to decline and say he was meeting a friend for a sandwich. Tómas wouldn't mind eating alone. He had to be used to it by now.

Ari Thór had another reason for preferring Natan's company over Tómas's. Natan knew Kristín, so Ari Thór could ask him if he had any news about her.

Ari Thór hadn't entertained the idea of a relationship with anyone else after Ugla and Kristín had both sent him packing in such quick succession. In all that time he had made only one false step – if you could call it that, seeing as he no longer had any responsibilities towards Kristín. The autumn after he and Kristín had parted, a friend from the police college had asked him if he felt like coming along to a country hop in Blönduós. Friend? Wasn't that too strong a word? An acquaintance, more like. In fact, Ari Thór had very few friends and had never acquired the skills needed to amass ranks of them around him. He found it difficult to open up and show others a warm, sensitive side. Since his parents and then his grandmother had died, there had only been two people with whom he had felt truly at ease: Kristín and then Ugla.

His acquaintance had just moved to Blönduós to take up a temporary post there and knew virtually nobody. He had told Ari Thór that he wasn't happy about going to this country dance on his own, and suggested that perhaps it wouldn't be a problem for Ari Thór to travel over from Siglufjörður. By then Ari Thór was so sick of his own misery and self-pity, having made such a mess of his relationships with Kristín and Ugla, he decided to go.

He had persuaded Hlynur to lend him a car, which was awkward seeing as they never met outside work and had little in common. However, Ari Thór had made himself do it. After all, there was no one else he could ask. Hardly Tómas, and certainly not Ugla.

⌖

When they had arrived at the dance, the noise was deafening and he soon lost sight of his friend somewhere in the throng. Songs he had never heard before were playing at full blast, blotting everything else out. What band was this, anyway? The booming bass beat was driving him nuts. He quickly decided he was getting too old for this.

Someone jostled him hard, and he spun around to return the favour. But he was too late, whoever it was had moved away. Instead Ari Thór's eyes fell on a stunning girl. Despite himself, he approached her, his body failing miserably to obey the rhythmic commands he was giving it, and his balance not everything he would have wanted it to be.

Over the din of the music, he introduced himself, telling her he was a police officer. He didn't catch her name, but, in case she hadn't heard him the first time, he told her again that he was a police officer. She was a petite redhead, outstandingly pretty, and definitely much younger than he was.

Almost before Ari Thór knew it, the last slow dance was over, and he was still with the same beautiful girl. They made their way from the dance hall, still clinging to each other, and before long he found himself standing outside a house in Blönduós. A red house. A red-haired girl who lived in a red house.

Inside, she handed him a drink, put some music on and turned up the volume, that endless damned noise. It wasn't long before her clothes were on the floor.

Sex with the red-haired girl was different to how it had been with Kristín, more daring, more urgent, colder. Yet all the time they were in each other's arms, his mind was on Kristín.

⌖

Once he had sobered up and was on the way back to Siglufjörður, he regretted the liaison. This was something that would be filed away under 'never happened' – if he and Kristín were ever to get back together, that was. *When* he and Kristín get back together, he told himself.

If it was all over between them, why the hell did he have the guilty feeling of having been unfaithful to her?

21

It was very quiet at the station. Hlynur had spent most of his time going through old obituaries. First Gauti's, and then Gauti's mother's.

He had been through his mailbox again and reread the threatening messages.

When would this end?

How could he make amends for his past misdeeds?

Could he ever?

He would have given everything he owned for a way out of this vicious circle, or for a voice that would tell him how he could put everything right.

He suspected, and feared, that the voice had already told him.

Next time I'll teach you how to die.

Whoever had sent him these messages, whether it was Gauti's sister, or some other person altogether, was waiting for the inevitable: for Hlynur to go the same way as Gauti.

The anger welled up again.

Why can't they leave me alone?

I regret it!

I regret everything!

22

Ari Thór walked through the square and up the steep steps leading to the old church and the churchyard, and finally arrived at Jónatan's house.

Jónatan stood in his doorway like a guard at a castle gate. Ari Thór recognised his face – someone he had seen around the town, although he knew nothing about him. So this was the man whose parents had farmed the place where Elías had spent time as a youngster. He was tall but stooped, his back clearly troubling him badly.

He took the measure of Ari Thór through a pair of thick glasses, looking down, as was inevitable with his stoop, as if he were handing down a verdict.

'What do you want with me?' he rasped, standing stock still. Jónatan's voice wasn't the dark rumble he had expected.

Ari Thór hadn't mentioned where he was going to Tómas, preferring to play his cards close to his chest. Neither had he called Jónatan in advance, and it was clear that this unexpected caller was far from welcome.

'Nothing special,' Ari Thór said trying to weigh the man up. 'A few questions, that's all.'

'I'm no friend of the police, as I presume you already know. They never leave you in peace,' he growled, but his voice lacked the volume to give it any depth or darkness. 'You're here to ask about Elías?'

Elías. So they knew each other. Presumably Jónatan remembered him from the farm.

'"As I presume you already know",' Ari Thór echoed, turning the words back on this irascible character. 'What's that supposed to mean? And aren't you going to ask me in?' he added.

'I don't ask anyone in,' Jónatan retorted. 'Nosy bastards everywhere.' He moved out of the doorway onto the steps, practically treading on Ari Thór's toes, and slammed the door shut behind him. 'I'm going down to the town, to the Co-op. You can tag along with me that far, young fella, and we can talk on the way.'

Ari Thór glanced towards the Town Hall Square. It wasn't a long walk from Jónatan's house by the old churchyard. There might be time for a few questions, but he'd have to choose them carefully.

'Fair enough,' he said crossly, although he saw with relief that Jónatan walked slowly, as if it was a struggle for him. That could make this informal interview a little longer.

'What did you mean just now?' Ari Thór asked.

'None of that crap, boy,' Jónatan snapped. 'You must know I did time. Otherwise why would you have come up here to pester me?'

Hell. That was a schoolboy error; going into an interview unprepared.

'I don't make a habit of checking for a criminal record every time I chat to someone,' Ari Thór said, hoping to sound convincing.

'I can imagine that wouldn't be the most pleasant of tasks,' Jónatan said, now seeming to struggle with the downward slope.

'What were you inside for?' Ari Thór asked, and immediately regretted wasting valuable time on a question he could answer for himself later by checking the records.

'Some stupid dope shit. Look it up for yourself. I was neither guilty nor innocent.' Jónatan hesitated, and then seemed to have decided to explain at greater length. It was Ari Thór's experience that everyone had extenuating circumstances of some kind. 'I did it for the money, all right? Smuggled some stuff from overseas. It wasn't my idea.'

'Did you know Elías well?'

'Well? No, I wouldn't say that. I remember him…' His voice failed him for a moment and he coughed before starting again. 'I remember him from the country, from my parents' farm. He never looked me up after he came to Siglufjörður, although I knew he was here before I heard about the murder. I'm not much of a one for mixing with people, so I don't keep up with the local gossip.'

'Have you lived here long?'

'Since father died. So that's five years. Mother had already gone. No point keeping the blasted farm going with half the animals dead and nothing to do but look out over the sea and remember … old memories.'

Judging by his tone, the memories were not pleasant ones.

'When did you get mixed up in that dope business?' Ari Thór asked, taking care to hide a cold smile. They were not far from the Co-op now.

'That was a long time ago,' Jónatan said, his voice wistful. 'Before my parents died. I moved to Reykjavík to learn something. Like everyone ought to do. Once I'd done my time I moved back north; nowhere else to go, you see. Then mother died. Father tried to keep the farm going, and then he died later the same year. Then I gave up. My brothers and sisters bought a place for me here; got it cheap.'

He stopped and with difficulty looked over his shoulder at his little house. 'My brothers and sisters are all down south, gone to live in some urban paradise.' He grinned. 'They never come to see me. There was cheap housing here and I reckon they thought it was best to keep me at a decent distance.'

'So what do you do?'

They were at the doors of the Co-op now.

'Well, young man, I suppose it's best to say I'm retired. I'm not a well man, you see.' He grinned again. 'I get a few sickness benefits now that I'm worn out and good for nothing. I get by, just about. I don't know what day it is any more, but I can tell the difference between a weekday and a weekend. You know how I do that?'

Ari Thór stood still, waiting for the answer to come.

'I look out of the window when I get up in the morning. If there are people about, then it's a weekday, otherwise it's the weekend.

That'll do me. Life's just so fucking simple when nobody gives a shit about you.'

And he limped into the shop without even one more look at Ari Thór.

23

Jónatan had no idea what he had come into the Co-op to buy. He didn't have much money to spend and, in any case, he had everything he needed at home: a little milk, some *skyr* and the leftovers of last night's dinner. The truth was he simply hadn't wanted to let that damned copper into his house, and a walk to the Co-op was the best idea he could come up with.

It was a real pain that he'd set off down the slope without taking his stick with him. In his haste to get out of the house he had forgotten it, and now he stood in the Co-op like a lost soul among the cruise-liner tourists, without any real need to make a purchase.

Why hadn't he wanted to let the copper in? He had to admit that part of the reason was that the place was a mess; he had long ago given up trying to keep it tidy. It wasn't as if he ever had any visitors.

The other reason was that he was terrified that he might ease his conscience and let something slip. Maybe that wouldn't be so bad, though; better than having to carry the burden of the truth on his bent back.

When he had seen the copper on the steps he had thought for a moment that it was all over; he almost felt a sense of relief. It had occurred to him to ask the copper in, to sit him down among all the junk and tell him everything.

He looked around the shop. There was nobody he knew, and nobody seemed to be paying him any attention, so he made his way to the checkouts and squeezed past them back out onto the street.

He felt like an idiot for going into the shop and then coming out empty-handed. Around the corner, he looked at the slope that awaited him. That stick would have come in handy now.

He had never been this forgetful when he was a younger man. He had been precise and thoughtful ever since he was a small child. He had been organised, reliable and conscientious. In such a large family, though, with so many brothers and sisters, and his parents having their hands full with the farm, he had received little encouragement to work hard. He had been the youngest of five in the farmhouse in Skagafjörður, yet there had never seemed to be any doubt that he would be the one to travel south to study. That had suited him; he didn't have the strength for heavy work and he had no interest in farming. So he went to Reykjavík, where he left college with top marks. It was after that that the problems that would plague him for the rest of his life had begun.

He had wanted to study medicine: a tough choice and a demanding course. He had already been preparing himself that summer, before the start of the first term. He had sat and read medical books, wondering if he could genuinely be a doctor. Could he handle all the patients that would come every day, and give each one a diagnosis and a prescribed treatment? 'Go home, there's nothing wrong with you.' How could he be completely sure he was right? How on earth did doctors manage to make so many decisions all day long? He imagined that each and every case would need to be examined thoroughly, looking up information in books and articles, and only after having carried out exhaustive checks could he say, 'go home, you're perfectly fit'.

And what if the person then became ill anyway? What if there was something he had overlooked? These were the thoughts that preyed on his mind.

Then the serious business of studying began.

⊕

He sat a desk in the library in the pool of light cast by the lamp. He stared at the book but was no longer reading; it remained open at the same page. He didn't know how long he'd been there. He'd started early. He'd been reading all night, doing his best to memorise every fact. The words were starting to fuse together. His days were dull and monotonous. Had he missed the first exam? Maybe; he wasn't sure any more. Well, perhaps he'd missed one or two exams … wasn't ready for them. Father had rung a few days ago and he hadn't been able to tell him the truth. He'd told him he'd passed, flown through every exam. That wasn't too much of a lie. He did know this stuff better than anyone. And yet he'd failed…

When his university studies had come to nothing, he looked for work. But finding something that suited him in Reykjavík was no simple task. He had never been robust enough to cope with the back-breaking labour on the family farm, but now he was reluctantly looking for the kind of work he knew his weak back would never let him do for long. Finally he landed a job at the docks, heavy work from morning to night. It was well paid, but he knew it couldn't last. He didn't have the strength to keep this up for long. He did his best to tough it out, but the pain in his back always returned and every time it did, it stayed longer.

Then there was the offer of a berth on a boat, where the pay was even higher; it was a chance to do better and put away some savings.

Life as a seaman was even worse that working on the docks, though. He forced himself to carry on for a couple of trips, fighting against the endless rolling, becoming grey and weak. That was where he met the devil in human form, a man who did his best to tempt him, and was successful in those efforts.

'Hard labour's for losers,' he had said.

Quick money was the best kind, and he had just the thing for Jónatan.

By this time his back was so worn out that he grasped any straw of opportunity.

Smuggling dope was easy enough the first time, and the second time.

Third time lucky?

He had been caught on the third trip, kept in a cell on remand for weeks on end and then shipped off to prison. That was when his parents found out he had given up on medicine months ago and had instead become a self-employed contractor in the practical chemical sector.

Prison wasn't too bad. He had a pretty large and comfortable cell. The worst part was having to move back up north once his term in prison was over, broken in mind and body.

Jónatan had finally made his way up the slope. He stopped to take in the mild summer weather, with none of the bitter winds that would lash the town during the long winter months. He stretched. The pain in his back was considerable, but it had often been worse.

He sneaked into his own house, that little detached shack that his brothers and sisters had clubbed together to buy for him. He saw the blessed stick hanging where he had left it on the radiator in the hall.

He lay down, exhausted. He had to rest for a while. He knew already that he would sleep badly that night. He couldn't stand the brightness of the light, the midnight sun that everyone else seemed to be so fond of. He had bought thick, heavy curtains, but somehow the light always seemed to find a chink it could get through.

In his mind the darkest nights were the brightest ones, and he knew all too well why that was the case.

24

It was getting on for evening by the time Ísrún arrived in Dalvík, although she needed the dashboard clock to tell her so. The placid June evening was bright and clear, the day even longer on the north coast than down south in Reykjavík. The landscape was rockier and more menacing here in the north, but, mercifully, she had left the poisoned air of the city behind her in the south-west of Iceland.

She pulled up outside the house where Elías's closest colleague lived. Svavar Sindrason. Forty-two years old. Lived alone.

Kormákur had called her when she was on the way north and asked if she had a scoop for the evening news. She replied, rather caustically, that she didn't yet, and that it would obviously take time. She took the opportunity to ask him to dig up anything he could about Svavar, saying she was going to meet him. She didn't mention her conversation with Ríkhardur Lindgren.

Kormákur had done well, calling her again a little later with a wealth of information about Svavar: his date of birth, family circumstances and much more. She grinned with delight at the thought that Kormákur was helping her, rather than her assisting him, as Ívar had wanted.

Despite Kormákur's efforts, however, there was little to be found about Svavar in the media or on the internet. His name had popped up on the sports pages of old newspapers occasionally, as he had played handball to a high level at one time. But otherwise he'd lived an uneventful life.

Handsome old houses were tightly packed along the length of the street. Ísrún rang the bell at Svavar's. These days she no longer needed to screw up her courage to disturb a stranger outside business hours. Journalism had helped her grow a hard shell. News took first, second and third place in her list of priorities. All the same, she took care to be professional, aware that she would sometimes inconvenience innocent people in the course of her work. Equally, she knew that if she were to start feeling too many twinges of conscience over this, then it would be time to look for a less brutal way of earning a living.

Someone finally came to the door: a man with a tired look about him.

'Good evening,' he offered in a low voice.

'I'd like to ask you a few questions about Elías,' she said, without introducing herself. 'I've come all the way from Reykjavík to talk to you,' she added, knowing that a little flattery wouldn't do any harm. 'I'd really appreciate five or ten minutes of your time.'

Svavar gave the impression of having been taken unawares.

'Come inside.'

She didn't hesitate.

'Aren't you on the news?' he mumbled a moment later, when she was standing in his living room. He stared at the scar on her face.

The room reminded her of an over-furnished summer house, with charmless, mis-matched furniture and a random collection of books in a bookcase, looking as if they had been left there by accident. The shelves were mostly empty, as were the walls. The only sign of life was the small television set in the corner – flickering images but the volume quite low. There was a difference between a house and home, she thought to herself.

Ísrún told him that, yes, she was on the news, and Svavar's gaze snapped back and forth.

'Where's … you know?' he muttered.

'Who?'

'Y'know – the camera guy.'

'I left him in Reykjavík. I'm doing some background research to start with, and then I'll do interviews if they're needed,' she said, taking care to leave out the magic words *off the record*. There would be nothing off the record about this interview; she was going to make use of every snippet of information she could get out of him, although not in any way that he might expect.

Svavar took a seat in the only chair, leaving Ísrún standing in the middle of the room, waiting for him to give some kind of response. After a few seconds of silence, she marched to the kitchen, fetched a stool, brought it back and sat down on it.

'I get it,' he said at last, the apathy clear in his voice. 'Background. I suppose you're doing this for the guy who was on the evening news just now.'

Hell. She should have chosen her words more carefully. She'd get nothing useful out of Svavar if he thought she was just Kormákur's assistant. That was something experience had taught her. People wanted to talk to someone with influence, and TV journalists have considerable influence.

'Not quite,' she laughed, with a tiny bite of conscience, although it was nothing she couldn't handle. 'He's assisting *me*. I couldn't bring him up here with me – someone has to stay behind in Reykjavík and put the bulletin together,' she said with a smile, and deftly redirected the conversation. 'You knew Elías well?'

'Yeah,' he muttered. 'Very well. Worked for him for years.'

'What sort of a guy was he to work for?'

He was silent for a moment. 'Pretty damn good.'

'A hard worker?'

'A really hard worker,' he replied.

'Were there many of you working for him?'

'Just the three of us, mostly.' He cleared his throat and wrung his hands. 'Me, Logi and Páll the Cop. They both live over in Siglufjörður. Elías was the man in charge.'

'And you had enough work?' she asked briskly, making an effort to avoid any long silences that might lead him to stray from the point.

'Yeah, more than enough. Plenty of night shifts. They want the tunnel finished. It's supposed to be opening this autumn.'

'So what happened to your friend?' she asked, coming to the point.

'Haven't a clue,' he replied, almost without thinking, and rubbed his bristled cheek.

'But I guess you'd like to know, wouldn't you?' Ísrún asked, leaning towards him.

'Of course I would,' he snapped. But his voice was so feeble, Ísrún was instantly convinced that he had his suspicions.

'Had he been in trouble with the law?'

'Why d'you ask?'

She could almost sense him sweating, even though there was, thankfully, some distance between them.

'Well...' she smiled, '... you know a journalist never reveals her source.'

'He was honest as ... as honest as the day is long, Elías was,' he said in a low mumble. 'And anyway, you shouldn't speak ill of the dead, should you?'

'Sometimes that's part of the job. So, no convictions ... nothing shady that you were aware of?'

'Hey, enough of this bullshit!' He raised his voice and looked ready to get to his feet, although he seemed to lack the energy to do so. 'I'm not being interrogated by the cops here. What the hell are you fishing for?'

'I think you know perfectly well. Did the police talk to you today?'

'Yeah, they were here today,' he muttered, apparently calm again. 'Told them the same as I'm telling you. I was at home all night. I didn't kill him.'

'That's not what I was asking,' she said cheerfully, satisfied with the nugget of information Svavar had let fall. The fact that he had been questioned by the police was something – a morsel of information she could pass on to Kormákur and Ívar while she carried on investigating the things she wanted to uncover.

'That'll do, won't it?' he said, a new decisiveness in his tone. It was as if he had finally summoned up the courage to behave as if he owned the place rather than looking like a visitor in his own home.

'That'll do nicely,' she said. 'But give me a call if there's anything you need to tell me.'

She wrote her phone number on a slip of paper and handed it to him. But as he took it from her, she regretted it. There was something about this character she didn't like and maybe giving him her number hadn't been a clever move.

Outside she stood by the red car and took out her phone. It was time to check in and buy herself some more time. If successful, her next stop would be an overnight stay in Akureyri.

Kormákur answered straight away. He was never without his phone.

'Hi. Up north, are you?'

She could hear traffic in the background behind him and guessed that he was on the way home after his shift.

'Yep, I'm in Dalvík, just been talking to Svavar. The police questioned him today,' she said.

'OK. That hasn't been mentioned,' Kormákur said, and she could hear the surprise in his voice.

Ísrún didn't doubt that Kormákur was right. It was uncanny how he managed to keep tabs on every media outlet, watching all of their competitors, reading newspapers and websites, and still doing a full day's work. Maybe that was what he had meant when he had once told her that he was married to his job.

'I hope it's of some use,' she said. 'I'll see if I can get something meatier for you tomorrow. How did it go today?'

'Not bad,' he said, although he didn't sound exactly overjoyed. 'It was at the top of the bulletin, even though there wasn't much new to report. We didn't have anything today that scooped the others, unfortunately.'

'That's something,' Ísrún said. 'I wish I could conjure up a scoop. Maybe tomorrow.'

'Your bit of information will also have to wait until tomorrow now. By the way, you were really lucky to leave town today. This damned ash cloud is still over the city like a blanket and it's got worse since you left. It's dark and gloomy in Reykjavík tonight.'

Ísrún could imagine the bright summer's night hidden behind a grey mist. It was like a vision of hell.

25

One year earlier

'It would have been good for you to know your grandmother,' said Katrín, the old lady sitting opposite me at the robust wooden table in her little house in Landeyjar.

That's true enough, I thought, but gave her a warm smile instead of saying anything. We were in her living room, if that's what you could call it. The house was so small that the living room and the kitchen were one. There was space to sleep upstairs, or so she said. The house was well heated; overheated, if anything. With every window shut securely the warmth was almost overwhelming.

Katrín was a distant relative of mine, and had been my grandmother Ísbjörg's closest friend; they had been close ever since they were children.

Now she was past eighty, about the same age that my grandmother would have been if cancer hadn't whisked her away at such a young age.

We sat by the window, looking out at the sea and towards the Westman Islands. The wind was blowing hard outside, even though it was the height of summer with the long days of sunshine stretching into light nights.

'There's always a wind blowing here,' the old lady had said as we sat down.

'I'll be damned if you two wouldn't have got on well together,' she said, after a moment's silence. 'You remind me of her.'

'Really?' I asked out of courtesy, having heard that said more than a few times before.

'Yes, you do remind me of her,' Katrín repeated.

It was bright outside, but she had lit a large candle in the middle of the table, giving the homely atmosphere of this little, old timber house, full of tales and old memories, a warm glow.

'We sat here often, at this table. That was back when we were both young and pretty, if you can imagine that! The house has been in the family for years, longer than the oldest of us can remember. That's further back than my memory goes, and God help me, my memory goes back a long way.'

'What did you do to keep yourselves occupied back then? Without television, I mean.'

'No television, no, you can be sure of that. I've never had much time for it, anyway. Don't have a set of my own,' she said and paused briefly. 'We used to talk. Or we'd play cards – sometimes just the two of us, sometimes more. There were a few of us in the district who were friends, to start with, at least. But our two best friends moved to Reykjavík and that left us here by ourselves.'

She sighed.

'What did you play?' I asked.

'Mostly marías. *You know the game?'*

'Never heard of it.'

'The younger generation doesn't sit down to play like we used to in the old days. Too much television,' she frowned.

I smiled to myself. I hadn't told the old lady that I worked in television.

'What sort of woman was my grandmother?'

'She was good,' Katrín said, without needing to think of what to say. 'You remind me of her,' she said yet again. 'She was as sharp as a knife, and warm-hearted. The kind of woman you could trust.'

I kept quiet, waiting to hear more. And after a little while, Katrín continued.

'She read a lot, but we all read a lot in those days. We girls would sit in a group and read together. Your grandmother wasn't much of a one for sitting alone in the dark. She was always a little afraid of it, of the night, of anywhere gloomy.' She smiled.

'Afraid of the dark? I guess it must have been easy to believe in ghosts – those dark nights and the long distances between the farms must have

brought all of the old legends to life,' I said, and realised that I had slipped into being the interviewer, trying to steer the conversation in the right direction.

'Believe in ghosts? Well, I can't answer for your grandmother. All I know is that she didn't like the dark. When there was the Hekla eruption in 1947, we were all scared – nobody had any idea how long it might last. But it terrified her. It stayed with her until she died.'

'Really?'

'Yes. She'd often talk about it. We were both about twenty when it happened. There was no warning and suddenly the air was filled with ash and the sky went black. That wretched ash destroyed all the pastures. It's unnerving when it gets dark as suddenly as that, when you least expect it. It was terrifying and it affected your grandmother very badly.' Katrín dropped her voice and leaned closer to me. 'She called it "the blackout". I remember that clearly. Afterwards, whenever she talked about the eruption, she'd use the same word. "Kata, do you remember the blackout?" she'd ask.'

I glanced out of the window.

A shudder went down my spine. It was as if my grandmother's world was coming to life, all her fears and the terrors that she had lived with had become real and immediate.

It was just as well it was bright daylight outside, in spite of that incessant wind, constantly howling, a reminder that Iceland, this isolated island in the northern part of the Atlantic Ocean, was always, in summer or winter, at the mercy of the weather.

'I was never as well read as your grandmother was,' Katrín continued. 'She had a word for everything. As far as I was concerned, darkness was just darkness. But these days, like her, I don't feel at ease in the dark anymore. I always feel that there's something sinister on the prowl – something that keeps itself hidden when it's light. But when the darkness falls … And that's when that word always comes to mind, "blackout".'

26

While Tómas went into the police station to pick up some papers, Ari Thór took the opportunity to put a classical piano CD into the stereo of the police four-by-four. He had no intention of listening to old-fashioned ballads from the herring years all the way to Akureyri.

Tómas seemed to have a burning passion for these old dance hall tunes, and Ari Thór didn't doubt that he'd taken his turn on the dance floor and had a few romantic assignations up in the valley at Hvanneyrarskál, above Siglufjörður, in his time. Maybe the music brought back memories of happier times. But now the car was filled with Chopin and Tómas didn't say anything when he returned. He was in a dark mood, as he so often was these days.

They would be in Akureyri in plenty of time. That suited Ari Thór perfectly, as he'd be able both to meet Natan and try to have a word with the poor man who had suffered at the former doctor's hands.

'I need to meet an old friend in Akureyri. Is that all right?' Ari Thór asked courteously.

'Of course. He can meet us over a burger.' Tómas said.

'I was going to go to his place, actually. I can get myself a sandwich on the way.'

Ari Thór saw that the bald inspector fought to keep his eyes on the road, as if he were barely able to contain his disappointment.

'Do what you like,' he snapped.

There was a chilly silence in the car until Tómas's phone rang. It was Hlynur, his voice echoing from the car's hands-free speakers.

'Where are you?' he asked without any preamble, his voice wavering and uncertain.

'We're on the way to Akureyri,' Tómas answered.

'Akureyri? What on earth for?'

'There's a conference about the murder case,' Tómas said, hesitating slightly.

There was a short pause. 'OK,' Hlynur said, and the call ended.

'That's very strange,' Tómas said, running a hand through the little hair remaining on his head. 'Extremely strange!'

'How come?'

'I told him that half an hour ago.'

Hlynur sat and stared at the phone.

He was alone at the station and he felt hot.

It was mild outside. In fact, it was unusually warm for early summer and he felt himself sweating in the close, still air.

With a flush of confusion, he realised that Tómas had told him where they were going before he and Ari Thór had set off. He shook his head as if to loosen his memory. He now clearly remembered looking up the computer when they had left, engulfed by a sudden sensation of discomfort … a strange feeling that he was completely alone in the world.

He felt as if Ari Thór and Tómas had vanished without a word to anyone. He had stood up and paced the entire station, calling their names, wondering where they could have got to. People don't just vanish, at least not in a little town like Siglufjörður.

He had snatched at the phone in a frenzy, and called Tómas to see if he could reach him. And was soon put straight. He cringed with embarrassment and more than a little concern.

What was happening?

How could he have forgotten?

He slumped onto the police station floor, deeply exhausted on every level; burying his face in his hands, thinking of Gauti.

He told himself that he had to pull himself together. What was in the past would have to stay there and couldn't be undone. He would have to make an effort, get a grip on himself and try to conquer the anguish that enveloped him.

Hlynur remembered that the event at the primary school was about to start. Tómas had made it plain that he was to attend and 'take some certificates' with him.

Maybe it would do him good.

He took a deep breath, stood up and straightened his uniform. Outside, the brightness of the sunshine took him by surprise after the gloom of the police station. And the fresh air went some way to helping him clear his head as he made an effort to pull himself together.

Before long he was standing at the front of a school hall crowded with youngsters.

As he looked out over the faces in front of him, he was transported back in time.

The faces of former classmates appeared from the crowd, and, yet again, a chilling discomfort swept through him. He caught glimpses of Gauti's pale eyes staring at him from the back of the hall. But when he looked harder, they would be gone, only to appear again somewhere else in the throng of schoolchildren in front of him.

He felt someone tap his shoulder and turned to see it was the headmaster. Hlynur realised he had frozen.

He did his best to get through the ordeal that the award ceremony quickly became without making a mess of everything, then hurried from the hall without a word; the ghosts of his past life had come all too palpably to life before his eyes. He headed straight for the nearest toilet and threw up.

27

Not in service read the illuminated signs on the buses that had driven past the waiting Ari Thór during his student years. After he had moved in with his grandmother following the deaths of his parents, Ari Thór had regularly travelled by bus. He had never had to do anything for himself while his parents had been alive, but once they were dead he had decided to make every possible effort to stand on his own two feet.

It was the contradiction in the bus signs that puzzled him. The bus wasn't servicing any route, but it shot past him, clearly on its way to somewhere.

He had been feeling just that way himself these past few months – constantly busy but without any obvious destination. Kristín had always been the lodestone that had kept him on track. Why the hell had he let her go?

'Have you seen Kristín? How is she?' he asked Natan as soon as they met. In some ways, he didn't want to hear the answers, but he couldn't stop himself from asking. They were in Natan's old Volvo, a vehicle that should by all rights have been on its last legs but which still seemed to be in working order.

Natan didn't answer right away.

'I meet up with her for a coffee now and then. She's doing all right,' he said, concentrating on the road, apparently reluctant to give anything away.

'Still single, then?' Ari Thór asked, hoping to sound uninterested but suspecting he hadn't managed it.

'Like I said, she's doing all right.'

'And what does that mean?' Ari Thór demanded, then immediately apologised for his abruptness.

'Since you clearly want to know, I'll tell you: she's been seeing some guy,' Natan said, just as abruptly. 'It's plain that you're still smitten, but you'll have to try and get over her. Don't you have enough on your plate right now, anyway, with dead people and whatnot?'

'It's my business what I get over, or not,' Ari Thór snapped back. Then he took a deep breath and made an effort to control his temper. 'I'm sorry,' he muttered again.

'Get over her, will you?' Natan said amiably. 'There are plenty more fish in the sea. Aren't there any pretty girls in Siglufjörður?'

'Yes, unfortunately.' His thoughts suddenly turned to Ugla. He regretted what had happened between them. Their relationship had destroyed what he had with Kristín. Even that smallest taste of forbidden fruit had been full of danger.

'So who is this guy?' Ari Thór asked. *Who's this bastard?* was what he had wanted to ask, but he restrained himself.

'I've never seen him, but she speaks highly of him. She met him playing golf. He's older and his wife died. I've never figured out what women see in older men. I almost take it personally when I see a woman my age on some old guy's arm.'

Natan pulled the car into the side of the road.

'We're here.'

Natan waited in the car while Ari Thór knocked at the widower's door. He lived in what had once been a farmhouse on the outskirts of the town, an old-fashioned, high-roofed wooden building clad in rusting steel sheeting, the garden around it unkempt and neglected, full of weeds and overgrown grasses. It must have been a prosperous farm in its day, but that wasn't the case any longer. There wasn't even a dog waiting patiently to run a check on unexpected guests.

When the old man opened the door Ari Thór quickly explained

the reason for his visit and realised straightaway that the man, who seemed to be close to eighty, had no objection to airing his strong and unfavourable opinions on the doctor.

They sat at one end of the building in the warmth of the evening sun, on an old blue bench that was as rusty as the house. The abundant long grass couldn't have been cut for a long time. In fact, the house, the bench and the land around them all seemed to have been treated badly by the passing years, as had the old man himself. His gaze remained on the lush, waving grass the whole time they talked. His eyes never once met Ari Thór's.

'You think the murderer may have made a mistake? He really meant to send that evil doctor off to the next world?' he asked Ari Thór, his voice faint.

'It could be. We aren't sure of anything yet,' Ari Thór replied.

'What he did can never be forgiven,' the old man said firmly. 'That's my opinion as a God-fearing man. He was drunk at work, and that is shameful. I miss her every single day, especially on a sunny day like today. She was my sunshine,' he said slowly. Clearly he was in no hurry to get rid of Ari Thór.

'Have you had any contact with … Ríkhardur, after everything that happened?'

'No, and I wouldn't want to,' the old man replied. 'We were awarded some damages,' he added with a sigh. 'But what am I supposed to do with compensation at my age?'

Ari Thór could see no way that this gentle man would plot murder, least of all such a brutal killing.

'Do you know if he was ever threatened?'

'No, my friend. I have no idea. I'm not saying I haven't thought about doing it myself. Your thoughts wander in all kinds of directions, you know? – take you to places you'd think you'd regret going. But I don't regret thinking like that, not at all,' he said and lapsed into thoughtful silence.

Ari Thór waited patiently for him to speak again.

'She deserved better. Such a warm-hearted person, thoughtful and kind, much cleverer than I am. She was the philosopher in this house. She had worked out the purpose of life, or so she thought. Her idea was that there was no simple answer. Every one of us needs to find their own purpose in life, what makes us happy. That's just as well, don't you think? If there was just one aim for each of God's children then we'd all be doing the same thing. That would be a dull sort of world, wouldn't it?'

He stared into the grass, seeming to welcome this opportunity to talk about his late wife.

'I'm afraid I have to be on my way,' Ari Thór said at last, standing up. He knew only too well what – or rather, who – brought him happiness in life. But he had made a mess of that opportunity to experience joy. Yet he couldn't get Kristín out of his mind. It had long been his hope that they would be together again, but today that seemed to be even further out of his reach than ever. He had lost his chance.

'Thanks for the talk,' he said.

'Thanks for coming. It's a shame that the victim wasn't Ríkhardur. That would have been some very welcome news.'

28

Ari Thór sat through the meeting in Akureyri in a daze. He tried to listen, but his thoughts remained firmly on Kristín the whole time. There was no tea on offer, so he drank the thin coffee and nibbled at the biscuits.

Helga, a young detective on the Akureyri force, explained that Elías had travelled to Nepal just a few days before his murder, with a stopover at Kastrup airport in Copenhagen. Previously, they had believed he had spent several days in Denmark. There was as yet no explanation for the Nepal trip.

The atmosphere in the incident room was heavy. The murder had attracted considerable attention and the press had been following it closely.

Still stunned by the news that there was a new man in Kristín's life, Ari Thór could hardly remember what the old man at the farmhouse had told him. But it was clear that he was no killer. Ari Thór was on the point of abandoning his theory that there was an angle that could involve Ríkhardur Lindgren, at least for the moment.

He made his best effort to follow the rest of the meeting and control the jealousy he felt rising inside him; but it was an emotion that he had not always been able to keep in check.

He thought back to the first time it had got him in trouble. How old had he been? Seventeen? Eighteen? He had started going out with a girl from another school. He thought he was in love, but the relationship lasted only three weeks, coming to a tumultuous end at a party.

The girl had gone without him, so Ari Thór had decided to

surprise her. He started the evening at a different party, with his classmates, drank too much punch and then took a taxi to meet his girlfriend at her party. He remembered the house – a smart villa in Hafnarfjörður, full of weighty, old-fashioned furniture that gave the place a gloomy, dark feel, although his memory may have been coloured by what happened next.

He couldn't see her right away and searched for her in the living room and the kitchen. He asked for her by name and someone jerked a thumb towards the passage. 'Down that way somewhere.' He peered into one room after another and in the last one he found her, enveloped in someone else's arms.

The emotion that gripped him was so strong, so unnervingly powerful, that he tried to avoid recalling it. But now, thinking about Kristín with this mysterious man, he felt much the same overwhelming urge to use his fists – and this time he was as sober as a judge.

The girl had looked up as he entered the room, had untangled herself from the boy's arms and looked at Ari Thór. She had said nothing, but the expression on her face was somewhere between 'sorry' and 'that's life'.

Ari Thór had lost control, there was no other way to describe it. He hurled himself at the boy and punched him. More by luck than judgement, the punch landed so strongly the boy fell sprawling back and hit his head on the headboard of the bed. Blood seeped from the cut. Ari Thór got out quickly, before the boy could get his bearings.

He never spoke to the girl again. What really surprised him, though, was that the boy didn't press charges. Maybe he had a guilty conscience? You don't steal another guy's girlfriend, or covet your neighbour's wife. Everyone knew that. It was one of the Ten Commandments, wasn't it?

29

It was late in the evening and Ísrún wasn't feeling at her best. True, she was exhausted after the long drive from Reykjavík, but there was something else. She couldn't blame the cheap guesthouse, which was fine for what it was: a tidy bed, a wardrobe and a chest of drawers that contained nothing more than a Bible.

Perhaps it was the memories that snapped at her heels now that she was back in Akureyri. She was disappointed in herself – she had thought she would be stronger than this. She had chosen a guesthouse even though she could undoubtedly have stayed for nothing with old friends. But she maintained nothing more than occasional contact with those friends in Akureyri since she had moved back south. And she'd left at very short notice, giving only weak excuses for leaving and without a single word to anyone about the real reasons for her hasty departure. Those facts she kept strictly to herself.

She drew the curtains shut and lay down to sleep. It wasn't late, but she wanted to make an early start in the morning, beginning with a visit to Elías's apartment, which, it turned out, was actually owned by his former wife. Then she would move on to Siglufjörður, a place she had never visited.

She was already asleep when her phone rang. A good news journalist never switches the phone off; news comes first. But she swore as she reached for it, telling herself that sometimes it would be worth breaking journalism's life rules to get a decent night's sleep.

Kormákur was on the line. He came straight to the point.

'You're in Akureyri?'

She rubbed her eyes and mumbled something into the phone that could be interpreted as a yes.

'Were you asleep? Get yourself up,' he chattered excitedly. 'There's a meeting at the County Sheriff's office about the murder case.'

'They're holding a press conference?' she asked, still dazed with sleep.

'No, nothing like that. Nobody knows about it except us – I have a contact. Get yourself down there.'

Ísrún sat on the bed, amazed, not just at the news that Kormákur had shared with her, but that he had such a reliable source in Akureyri. It was unbelievable what the man could come up with.

'I'm on my way,' she said. 'Do I get a cameraman?'

'He's on his way too. We'll cover his call-out fee.'

'And can I take him to Siglufjörður in the morning?'

'You seriously expect Ívar to agree to that?'

There was no mistaking the disbelief in Kormákur's voice. He was right, she couldn't imagine that.

She forced herself to her feet, although ever fibre in her body fought against being dragged out of bed. She longed to pull the covers up over her head and close her eyes, but instinct told her that news had to come first and a lead had to be followed up, even if it was likely to take her nowhere.

The cameraman, who doubled as the local stringer, was waiting for her outside the County Sheriff's office.

'Nobody's come out yet,' he said.

They waited for half an hour for something to happen. A slight night-time chill had descended on the town. Ísrún shivered. But, looking up into the sky she found it bright and cloudless. No trace of ash here. She laughed grimly to herself, thinking how shrouded in mystery and shadows this case seemed to be. She glanced at the glass doors of the building. Did everyone inside feel like they were groping through the darkness too?

Finally they saw some movement. People were coming out.

The meeting must be over. The first out was a middle-aged man in uniform who Ísrún didn't recognise. He was somewhere over fifty, and almost bald. Behind him followed another officer – younger, probably not yet thirty, taller and well built.

She walked towards them and was about to drop her first question when she saw a face familiar from news bulletins: Helga, one of the senior detectives in the Akureyri CID.

'So the newshounds are already on the trail,' said Helga with an amiable smile. 'There's no information right now. There might be a statement later tonight,' she added, although her expression told another story. Ísrún knew that the camera was running and stuck to her guns.

'What's the status of the investigation?'

'No new developments,' Helga said.

'Have you questioned Svavar Sindrason in connection with this case?'

The question clearly took Helga by surprise.

'We have interviewed a great many people as part of this investigation. We don't have a suspect at present,' she said crisply.

'Does this investigation have any connection to Ríkhardur Lindgren?'

'Definitely not,' Helga replied.

Ísrún was about to ask about Elías's apartment in Akureyri when Helga cut her off.

'No more questions for the moment,' she said.

Ísrún was too tired to pursue the point.

30

A summer night in Siglufjörður.

Jónatan turned his TV off and peered out of his window. There were few people about. The cruise ship had presumably departed, taking its tourists with it.

On the news they had said that in Reykjavík it was dark and the air choking, the city covered by the ash cloud. There was no evidence of it here. Not yet anyway. The little town was bathed in a luminous glow. But for how long?

He wasn't happy with the changes to the town: new buildings, coffee shops and restaurants, a new tunnel. No more peace and quiet. That lousy tunnel was nothing but a curse. The tranquillity and the isolation of the place would soon vanish.

The policeman's visit was troubling him.

Jónatan had done his best to avoid thinking about the past, his parents and the 'good' old days.

And the violence. Violence in its clearest and most basic form.

It had been inflicted on him as much as on the other boys, even though he had been a few years older than them.

It was difficult to put a finger on where it had come from, that pure, unmitigated violence. An addiction to power, maybe?

He was sure that power had something to do with.

Had it been an urge to demonstrate just who wielded it?

Despite having been a victim rather than a 'wrong-doer', he still felt that he bore a certain responsibility; especially later, when he had remained quiet. If he had come forward maybe he could have helped some of the unfortunate children, if not himself.

He had thought, or hoped, that the whole thing had been long forgotten.

Now he had the feeling that wasn't the case.

Poor Elías. He had been one of the victims.

Jónatan hoped that those events – events that should have stayed buried deep in the past – hadn't led to his death.

That would be a heavy cross to bear.

INTERLUDE: EARLIER THAT SUMMER

A little boy stood by the roadside. He was dressed in some sort of school uniform, a white shirt and grey trousers, a colourful belt and a striped tie. On his wrist was a digital watch and there was a schoolbag at his side. His hands were clasped tightly together, held up to cover his mouth and nose. Maybe his hands were held this way to protect him from the dust and fumes that were everywhere. Maybe he was just thinking. Maybe he was praying.

Everything around him was grey. Sand and stones surrounded the houses, and there was some scrub grass by the roadside. But even this wasn't as green as Elías was used to seeing in Iceland; its green was diluted by a heavy, dusty grey.

Elías sat in the back of a rundown taxi, stopped in a traffic jam. He stared out of the window and waited. He looked straight into the boy's eyes, before he looked away. Then the taxi moved on a short way before coming to a halt again, and the little boy by the side of the road was out of Elías's sight. There had been an aura of innocence about him, sending Elías's thoughts back decades, to a time when his innocence hadn't yet been stolen away by the monster in the farmhouse.

There were two brick buildings behind him, one of them a supermarket of some description, its window display decked with canned food and on the wall a brightly coloured advertisement for soap. Sacks and boxes were stacked outside the shop, and an older woman waited in the doorway for customers. The other brick-built place sold paint. An old motorbike was parked outside.

Elías wondered, and not for the first time, if this trip was worth it. He was in a foreign country, commissioned to do a strange job for some rather dubious characters.

He had never been outside Europe before. Normally a week or two drinking beer on a coast somewhere was enough travel for him. That's the way it ought to be, a break from the endless daily grind back home in Iceland.

But he was aware that the men with whom he was involved could make him rich. He had been given the opportunity to prove himself. First, there would be this job and, if it went well, they'd promised it would be followed by something bigger. But he knew he had to be careful not to let himself be taken for a ride. He had to have eyes in the back of his head.

He had told Svavar about his new friends and mentioned that he was thinking about bringing him into the business. He was even thinking about taking another person into his confidence, cut him into this operation. There was room for one more if there were other jobs like this.

He could hardly wait to get away from that lousy rented apartment in Siglufjörður. He was going to move as soon as the tunnel was finished, but he'd be sure not to let the charity business go. That had proved to be a brilliant outlet for laundering dirty money.

The taxi inched forwards. There was heavy traffic in both directions. Elías had seen a few clapped-out buses packed with people, so full that some passengers had taken the drastic step of hanging on to the outside rather than be left behind.

The sweltering heat was oppressive and there didn't seem to be any way of opening the taxi's rear windows.

He had spent the first night of his trip in Kathmandu, followed by another flight the next morning. He had never been particularly afraid of flying, but the flight from the capital in the rattling light aircraft had unsettled him. Now he was at his destination, a small rural town.

He had been in the taxi for half an hour. The taxi driver didn't spare the horn and now and again he'd look over his shoulder at Elías and shrug as if to say there was nothing else he could do.

Maybe it was as well that Elías couldn't open the taxi's windows. The air outside had to be stuffy in this heavy traffic. He understood from the driver that there were roadworks somewhere up ahead and a road had been closed, the likely explanation for the delay.

Was travelling to the far side of the world on behalf of some men he hardly knew too dangerous? All this to collect some woman and bring her to Europe?

'It's a fantastic scheme. You won't regret it,' one of the men, a go-between who was organising the woman's visa, had told him in English.

He had hinted that Elías wouldn't be forced to do many more such trips. There was something bigger waiting for him. Then other people would have to do all this tiresome travelling.

This trip was a test and he had every intention of passing with flying colours. He just had to try not to let the effects of the long journey fray his nerves.

They drove slowly past a lively outdoor market in the shadow of a red-brick block, fronted by little handcarts laden with garishly coloured fruit. There was business going on here. Sellers chatted to customers, apparently unaffected by the constant hum of traffic.

The tangle of traffic finally seemed to be clearing a little and the driver pushed the taxi up a gear. In the distance Elías could see more brick buildings, mighty trees and, in between, the occasional hoarding with English adverts for European beer.

Elías could have done with an ice-cold one right now.

The houses grew sparser, the few they saw now looking close to collapse.

Maybe he'd be doing this woman a favour, taking her away from the poverty he could see all around him. He didn't know whether she knew what was waiting for her in Europe. Not that he cared one way or the other. Some woman he knew nothing about from the other side of the world wasn't his problem. He was ready to sacrifice her for his own ends. More than ready in fact; he was delighted to do it.

Elías stood outside the cluster of houses with the girl and her family. He had been invited into their apartment but had declined. He had neither the interest nor the time.

He was impatient to get back to the airport, back to Kathmandu and from there home to Iceland, as soon as possible.

The girl was a beauty. There was no doubt about it. His new employers would be pleased with him once he had delivered the girl to her destination in Iceland.

Would the family never finish saying their farewells? He noticed a woman who had to be the young girl's mother, her eyes brimming with tears.

For crying out loud. That's enough, surely?

His mind wandered while he waited. It occurred to him that they would probably never see her again, but he didn't allow himself to contemplate, let alone feel, any emotion. The world is a hard place; he knew that himself from bitter experience.

The girl had said farewell to everyone but her mother.

And she's taking her time over it…

She turned to her mother, tears streaming down her cheeks, and was about to embrace her. Elías sighed. He put a hand on her shoulder, as courteously as he could, and told her they would miss the flight.

The girl was startled, tearful. But she nodded and followed him to the taxi.

He hadn't exactly been truthful. They had plenty of time, but he hadn't the patience to watch one more wailing farewell.

⌖

She stood under a fan at the little domestic airport, wearing her best blouse, the pale pink one. She watched the strange Icelander who had come all this way to collect her. He marched back and forth around the terminal building, without any obvious destination. She had a little sympathy for him. It couldn't be easy for a foreigner to work out how to find the plane that would take them to Kathmandu. She had stood at the window and watched the aircraft landing and taking off, one after another. This would be her first time in an airplane. Flying was expensive, something her family had never been able to afford. Not that they had anywhere to go.

She could hardly believe that this opportunity had presented itself, the chance to go and live in Iceland. She was sure that it would be freezing cold so far north, but the pay was good, and she was excited about the prospect of travelling to Europe. Nevertheless she couldn't quiet her nerves. She was already missing her family. They were the real reason she was doing this: to ensure their future.

The job description had been clear: work in a large hotel. That sounded fine to her, as did the offer of free board and lodging, which would allow her to save all of her earnings. It was just as well that she spoke some English. That was how they had found her – on a website where she had registered to find work. The Icelander assured her that she wouldn't need to worry too much about language skills in her new job.

The little aircraft was packed with people and Elías felt another surge of disquiet. He hoped he'd get out of this damned place in one piece. At least it was a relief to get away from the countryside and back to the city.

In the rural area where the young girl lived he had found his thoughts taken back to the farm in Skagafjörður, where his own childhood had been made a perfect hell.

He had been six years old and excited at the prospect of spending a summer away from the city, as so many children did every summer, their parents' keen to let them see the Icelandic countryside, which they had left behind them when they moved to the city in search of work or education.

But the rural dream had rapidly become a nightmare.

To begin with, the abuse had been verbal. There was nothing casual or playful about it; it had been pure and simple malice.

And it didn't stop there, instead getting steadily harsher. Soon he began to suspect that everything that his parents sent to him during the summer was being stolen. Then blows took over from words.

The beatings weren't heavy. Care was taken to leave no marks. But even that wasn't the worst of it. That was something he couldn't speak of. It was impossible to describe in words the simple enormity of the violence perpetrated against him. The boys didn't even talk about it among themselves, although he was sure that they had all been forced to endure the same treatment; even Jónatan, the old couple's youngest son, who was quite a few years older than Elías. He had probably suffered the most – and he didn't get to go back south in the autumn.

Elías returned to school a shell of himself after that first summer. But he took care to not let anything show. The threats had been barely disguised – heavy hints that 'accidents' might befall his parents unless he promised two things: first, not to whisper a word of what had happened that summer; and second, to return the following summer.

'We can't do without our summer kids here to help out with the heavy work,' he was told in no uncertain terms, knowing also that the parents paid a hefty sum for sending their kids there.

Elías had no intention of discussing the summer's events. He was deeply ashamed of what had happened, certain that he was somehow to blame. He had never breathed a word of it, managing to come to terms with it in solitude, although even now he was not sure quite how he had achieved this.

All winter long he had dreaded the coming of summer, sleeping badly and frequently waking in the night, bathed in sweat, shivering and terrified. His parents didn't understand what was troubling their much-loved son, but he never broke his promise, never mentioned a thing. As spring approached and the winter darkness gave way to light, each day the sun reaching a higher point in the sky, his parents told him that they had made arrangements for the summer and he'd be going back to the same farm as before.

'You're looking forward to it, aren't you, Elías?'

Looking forward to it? Nothing could be further from what he was really feeling. The experience had deadened him, and he was unable now to look forward to anything – not summer or winter, not even Christmas or his birthday. The fear overwhelmed everything, its tentacles taking hold of him.

He managed to survive a second summer at that place, but wasn't sure afterwards how he had managed to get through the whole stay. The previous summer's group of boys had changed, with two new lads making their appearance. Elías longed to warn them, tell them to run, to go home before it was too late. But his courage failed him. The abuse began again, just it had before, although now the boys were punished for the slightest infringement and it became impossible to behave in a way that conformed to a set of rules that could only have been created by a sick mind.

It was as if Elías had lost all zest for life that summer, as if something inside him had died. The following summer he was taken ill just as he was due to travel north to the farm. He had been ill for days on end, and became weak and pale. The doctor was at a loss to diagnose precisely what was wrong with him and there never was any satisfactory explanation.

Elías's condition improved as the summer advanced, and in the end it was felt that it was too late to send him away. Still perplexed, the doctor suggested that he stay in town, where his condition could be monitored.

Decades passed before he set foot in Skagafjörður again. When he finally had reason to travel to that part of the country, it was as if everything that had taken place there had been part of some different life, as if it had all happened to some other boy. The sole emotion he felt was hatred, a need for vengeance. But it was difficult to seek revenge on someone who was now six feet under.

His need for retribution took other forms instead.

They had to spend a night in Kathmandu, so they went straight from the airport to the hotel. Elías had booked a small room for her and a suite for himself – having found that, in spite of the Icelandic króna's fall from grace, his money still had plenty of purchasing power in this part of the world. The hotel wasn't short on luxury, with opulent fittings and furnishings, and a suitably cordial welcome from the staff. He felt comfortable there. The girl didn't say much; she seemed grateful and remained courteous. He told her they could have dinner together. There was no need for him to do so, but he couldn't be bothered to eat alone. It certainly helped that she was young, not yet twenty, and outstandingly pretty.

He lay down on the bed and closed his eyes for a while, and then took a walk through the centre of the city. The density of the crowds was overwhelming, with noise and bustle everywhere in the narrow streets. Colourful signs advertised everything from restaurants to laundries to internet service providers and phone companies.

His mind wandered back to Iceland – to Skagafjörður, and to Siglufjörður.

He hadn't hesitated when the tunnel job had been offered, even though it meant living in Siglufjörður. He had known he'd do well for himself there, and he needed to get some serious money together so he'd be able to get off the island for good. He had lived in Akureyri at one time, and the proximity to Skagafjörður hadn't troubled him at all.

It wasn't until a few months after he had come to Siglufjörður that he discovered that Jónatan was living in the town. The son of the farmer and his wife, he was the only member of the family at the farm who had not moved away from the north of Iceland. He saw him about the town several times, but never spoke to him. They had nothing to say to each other, no reason to share the misery of a past that was now so far away. Jónatan didn't look well, a limping old man long before his time, his face thin and his back bent.

Elías felt so much better for seeing the other man's clear ill-health. Maybe he had come out of those summers in the country relatively unscathed after all.

It wasn't easy for Elías to cope with the hotel restaurant's low table and he sat in awkward discomfort with his legs crossed. The girl sat opposite him, seeming more at ease. He ordered the six dishes the waiter recommended. The menu was in English, but Elías still found himself confused by exactly which of these unusual dishes was which course – a soup, a rice dish, spiced chicken, a pudding and something else that he wasn't able to identify were all brought to the table at once.

They didn't speak during the meal. It seemed that she didn't dare say anything, and he wasn't interested enough to ask her anything about herself. He was just there to bring her to Iceland, where she would undoubtedly find out the stark truth of what was awaiting her.

What he really wanted to do was take her up to his suite and get to know her in his own way, but he didn't want to take any risks. It had been made distinctly clear to him that he must not touch her, just deliver her to Iceland. He'd get part of the payment on arrival at the airport and after that he'd have to hide the girl for a few days. Then they would take over. After that there would be more lucrative work for him.

Not bad.

He looked across the table at her and smiled. The temptation was hard to withstand.

She smiled back at him, her eyes innocent and full of anticipation.

She gazed out of the window of the little hotel room that she found so delightfully spacious. It was getting dark outside, with the lights switched on in the hotel grounds. She could see the outlines of the striped hotel chairs by the swimming pool and the magnificent trees.

A new chapter in her life was about to begin.

This would be an opportunity to make her contribution to the family and she felt profoundly grateful to her new employers who had gone so far as to send someone all the way from Iceland to bring her to her new job.

She lay down on the wonderfully comfortable bed, closed her eyes and was soon asleep.

PART II: DAY 2

1

She woke up in darkness. A faint gleam of light made its way in through a crack that also brought her air, but there seemed to be little difference between day and night. She had no idea how long she had been asleep this time.

It was a long time since she had seen the man and she was past trying to understand what was happening. Had he brought her to Iceland to let her die, locked away in here?

Why would anyone do such a thing?

And he had seemed to be such a good man.

She had been delighted when the aircraft finally landed in Iceland after the long journey. The landscape that greeted her was unlike anything she had ever seen before. They landed at midnight, but it was still strangely bright. She had the feeling that this strange country would be a good place for her.

At the airport the man had had a short conversation with another man, who had handed him a sports bag. There was something about the way they approached each other that felt wrong to her; it was as if they were awkward around each other. However, she was so optimistic and excited that she didn't feel suspicious at all, she had no reason to believe that there was anything to worry about.

The trip in the car from the airport took several hours. She expected it to end at the hotel, where she would be put straight to work. But when they finally stopped, the building they were in front of didn't look at all like a hotel to her.

To her complete surprise the man grabbed her, pushed her through a door and locked her in, enveloping her in darkness. She tried to call him, to ask what was happening, to beg for mercy. But there was no response.

It was then that she finally understood that she had not been brought to Iceland to work in a hotel.

Later he returned with food and water. She tried to attack him, to break out, but they both knew that she was no match for a man so much bigger and stronger than she was.

So she had no choice but to wait. She was ravenous when he finally appeared again with another portion of food. Again she tried to break out and get past him into the Icelandic daylight beyond. But by now she was even weaker with hunger. He pushed her back easily.

'Stop it,' he ordered in English. 'Or no food.'

She wondered now if he had meant it. Was he punishing her for resisting? How long was it since he had been here? A day? Two days? She had finished the food and water long ago.

It was a cramped space – barely large enough for her to stand upright and a couple of steps from one end to the other. There were no windows and she sat in darkness with nothing more than a glimmer of light making its way in through the gap where the door did not quite meet the floor. Worst of all was there was no toilet; the smell of her waste was overpowering.

She closed her eyes, and sat with her head in her hands, waiting, overwhelmed with fatigue. Cramped by the long confinement, there were shooting pains in her legs, and she was incredibly thirsty. There wasn't a drop left in the bottle; she had tried to suck the last vestige of water from it more than once. She was surprised that she was no longer hungry. It was as if the thirst was all-consuming.

She was sure now that if he didn't return, nobody would come to her rescue. Nobody would come looking for her. She would die here, in a place she didn't know, in a distant land.

Her thoughts were of home. She knew that her family would not expect to hear from her for some time. She had promised to call or write when she could. It would be a week or more before they would start to worry about her, maybe several weeks, and by that time she would be long dead.

She had no idea how long she could survive without food or water. That was something that had not been taught at school. But she could feel her strength ebbing away with every minute that passed.

To begin with she had been gripped by the terror of being locked away, being someone else's prisoner, unable to escape, and without fresh air or sunlight. The feeling was oppressive. For a while she struggled to breathe, almost expecting to faint with fear. But gradually she had been able to steady her breathing by trying to think of something beautiful, directing her thoughts to a fine summer's day at her parents' home.

Then she started to call for help, shouting as loudly as she could. The ensuing silence was deafening. It seemed that there was nobody to hear her. She rested her voice for a while, trying to conserve her strength, and then started again. By the time she had managed to sleep, her voice was so hoarse that it had almost gone.

Now she had given up shouting. Her voice was spent. Her tongue so dry she could barely mouth a word.

But she was determined to keep trying, to do her best to stay awake even though she longed to sleep again. She had a crystalline vision of what would happen if she let herself sink into slumber. And there was no way she was going to allow that.

2

In Akureyri, Ísrún was awake early, looking at a dilapidated old house.

There wasn't much to see. It was some distance from its closest neighbour and it looked as if a business of some kind had been run on the ground floor – a shop or a workshop, perhaps, but the big windows had now been boarded over. Elías's apartment had to be on the floor above. There was no sign of life; the curtains were drawn across every window.

She felt a chill. This was a house she wouldn't want to live in; the whole place had a ghostly feel to it.

It occurred to her that she should take a walk around the house, look more closely and see if she could get inside. There could hardly be repercussions, considering the owner was dead. He wouldn't be able to complain, anyway. But the prospect of poking around that man's apartment was too uncomfortable, even if she did find something useful to the story. She pondered her options a moment and decided against entering.

Back in the car she didn't even look over her shoulder as she put her foot down and headed for Siglufjörður.

⌖

Svavar had slept badly. All of a sudden he had found himself at the centre of attention, with visits from the police and that television woman. He reckoned he'd come out of both without having said too much, though. He hadn't betrayed Elías or tripped over his own feet.

During the night, however, he began to be assailed by doubts. How long would he be able to keep this up?

He had managed to get off to sleep a few times, but had woken each time sweating with anxiety, thinking about *her*. The woman he had never seen. The woman from another country, from the other side of the world.

All he knew was that she was young and pretty. That was how Elías had described her, although those weren't the words he had used.

Now though, since the moment he had heard of Elías's death, Svavar had been unable to think of little else *except* her.

He thought of her all day, and thought of her at night when sleep refused to come to him. And when he did sleep, he dreamed of her.

Time must be running out.

Maybe he was already too late?

To begin with he tried to convince himself that she was not his concern. He couldn't be responsible for every person in the world.

People die all the time.

What difference does it make if one unknown woman dies today?

He sensed the emptiness of this argument as soon as he put it to himself. Elías wouldn't have let it worry him, but Svavar wasn't Elías. They were very different, even though they had been friends for so long. Svavar was well aware of Elías's darker side. Sometimes he struggled to comprehend just how ruthless Elías could be.

Svavar would have been the first to admit that he was no angel himself. Neither of them had been known for sticking to the letter of the law. Brothers in arms, they had been through thick and thin together.

So when Elías had been given this assignment, it was natural that he sought Svavar's help, telling him that he was in contact with people with a wide network of activities that stretched all around the world and back to Iceland. Their business included trafficking and prostitution, and there was a possibility of bringing women from Asia to mainland Europe via Iceland. They had established contacts with individuals in Asia and were preparing to transport young women who had expressed an interest in seeking work in Europe. Once they had arrived, the grim reality of what they had signed up for would become evident. Or that's how Elías had worded it, with a grin on his face.

'But that's not my problem,' he had added. 'This looks like it's going to be a profitable business, and I need someone I can trust to come in on it with me, someone who can do a few trips to bring them here and keep them somewhere quiet until we move them on. Are you up for it?'

Svavar had nodded his head and thought of the pied-à-terre he dreamed of owning somewhere in southern Europe, maybe in Italy or Portugal, somewhere a long way south. There was nothing he could do to prevent human trafficking – it went on everywhere – so why not make a little money out of it?

Now, thinking back on it, he wasn't as convinced as he had been.

Elías's first assignment had been to fly to Nepal, fetch some young girl and bring her back. Then someone else would take over from there. It had been an easy, straightforward job, he said. Svavar half expected to be sent on the next trip himself, and he even looked forward to the opportunity of visiting a distant part of the world.

But those dreams had now turned into a nightmare. He felt physically sick when he thought of Elías's plans. He thanked God he hadn't had to travel himself to fetch this unfortunate woman, who can't have been expecting that anything so horrible would happen to her.

'I need to hide her for a few days,' Elías had said. 'Don't worry, I'm not going to keep her in your cellar,' he added when he saw Svavar's expression.

Svavar got out of bed and looked out of the window.

It was a beautiful day in Dalvík, a place he still regarded as a temporary home until he could realise his dream and migrate southwards, like the birds in autumn. Once he had moved, he was certain that he'd never return. Maybe he'd already left it too late, though, missed the bus? Maybe he ought to be on his way as soon as he could; sell the house and use the savings he had put by, get hold of some foreign currency and find himself work somewhere warmer. It was not quite the lifestyle he had dreamed of, but it was a step in the right direction. At any rate, he'd be free of the miserable daily grind in Iceland, and even though he wouldn't be able to retire right away, he'd be somewhere warmer and brighter.

The sky outside was a clear blue. He missed his friend; but at the same time he was relieved to be free of him. It was as if a burden had been lifted from his shoulders. In a flash of insight he saw more clearly than ever the lines between right and wrong. His conscience was making its presence felt in the most uncomfortable way.

Thinking of the girl was painful.

He wanted to save her, but he also had no desire to go to prison.

Hell and damnation.

Should he save the woman's life and clean up the mess his friend had left behind; or stop thinking about it and leave her to die?

How many more sleepless nights would he be able to endure?

Svavar didn't know much about the girl other than that Elías hadn't told his foreign collaborators exactly where he was keeping her hidden. Elías had never been a man who found it easy to trust others, and he wanted to be sure of his final payment. But Elías had been murdered more than twenty-four hours ago. God only knew when the girl had last had anything to eat.

Wracked with doubt, Svavar did his best to convince himself that she was no concern of his.

They didn't know each other. They were two different people; one would die and one would live.

Was this part of what Elías had described as the 'grim reality'? Things like this could happen to people like her.

The worst part was, he had no idea where the girl was.

On the other hand maybe it was just as well. Maybe it was best, after all, to let things take their course.

3

Ísrún had driven out along the coast, taking the Eyjafjörður road past farms where the summer's haymaking was in full swing and the air was full of the scent of newly mown hay being gathered for the winter. She drove through the quiet fishing village of Ólafsfjörður, which clung to the shore of the bay, the houses clustered around the harbour. From there she took the Low Heath route, a poorly made gravel road that called for constant vigilance. She drove slowly to spare her old car the worst of the potholes, expecting it to give up the ghost at any moment. The mountains here were close, looming high over the road. There was still no shortage of snow to be seen. She wanted to stop by the side of the road, walk the short distance to where a sheet of snow, brilliant white in the sunshine, covered the side of a mountain, and lie in it to rest her tired bones. These days it was so difficult to find time to relax. And yet a pressurised trip like this was still better than listening to Ívar's constant droning in the newsroom.

She also felt her revenge was long overdue. There was no way around it – she was fascinated by the case and what had actually happened to Elías.

The driving didn't improve much when she finally reached the end of the mountain track and the Siglufjörður road took over. Although this was a surfaced road, it was still too dangerous for Ísrún's liking. She didn't feel completely safe until she had finally made it through the Strákar tunnel and the fjord beyond opened up in front of her, the town itself welcoming her into its embrace.

Her intention was to use the day to talk to Elías's workmates, Logi and Páll, and to visit the woman who, according to the national registry, had shared her house with him. Ísrún slowed down as she tried to get her bearings, and, looking at a street sign, realised that she was on Hvanneyrarbraut, the street where Elías had lived.

It didn't take long to find his place, a striking detached house down by the water. This was just the kind of house Ísrún could imagine living in if she were ever to decide to leave Reykjavík for somewhere smaller. A view like this, over the water, would be one of her key requirements.

There was something restful about the proximity to the clear, cobalt-blue sea; maybe it was something in her genes, a little salt water flowing through her veins. Her Faroese grandfather had been a seaman, as his forefathers had been before him. Ísrún herself had no interest in seamanship and avoided covering news stories about quotas and fishing. So maybe it was the sea itself that held an attraction for her, rather than the fish that lived below its surface.

Ísrún rang the bell, which was marked with Nóra Pálsdóttir's name in neat, decorative lettering. Nothing happened. She waited and rang the bell a second time, knocking on the door as well to be sure of being heard. Finally, behind the tissue-thin curtains obscuring the little window in the door, she saw signs of life.

The door opened and a woman swathed in a bright-yellow dress gave her a welcoming smile, her teeth a perfect white. A too-perfect shade of white, Ísrún thought, for a woman who looked to be around sixty.

'Good morning, and apologies for keeping you waiting,' said the woman smoothly.

'Hello, I'm Ísrún. You're Nóra?'

'Yes, quite right.' The broad smile returned and she pointed to the name under the bell. 'Nóra Pálsdóttir. And you're from the TV news, aren't you?'

Ísrún nodded.

'Come in. Please excuse the mess. I wasn't expecting anyone today. I've been so upset since poor Elías died.'

Ísrún followed her into a living room looking over the sea, conscious of the mud on her shoes. She tried to see where the mess she had to excuse might be; but as far as she could tell, both the house and its owner were clean and tidy, as if dressed up for Christmas at the height of summer. She couldn't avoid, however, the powerful scent of perfume. Perfume was something Ísrún preferred not to use herself, while it seemed that Nóra had decided that there was no point applying it sparingly.

'I'm devastated,' Nóra said with a sigh. 'Completely devastated. I still can't believe that it's really happened. Sit down, won't you? I'll see if there's anything in the fridge.'

She trotted out of the room, leaving Ísrún to make herself at home in the most comfortable-looking chair.

'I do hope you're not going to quote me on the news,' Nóra called to her. 'But I'd understand if you did. You have a job to do, just like the rest of us,' she added before Ísrún had a chance to reply.

There was a silence and Nóra returned, a lavish chocolate cake in her hands.

'I don't work. I'm retired now, you see. Maybe I gave up work far too early. Anyhow I've found a calling, if that's the right expression, and nowadays I'm up to my ears in charity work. You've heard of Household Rescue?'

'I'd like to ask a few questions about Elías if that's all right,' Ísrún said firmly.

Nóra placed the cake on the table.

'I had completely forgotten I had this one. It's rum and chocolate; quite delicious, if I do say so myself,' she said in a dramatic voice.

Ísrún declined to comment, and waited instead for an answer to her question.

'Yes of course that's fine,' Nóra said at last. 'Ask away. I'll do my best to tell you what I can about Elías.'

She stood completely still, as if the yellow dress had to remain pristine.

'As you can imagine, I'm working on a report about the murder,' Ísrún said and paused, trying to squeeze out a smile. 'But not just the murder. I want to find out what kind of man the victim was. I was hoping you could help me get an angle on that side of all this.'

'Of course. A pleasure and a duty. How do you want to do this? Do you want to take notes and come back for the interview itself?' she asked, her excitement obvious.

'That's right. Anyone would think you'd been a journalist yourself.'

'It's something I used to dream about doing but never did. I trained to be a dentist instead. You'll have seen my work everywhere down south, without knowing it,' Nóra said with a laugh. 'It's a shame I can't show you his apartment. He lived upstairs, but the police have sealed it and taken the key away. They found something up there and a policeman took a sports bag away with him. That's all I know.'

Wrinkles appeared around her eyes as she smiled.

'That's fine,' Ísrún assured her. She looked longingly at the cake. 'Maybe I'll have a slice of this, please. You really baked it yourself?'

'*Oui*,' said Nóra, the theatrical tone returning. 'It's a French recipe that I picked up on my travels.' She cut a thick slice, laid it on a plate and handed it to Ísrún. 'Coffee? There's some already made.'

'Thank you.'

Nóra hurried from the room and returned with a steaming cup.

'You're clearly ready for anything these days. Plenty of visitors since the murder?' Ísrún asked. She immediately regretted it; Nóra looked embarrassed. 'Tell me more about Household Rescue,' said Ísrún hurriedly.

It was the best she could come up to salvage the situation. It worked. The pained look on Nóra's face was immediately replaced by a smile and she launched into a long description of the movement's background. Only the cake, which was wonderful, made the account bearable.

Right at the end of this diatribe, when Ísrún had nearly stopped listening, she found herself suddenly interested again. Nóra mentioned how Elías had practically taken over the running of Household Rescue.

'It was all down to his sheer energy and his exceptional concern for those less fortunate than himself,' she said with great seriousness.

'So yours was just a business relationship? Was there any more to it? Apologies if that's too personal a question.'

'Good grief, don't worry about that. I've heard all sorts before now,' Nóra squeaked. 'The answer is no. The relationship didn't go in the direction you're hinting at. Not that it would have come as a surprise.' Nóra played with a sleeve of the yellow dress. 'I couldn't miss him eyeing me up, if you know what I mean, and we were much the same age.'

Much the same age ... Ísrún stared at Nóra. Elías had been in his mid-thirties, while Nóra looked old enough to have been his mother.

'How long did he live here with you?'

'He moved in just after New Year. Before that he had rented a room from his colleague, Logi.' Nóra paused, thinking. 'I was wondering,' she went on, 'maybe we should record the interview at Household Rescue's office? With our logo in the background, perhaps?'

'That's an idea,' Ísrún said, hoping that Nóra wouldn't notice her lack of enthusiasm. 'Was Elías involved with any of the local women?'

'I don't think so,' Nóra answered, seeming a little piqued. 'I suppose he must have had a girlfriend somewhere. Perhaps he preferred to keep her clear of small-town gossip. Men like him – handsome men, I mean – tend to have a girl in every port.'

'I suppose so,' Ísrún agreed, putting her final forkful of cake down, having suddenly lost her appetite.

'When do you think you might record my interview?'

Nóra hadn't even sat down. She still stood like a queen in a yellow dress, overseeing her realm from her vantage point in the middle of the living room.

'I need to work through all the material and check with the desk editor on what sort of angle he wants to take. Then I'll see if I can get a cameraman here from Akureyri. If I can, then maybe we'll film it later today, if that's OK?'

Nóra smiled again and her white teeth shone.

'Wonderful. Can I have your number, just in case?'
Ísrún smiled back.
'Don't worry about that. I'll give you a call later.'

4

Ari Thór was at work early the morning after the meeting at Akureyri. It was the second day of the investigation, and judging by the effort that went into the first day, he knew that this one wouldn't be any easier. At least he felt thankful for the fresh air here in the north, after having seen the news of the ash cloud over Reykjavík and the south. His mind had gone back to his days at school when his class had learned about the famous Skaftáreldar eruption in the 1700s. It had not only caused a mist over Iceland and around Europe as well, with the sun appearing blood-red and temperatures suddenly dropping, but had also resulted in the deaths of perhaps two in ten Icelanders.

Hlynur was already at the station when Ari Thór arrived, but he seemed as listless as ever, staring at his computer screen as if he were deep in a case, although Ari Thór knew that he had nothing serious to work on at the moment. He hardly seemed to notice when Ari Thór walked in.

It was almost eleven when Ari Thór realised that he hadn't eaten, either in Akureyri the night before, or at breakfast time that morning, so he took a walk to the shop to buy himself a bag of dried fish. A fresh sea breeze welcomed him outside, but the sun was nowhere to be seen in the cloudy sky.

On his way back into the station, Ari Thór met Tómas in the doorway.

'Let's take a walk,' Tómas suggested, and headed off down the street, Ari Thór walking in silence at his side.

'I'm ready to give up on all this,' said Tómas moodily. 'I can't get through to Hlynur at all. And Ómar the Skipper was here while you were out. He's only just gone, or rather, I told him that I had a meeting and he finally left. I guess he didn't want to stick around there with Hlynur, looking like he's seen a ghost. I've had a bellyful of Ómar as well, I can tell you. That man can really talk, you know.' Tómas sighed.

'He's pretty harmless,' Ari Thór said.

'He was a proper hell-raiser in his younger days. My parents knew him. Sometimes he'd come knocking at our door in the evenings, dead drunk. I should have been fast asleep that late, but I clearly remember the damnable racket he made. The old boy's dried out now, but he's no less of a pain in the neck.'

They crossed the street and walked towards a newly refurbished building by the small boat harbour, which was now home to the town's tourist information centre and a new bistro.

'This place is changing,' Tómas said, apparently less than pleased at the prospect.

They sat on a bench by the building and Ari Thór chewed a piece of dried fish.

'There are changes everywhere,' Tómas continued. 'Restaurants, maybe a new hotel, more visitors, more tourists, and the tunnel. Siglufjörður will be practically on the main road. We'll need more officers to cope. There'll be all kinds of people coming here ... drugs and I don't know what. There are as many cons as there are pros to making the place easier to reach, my boy.'

'What do you make of the Elías case?' Ari Thór asked, feeling slightly uncomfortable with Tómas's depressive stance.

Tómas sighed. An elderly lady walked slowly past, supporting herself with a stick. She nodded to Tómas, clearly surprised at the sight of two of the town's three police officers sitting on a bench in the middle of the day, and not even a particularly sunny one at that.

'I can't say for sure,' Tómas said at last. 'It strikes me that it's out of our hands. You've done a good job on it and we've done what we can. Now it's up to the crime-busters at the station in Akureyri to see if they can solve the puzzle.'

'Can't we check on their phones?'

'Phones?' Tómas asked in surprise.

'Yes. Look at the phone traffic for those who knew Elías best: Páll and Logi, and that Svavar over in Dalvík. And maybe Nóra, and Hákon the foreman. Can't we check and find out if any of them were over in Skagafjörður that night?'

'Don't forget Jói,' Tómas said with a wry smile. 'But no. We can't do that. None of them are suspects. We can't barge into people's personal lives just because they knew Elías, even if it is a murder investigation. Our lawyers would have a fit if I were to even suggest it.'

'Nothing but trouble, these lawyers,' Ari Thór said.

'You're right on that one, my boy,' Tómas said and yawned.

'Tired?'

'Not really. But I did sleep badly last night,' Tómas replied, sounding exhausted, despite his denial.

Ari Thór hesitated, unsure if he should mention the subject that was so obviously troubling Tómas. He was half the man he had been before his wife had moved south to Reykjavík to study. Ari Thór was reluctant to step into what could be a minefield, but decided it had to be done.

'It must be a big change for you…'

'It is, my boy,' said Tómas, and repeated what he had said earlier. 'Changes everywhere,' he said, his mind elsewhere.

'How's she doing? Your wife, I mean.'

'She's doing well, or so I hear,' Tómas muttered. 'I get a call now and then, and she tells me she's fine. She's finished the first year at college. She's always talking about people I've never met. She seems to spend a lot of time with them. Other students, younger than she is. I can't fathom what made her want to up sticks like this at her age. We had it so good here; everything was just fine.'

'Why don't you go south as well?'

There was a long silence. Ari Thór wished he could take his words back, but they hung there behind their silence.

'Perhaps I should. What do *you* reckon?' Tómas asked, taking him by surprise.

'Me?' Ari Thór asked.

'I never thought I could move away,' Tómas said. 'But now I'm not so sure. Maybe I could do with a change.' He lapsed back into silence for a long moment. 'I don't know. Perhaps I'm too old now. You can't pull up a tree when its roots have grown so deep.'

'It might be worth thinking it over.'

'Don't you worry, my boy. I don't seem to do much more than think this over. And if I go, then you can take my place. The station will be fine in your hands.'

Ari Thór couldn't deny that the thought of a step up the career ladder was tempting. An achievement like that in his professional life might go some way to making up for the shambles of his private life.

But now that he heard Tómas say the words out loud he had the sudden feeling that the mountains were closing in on him, just as they had done during that snow-heavy winter when he had first moved north to Siglufjörður. It was uncomfortable to be reminded of it, just when he had been sure that he had conquered his claustrophobia.

He'd thought he'd become used to the little town, had even developed a fondness for it. Could it be that he still hadn't come completely to terms with the isolation and the sparse population; not enough to consider staying in Siglufjörður for good?

It didn't take Ísrún long to find the police station. She parked outside and breezed in, as if buoyed on the cloud of confidence that came with a journalist's job, something that was absorbed with the newsroom coffee.

The police station seemed quiet, with apparently only one officer on duty. He sat engrossed in a computer screen and didn't move, even though she had almost slammed the door behind her.

'Good morning,' she offered, but the man remained immobile.

She took a few steps closer and repeated her greeting.

'Good morning?'

Finally he looked round and stared as if he had been woken from a painful dream.

He gazed intently at her, and for once she saw someone taking in her eyes before noticing the scar on her face. But his look was alarmingly blank and distant. It was as if his soul had been left behind in the computer, she thought, forgetting for a moment that her long study of psychology had banished any belief she might have had in the existence of the soul.

'Are you here about the emails?' he asked, his voice almost robotic in its monotone.

'Emails?' she replied, wondering what he was talking about. 'I'm looking for someone called Páll the Cop.'

'Páll?' It was as if the policeman had regained consciousness. 'I'm sorry. My name's Hlynur. Páll left the police a long time ago. But in a place like this that kind of nickname can stay with you for the rest of your life.'

'Do you know where I could find him?'

The policeman thought for a moment.

'No idea. His name's Páll Reynisson. Look him up. He's bound to have a mobile phone.'

He turned and his attention went back to his silent study of the computer screen. Ísrún made her way out. She didn't think it was worth saying goodbye to this man, who had the look of someone who might be dangerously unstable.

5

It turned out that Páll Reynisson did have a mobile phone. When Ísrún rang it he seemed happy to announce that he had 'nothing to hide', and agreed to meet her.

Now she stood outside the house on Hafnargata, where he had said he was working. A young man with longish hair, wearing jeans and a checked shirt, peered out from the basement doorway at the front of the house. He had red cheeks and greeted her with a smile.

'Hello there. I'm Páll.'

'Ísrún,' she said warily.

'Come inside, will you? That way I don't have to stop work. I don't get paid for standing around.'

'What are you working on?'

'Re-wiring this old place. A local boy who moved away years ago has just bought it to use as a summer house. He's not the first and he won't be the last. The whole of Siglufjörður is becoming second homes.'

'It's a magnificent place,' she said to keep the conversation alive.

He laughed. 'That's not going to win you any bonus points from me. Come on in, or rather, come on down. I have to get back to work.' And he disappeared back inside.

She stooped to go through the door. Inside the basement the ceiling was so low she could hardly stand up straight.

'Not the easiest place to work,' she said, looking around.

'It's not the worst place I've had to work in,' he replied with a grin.

There were three rooms in the old house's basement. The one they stood in was scattered with tools, rusted garden shears, an old lawnmower, a wheelbarrow and even a stack of old paving slabs. In the little room to the right Ísrún saw the glitter of light falling on empty jars of all shapes and sizes. But what caught her eye was the line of old milk bottles that filled one shelf. She had heard about these bottles but had never seen them before, cartons having long replaced milk bottles by the time she had been growing up.

'I wouldn't mind one of those,' she said, pointing at the row of empty bottles. 'It'd make a lovely flower vase.'

She was half hoping that he would hand her a bottle, so his answer was not what she expected.

'You can probably buy bottles like those in some antique shop down south,' he said.

'What's in there?' she asked, pointing to the left to steer the conversation in a different direction.

'Just some old junk. This was a sort of cowshed in the old days.'

'A cowshed?' she asked in amazement.

'That's right. The people who lived here had a cow in the basement, or so I hear. They were allowed to do it when there was scarlet fever about so they could produce milk for their children. That was a long time back.'

'A house with a story to tell?'

'That's true enough,' he said.

'And you're an electrician?'

'That's right. Been working with Elías and the guys until now.'

'And now you're out of work?' she asked in a tone that bordered on caustic.

'Does it look as if I'm out of work?' he said, his attention on the job in hand. 'In a way I suppose you could say I am. The murder has really shaken me up. But I've been in touch with the foreman at the tunnel and he wants to work things out to keep us on – me, Logi and Svavar.' She could hear from the tension in his voice that it was important to him that this should come together.

'But now you're working here,' she said.

'Well, this is a job that I should have done a while ago,' he replied and turned to look into her eyes. 'The problem is that nobody can get hold of Svavar. He was the one who was closest to Elías, and the foreman will only let us continue the tunnel job if he's part of the team.' Páll was unable to hide his concern. 'At the moment Logi's doing some shifts to keep our side of the work up to date.'

'And you can't reach Svavar?'

She resisted the temptation to say that she had spoken to him the night before.

'No. He's not answering his phone. I might drive over to Dalvík later today and bang on his door. He and Elías were good friends, so I wanted to give him some space. But enough is enough. I didn't expect it would hit him so hard, but we can't afford to lose this opportunity. If we drag our heels too much they'll find other contractors. Unemployment here is just the same as everywhere else. You should know. You're always telling us on the TV news how deep the recession is.'

He snorted as his attention went back to his work.

'You said on the phone that you have nothing to hide.'

There was a surprised expression on his face as he looked up from the wiring, but he still wore the same amiable smile.

'I did.'

'What did you mean by that? Did Elías have anything to hide?'

'I can tell you know the answer to that already.'

'I have my suspicions,' she said, looking away.

Páll didn't react, focussing on his work instead.

'I want to know more about him,' she said when she felt the silence had lasted long enough. She was uncomfortable, unable to stand properly upright, and with no chairs in the room, unable to sit down either. 'What was he up to? Do you know if he had any tendencies towards … well … violence?'

'Not asking for much, are you? You think I'm going to blab to some reporter from Reykjavík? Does it matter, anyway?'

'It might.'

'I suppose I should be happy that I'm not under suspicion. At least you're not asking where I was when he was murdered,' he said lightly.

'So where were you?' she asked, taking the bait.

'In Reykjavík, on the pull. You hacks probably don't do that kind of thing, too busy looking for the next scoop.'

'I've given that up,' she said truthfully. And then decided to add a story that had a grain of truth behind it. 'I gave up when I met a guy in a bar who said I looked like a pitcher.'

'What?'

'He said I was as pretty as a pitcher,' she said. 'He seemed to think it was something to do with Ming vases. What he meant was, "as pretty as a picture". We argued about it for ages. I gave up going out on the town after that.'

Páll laughed, but she didn't join him.

'Did you kill him?' She interrupted his laughter, hoping to take him unawares. She didn't succeed.

'No. I've no idea who did it. Elías was no angel, but don't quote me on that. This was a guy who had no conscience.'

'Could you give me an example?'

'I'd rather not,' he replied and looked away, the smile still on his lips.

You could get away with anything with the right smile on your face, she thought.

⌖

Every two months Nóra had her hair done at a little hairdresser in Siglufjörður. It was hardly even a salon, just a chair in front of a mirror in the house of a retired lady who cut hair when required; a place that was open by arrangement, as the saying goes. Nóra had been there a month or so ago, but she called and booked an appointment for later that day. The TV journalist could arrive at any minute with a cameraman, and she was determined to look her best.

Her main concern was that the woman might turn up just as

she was having her hair done. If that happened, she could miss her chance, and that would be a disaster. There was no certainty that this woman, Ísrún, would call ahead. After thinking it over, Nóra decided that she would have to get in touch with her, and tell her when to come round.

Without a mobile number to call, however, Nóra had to dial the newsroom directly. It wasn't something she had ever done before. Nothing newsworthy had ever happened to her.

'Newsroom. Desk editor,' a stern voice answered.

'Good morning. My name's Nóra. To whom am I speaking?' she asked, absurdly formal.

'Ívar,' the voice snapped.

She could almost see him before her. She had seen him many times on the screen; a rotund but handsome man, masculinity personified, she thought.

'I need to get in touch with Ísrún,' she said at last.

'Ísrún isn't here at the moment. Can I help?'

He was already impatient, even though the conversation hadn't been a long one. But Nóra sympathised. Journalism had to be stressful with the deadlines all day long, or so she imagined.

'No, I just need her mobile number. We were going to meet up later today in Siglufjörður.'

'Oh, right?' Ívar said, no longer in a hurry. 'What for, if you don't mind me asking?'

'Well, she spoke to me this morning and was going to come back later with a cameraman,' Nóra said, pleased with herself.

'Right…' Ívar repeated. 'A cameraman, you say. What for?'

'The late Elías Freysson lived with me … that's to say he was my tenant. I understand that Ísrún is doing a programme about him, looking for a new angle, or so she said. The man behind the victim, that kind of thing.'

Nóra hoped that she had managed to get everything right. Not that it mattered to her. What was important was that she would be on television.

'Right!' Ívar said once more, and Nóra detected a note of derision in his voice. 'The man behind the victim, is it?' But he didn't give her an opportunity to reply to his question. 'I'll give her a message. What do you want me to tell her?'

'Would you please just tell Ísrún that I won't be at home until after four today? I've an appointment with the hairdresser. It's something that was booked ages ago and I completely forgot about it when I spoke to her this morning.'

'I'll let her know. Bye.'

He had put the phone down before Nóra could say another word.

6

She was determined to stay awake. She wasn't sure how she was managing it, but she was sure that if she allowed herself to fall asleep, she wouldn't wake up again.

Maybe that wouldn't be so bad.

She wanted so much for her thoughts to carry her all the way home, where her family would welcome her, and the old puppet that hung from the ceiling in their living room would come to life and do the same.

She felt so small, alone and abandoned.

Each time the fear returned, she wept, or tried to, but it felt as if she had no more tears to shed.

Her head hurt. She would close her eyes for moment, try to relax and make the effort to calm herself. Then she would open them again, determined not to take the risk of falling asleep. She wasn't sure what was causing the blinding headache, although she suspected it was probably dehydration. That and the smell, which was becoming almost intolerable.

To begin with she had sat in the corner, the wall at her back, and tried to put herself in a position that would ease the cramps in her legs. But frightened of sleep, she moved about, careful not to give herself too much comfort.

Maybe it was all for nothing, though?

She knew that death was approaching. She had lived well and honestly. It would be wrong to let fear and fury gain the upper hand now. She had to think of something positive: her family.

But then maybe it was time to lie down, after all. Time to relax. Time to give in.

7

A year before

I got on well with the old lady, Katrín. I identified something of my grandmother Ísbjörg in her friend – their shared memories, some habits and mannerisms, phrases she used. I let myself dream that for a moment I was sitting with my grandmother, and not with this stranger out here in Landeyjar.

'Can I offer you anything, my dear? I don't bake anymore, unfortunately.' She looked down at her bony fingers. 'I'm not sure I trust myself to do it these days. My hands aren't as steady or as strong as they once were. That's what age brings us, I suppose.'

'I'm fine, thanks.'

'Nonsense! You look so pale, washed out. Can't I even offer you a glass of milk?'

'That would be lovely,' I said, if only to show a little courtesy.

It was stuffy inside the little house, with all of the radiators turned on even though it was summer. I could feel a tranquillity gradually coming over me. Maybe the old lady was right and I wasn't well. I had felt a little nauseous earlier, and a few aches and pains, as if I had a bout of flu that refused to go away. Working too hard, I suppose. Bastard journalism.

All these shifts were becoming ridiculous, all the endless stress.

Katrín had gone to the kitchen with painfully slow steps. I should have offered to fetch the milk myself.

'Would you like some biscuits with it?' I heard her call from the kitchen as loudly as those old vocal chords would allow.

'Yes, please.'

She came back with a glass of milk in one hand and half a packet of biscuits in the other. She sat down at the wooden table with difficulty; the journey to the kitchen seemed to have aged her. The marks of the passing years were clear to see on her face; there must have been hard times.

'Do you remember her diary?' I asked, in a voice so low that I wondered deep down whether I really wanted to ask the question out loud.

'What did you say, my dear?' Katrín asked, and leaned forward over the table.

It was an opportunity to leave the words alone, to pretend they hadn't been spoken after all. But I decided not to take it.

'Do you remember if my grandmother ever kept a diary?' I asked again, my voice stronger and clearer.

'A diary, yes, I remember that. She didn't always write in it, not every day. It wasn't that kind of diary. But I saw her note things down in it sometimes, normally when something particular had happened – around the time of the eruption, for example.'

'Did you ever see what she had written?'

'Goodness, no. I certainly did not. It was for nobody's eyes but her own. I did have a glance at the occasional page, but it was written in such tiny handwriting that it was probably not something anyone else could have read.'

'Was it just the one book for her whole life? Or more than one?'

'I'm fairly sure there was just the one book. She didn't start to keep a diary until she was in her teens and I think she stopped when she was around twenty. But I know she picked it up again when she was taken ill. She used to say that she told the book how she felt,' recounted Katrín, her voice laden with sadness.

She gazed into space as if she was being transported back into the past.

'I hope the milk tastes right. It's not getting old, is it?'

'It's fine, thank you,' I said, even though the milk was certainly past its sell-by date. It was good enough to add to coffee, but not much else.

'I wonder where the book is now?' the old lady said, unexpectedly.

'It's lost, I expect,' I said, giving her a half-truth at least.

We sat on in silence.

The wind could still be heard outside, blowing half a gale on this summer's morning. Nothing unusual about that, being so close to the sea and with no hills that could provide even a semblance of a windbreak on these flat lowlands. The only mountains were the distant volcanoes, and they were of no help.

And then came the thing that changed everything.

8

This wasn't an opportunity Ívar was going to let slip through his fingers.

He was a pragmatist by nature, and he hadn't got this far in life by being considerate to others. The station had poached him from a rival company, and paid him well to make the move; he was certainly better paid than most of his colleagues.

He had done well for himself, but he still had his sights set on higher things. Of course, the news editor's job was what he had his eye on, but the post was already taken by María, a woman with whom he got on well. Like him, she had been head-hunted from a daily newspaper. He guessed that was why they liked each other – both of them outsiders trying to work things out for themselves as they did their best to negotiate the station's cliques, while still keeping them at arm's length. She did this because of the position she was in; he did it because he hoped one day to be in that same position. María had a reputation for not staying long in any place and he reckoned that she wouldn't be here more than three or four years before moving on. Then it would be his turn.

There were a few challenges to be met before then, though. Not least among them was ejecting those news team members who seemed to distrust him. Ísrún was at the top of this list. Everything about the woman grated on his nerves. She was annoyingly independent and competitive, plus she had a long background at the station, despite the extended breaks in her career. She was part of that irritating little clique of colleagues who had been together for years, all of whom trusted her. It was as well that Ívar had managed to make a few allies of his own, such as Kormákur; but he knew that he would have to isolate Ísrún.

He suspected that she would be bold enough to apply for the news editor's job herself when the time came. Fortunately he was one of the regular desk editors and she wasn't. As desk editor he could frequently arrange things to his advantage and her detriment. The desk editor was the person who took decisions on the fly, allocated assignments and had the deciding vote on what news would be included and in what order. This meant he could assign Ísrún minor stories that normally ended up in the late bulletin. And Ívar knew the late bulletin was no route to stardom.

Ever since the unexpected phone call from Siglufjörður, he had been keeping an eye on María's office, so he noticed the door open and a man he recognised from the accounts department left. Now was his chance, although he knew that María was rarely at her most agreeable after a visit from one of the bean-counters.

'Not interrupting, am I?' he asked cheerily, as he put his head around the door.

'No, it's all right.'

María took off her reading glasses and her sharp eyes stared at him. He had often thought that she was the last person he would ever want to be interrogated by, especially if she wanted her interviewee to confess to some indiscretion.

'Sit down.'

With María this was always an instruction and never an invitation. Words were never wasted inviting anyone to take a seat.

'It's about Ísrún,' Ívar said, unconsciously speaking in a lower voice than usual.

María said nothing, but waited for him to continue.

'She went up north to investigate the murder story.'

María nodded but still said nothing.

'I wasn't happy about letting her go; we're not in a position to allow someone to focus on one story like that, but she said she had a source that linked Elías, the victim, with dope smuggling. I was hoping she'd come back with some fantastic scoop. Every now and then you have to let the kids off the lead, you know? Not that she's done all that brilliantly recently.'

He used the word 'kids' for good reason, preferring not to remind María how long Ísrún had worked at the station.

'Really?'

'Her stuff has been pretty mundane, and I've had to put it at the back of the running order. I've even had to ask her to go back and re-do some material. She seems to have lost interest,' he said, trying to assume a look of pained concern.

'She does look pale on screen,' María said thoughtfully.

'Tired maybe, or just bored. I've a feeling she's been hitting the nightlife as well. She's used up all her sick days these last few months, and it's as if she's trying to do as little as she can get away with.'

'Interesting,' María said.

'So, anyway, she went up north. Now I gather she's working on some item about "the person behind the victim". That wasn't what we agreed.'

'And what do you expect me to do?'

María's tone was sharp and her eyes bored into him.

'I reckon she's lost her enthusiasm completely. Perhaps it's time to consider letting her go…?'

'We'll see.' María picked up her glasses again.

He decided to let the matter lie there. He could bring it up again soon. A slow drip-feed would do the trick.

Tómas and Ari Thór were back at the police station. Neither of them spoke a word to Hlynur, who sat at his computer, deep in his own thoughts. He didn't need them, though. They had both betrayed him, made him impotent, as useful and as colourless as the police station's furniture.

It had been a day of contrasts. Sometimes he had been present, there at the station, trying to keep on top of things. At other times it was as if he were elsewhere, somewhere Gauti and his mother were still alive and well, where he had been able to atone for his misdeeds, where there were no wretched emails tripping him up; somewhere email hadn't even been invented.

Now, for what it was worth, he was definitely back at the station, where he couldn't think of anything other than the message contained in all the emails.

Next time I'll teach you how to die.

He longed to go home, tell them he was coming down with flu, however unlikely that might sound in the height of summer. But he hardly had the energy to do even that. Apart from anything else, he had no wish to play into Tómas's hands.

No, he'd stick it out. He'd stay until his shift was over, but try to drift off for as long as he could into the warm, pleasant world where he didn't have anyone's death on his conscience.

Ari Thór glanced over at where Hlynur sat engrossed in his computer. He and Hlynur had never hit it off. They had little in common other than the job and he saw no reason to talk to him, to find out what the problem might be. Any conversation was bound to be superficial and uncomfortable.

It was for a similar reason that he had so far avoided calling Kristín. While he desperately wanted to hear her voice, even arrange to meet her, he dreaded the awkward moment when she would pick up the phone.

The awkward moment. Was this genuinely the only reason he hadn't called her? Or was jealousy, that old spectre, rearing its ugly head again? Was he scared that he might lose his temper if he called and her new relationship came up in the conversation?

He looked at the phone in his hand, wanting to dial her number, but still holding back.

Then the phone rang.

⌖

It was a slow day, the same as every other day at the hospital; far too slow. All the same, there was plenty that needed to be done, even if it was monotonous.

Kristín was looking forward to the evening, a cosy night and a glass of red with him at her place. It was going to be their first proper date at home – away from the neutral ground of a public place. But this wasn't the main reason time was passing so slowly. Work bored her – it was as simple as that. None of the tasks she had to deal with genuinely sparked her interest, and this was becoming intensely irritating.

Was it too late to change course now? All that study and work would be wasted if she were to give up now. And what would her parents' reaction be? Common sense would also have to be part of her decision; it would be ridiculous to turn her back on the chance of secure employment and respectable earning potential in the middle of a recession.

Then there was the question of what else she could do. It wasn't as if there was anything else that particularly inspired her; nothing that set her heart racing. She got up every morning and played a round of golf if there was time; worked like a robot until the end of each long shift; and went home, where she did nothing much other than sleep until the cycle began again. The pattern had been the same all through her student years: wake up, study, sleep.

She knew she had to do something to break free of the routine. Maybe she should follow her instincts, enjoy tonight's wine and for the moment forget her immediate problems – instead make the most of an evening and a night in the company of that unfamiliar yet fascinating man.

⌖

Helga from CID in Akureyri had called Ari Thór to ask him and Tómas to come in for another progress meeting that evening, a conference to round up the second day since Elías Freysson's body had been found.

'You'll be very welcome,' she had said, although it was obvious that this was not in the least bit true; in her eyes they were a pair of uniformed bumpkins getting in the way of the work of real police officers. Ari Thór said that he would be there and expected that Tómas would do the same.

On the phone, Helga gave Ari Thór a brief status report, including the information that Elías had been involved in some shady business, which included fencing stolen goods and even organising break-ins. The charity's accounts were also raising a few eyebrows, with ill-defined costs and revenue from unidentified sources.

All of this meant that Ari Thór would be on his way to Akureyri again.

Maybe this time he would call Kristín, or send her an email. He had nothing to lose, after all. He was already mentally composing it.

Hello. No. *Hi*. That sounded better. *Hi, hope you're well. I'm going to be in Akureyri this evening. I'd love to see you if you have time to meet. Do you have a spare ten minutes?* That would do. Ten minutes. She could hardly refuse him that.

He called over to Tómas.

'Meeting in Akureyri tonight. We'll have to leave around half-five.'

'Excellent,' Tómas replied. 'And we'll have time for a burger and a plate of chips on the way back, won't we, my boy?'

Ari Thór nodded and grinned.

He clicked on his email, wrote his message to Kristín, then quickly pressed 'send' before he had time to change his mind.

⌖

Ísrún could feel fatigue taking hold of her. It had been a tough couple of days: Dalvík, Akureyri and then Siglufjörður.

Against her better instincts, she decided to call Kormákur to tell him what she had been doing. It wasn't even as if she had much to say. There was the attention-seeking woman Elías had rented an apartment from; or she could tell him about Páll Reynisson. Páll had said he hadn't been in Siglufjörður the night Elías had been murdered, but down south in Reykjavík – although he could just as easily have been in Skagafjörður committing a murder. But he didn't seem like a man with anything to hide. He was a very unlikely murderer and she had no desire to drag him into the news spotlight.

She still had one more person to talk to about Elías, though: his workmate, Logi.

She had found out where he lived. But before paying him a visit, she needed to rest. She took a room at a local guesthouse, mainly to give herself a chance to close her eyes before driving south that evening. With no expectation that the station would reimburse her costs, she opted for the cheapest room available.

Once inside, she drew the curtains and lay down without bothering to pull a blanket over herself. Then she remembered her phone and decided, just for once, to break her own rule. She stood up, picked up the phone and set it to silent. Nobody knew precisely where to find her, nobody could disturb her and that was just how she wanted it.

She lay down again and her eyelids drooped as her thoughts began to wander. But it was not long before they came back round to reality, and she thought about what she was expecting to achieve with this particularly private investigation.

Kristín's longed-for break arrived and she poured herself a strong coffee, hoping it would be powerful enough to jolt her back to alertness while she leafed through the papers and checked her emails. Taking a seat in front of the office computer, she clicked on her account.

He heart skipped a beat. There was a message from Ari Thór.

She hesitated, wondering whether or not to delete it unread.

He had sent her many messages in the weeks after they had parted company and often tried to call. But she had never replied, adamant that he didn't deserve a response. Now her feelings were different. She had met another man. It wouldn't do any harm for Ari Thór to be aware of it – proof, perhaps, that she could stand on her own two feet.

She read his message; it was short and straight to the point, suggesting they should meet.

She chose her words with care as she typed a reply.

'Sorry, I'm not free this evening. I'm expecting a friend.'

9

How could she have let herself be taken in by the offer of working in Iceland?

She had seen stars, their light so bright that she had not seen the sinister shadow they cast – a shadow she should have taken care to avoid.

She could feel death coming closer.

She didn't fear it anymore.

Death was simply a part of living, or so she had been brought up to believe.

What worried her most was that her body would probably be buried in the ground instead of being cremated according to the beliefs and customs with which she had grown up.

She tried to stifle her negative thoughts, and fought hard not to dwell on her terrible thirst.

10

It was a long time since Ísrún had slept so soundly. Normally she dipped in and out of slumber, waking several times every night. Occasionally she managed something deeper, a sleep of dreams, but then the nightmares they turned into ensured that she still slept badly, waking with her heart beating wildly, her body drenched in sweat, drained rather than rested.

And now she was awake. She stood up, felt a moment's dizziness so overwhelming that she sat down on the bed again and took a lungful of air, closing her eyes and making an effort to take steady breaths. She checked the time on her phone and saw with satisfaction that she had slept for almost an hour. But she also saw that she had missed a call. From María, the news editor.

What could she be calling about?

Ísrún didn't have the energy to talk to her right away, so she dropped the phone in her handbag and ventured out into the bright Siglufjörður sunshine. Having already paid for the night, she decided to keep the room.

María sat in her office, contemplating the advantages of being able to shut the door. Open-plan offices were usual for newsrooms, something that journalists had adopted long before the economic boom years had made them standard practice everywhere else – in banks and finance companies, who had taken on huge numbers of staff to fill their open workspaces. It was the magic solution that was supposed to promote tight-knit teamwork, lower overheads and ultimately result in higher profits.

María herself had had a couple of offers from the financial sector, but she had withstood the temptation to leave the media. The money on offer had been very attractive, but news was deeply ingrained in her. When it had come to making a decision, she had been unable to leave behind the environment she had thrived in all these years.

The news editor's job came with pros and cons, however. She was free to concentrate on the big picture and had the opportunity to put her own stamp on the newsroom, but part and parcel of the job were the endless meetings about staffing, budgets and management. The worst part was having to lay people off; this was something she avoided as much as she could, although if it had to be done, she wouldn't shy away from it.

She couldn't help thinking there was something in what Ívar had said. There was no doubt that Ísrún was a talented journalist, but she seemed to have lost her spark. She could be resourceful and determined, sometimes a little too determined, if truth be told. But something had gone wrong. There had been too many absences and, as Ívar had pointed out, she had claimed every available sick day recently and often appeared out of sorts at work. Six months ago María had called her in for an appraisal and asked if everything was all right, tactfully pointing out that she had been off sick unusually often.

'I've just had one cold after another this winter,' Ísrún had replied. But she'd seemed so uncomfortable that María didn't need any special insight to see through the lie.

Nothing much had changed after that conversation. On top of which, Ívar didn't trust Ísrún. This was nothing new; sometimes people just didn't get on. But Ívar was the more valuable member of the news team, a man with plenty of experience who had been headhunted from a competing station. She couldn't afford to lose him. It looked like she was going to have to sacrifice Ísrún.

María knews this situation had been brewing for some months, yet it remained a difficult decision to take, all the same.

Once María had made up her mind, though, not least when the decision was a tough one, she habitually wanted to push it through right away. And there would be little that could persuade her to alter her course.

11

The pregnant woman standing in the doorway was around Ísrún's own age. Ísrún immediately saw there was something troubled about her, though she found herself unable to pin it down. Tiredness? Maybe. A reticence about her? Yes, more than likely. Some kind of pre-natal depression? It was possible.

'Hello,' Ísrún said, not yet sure how she was going to talk her way into this house.

'Hi,' the woman replied curtly, seemingly intent on showing only the minimum of courtesy.

Ísrún's plan was an as-yet-uncertain mixture of honesty and white lies.

'My name's Ísrún,' she opened.

You might recognise me from the television, she wanted to say, but saw right away there was no need for that.

'We're making a short news item about Elías Freysson, the man who died the other night. He had been prominent in charity work locally, as you probably know, and we thought it would be worthwhile to talk to some of his friends and acquaintances.'

The surprise on the woman's face was clear; she remaining in the doorway staring, apparently wondering what to say.

'I've spoken to his friend Svavar, over in Dalvík, and with Páll here in Siglufjörður. I imagine Logi would want to say a few words as well, don't you think?'

'What? Well, I guess so,' answered the woman, clearly unconvinced.

'Is he at home?'

'No, he's at work. I expect he'll be back soon, though,' she mumbled.

'That's great. Could I wait for him? My cameraman is on the way and I asked him to meet me here.' She put out her hand. 'My name's Ísrún,' she repeated.

'Yes … Sorry. I'm Móna.' She tried to smile as she shook Ísrún's hand. 'Won't you come inside?'

'Thanks,' Ísrún said, quickly stepping inside before Móna could change her mind. She followed her into a large kitchen where a glass of milk stood on the table next to an open newspaper.

'Sit down,' said Móna. 'Can I get you something to drink? I don't have any hot coffee right now.' She patted her swollen belly. 'I've given it up for the time being.'

'A glass of milk would do fine,' Ísrún said and thought back to old Katrín in Landeyjar and the glass of milk she had been given there. That was a day she would prefer to forget. 'How far gone are you?'

'Five months,' Móna said, fetching a carton of milk from the fridge and placing a glass in front of Ísrún, as she took her seat back at the table. Ísrún sat down opposite her and looked around the kitchen. The white of the cupboard doors shone in contrast to the black stone of the worktops. The kitchen table was black and surrounded by white chairs. A couple of monochrome photographs hung on the walls. The unwashed dishes in the sink, in rainbow colours, struck a jarring note against their stark surroundings. Everything seemed to be hidden away in cupboards, with little to be seen on the worktops. A row of white cups stood on a narrow shelf above a magnificent coffee machine.

'Congratulations,' Ísrún ventured.

Móna nodded and smiled, saying nothing in reply.

'Do you and Logi have many children?'

'What? Me and Logi?' Her voice rose and there was a note of determination in it that made Ísrún quail for a second. 'This is Jökull's baby.'

'Jökull?'

'That's right. Logi lives in the apartment upstairs. My husband is Jökull, Logi's brother.'

'I'm sorry,' Ísrún said in embarrassment. 'I hadn't realised. Should have done my homework better.' She smiled to try and lighten the atmosphere, but with little apparent success. 'This is your and Jökull's first child?'

'Yes.' The reply was short and sharp.

'OK. Some people start having children later in life, or like me, not at all.'

Móna was silent and stared into her glass of milk.

When the silence began to become almost unbearable, Ísrún decided to try and break it.

'Did Jökull work with Elías as well?'

'He certainly did not. He works at the Savings Bank,' said Móna, her voice still sharp.

'You're both locals?'

'Yes.'

'Born and bred?'

Ísrún glanced at the black-and-white photographs on the walls, all of which looked to be Siglufjörður scenes, landscapes or old pictures taken in the town.

'Pretty much. When's this cameraman going to be here?' Móna asked, her impatience clear. 'Shall I give Logi a call? He might have been held up.'

'There's no hurry,' Ísrún assured her. Nóra had mentioned that Elías had rented a room from Logi before he moved to her house. Ísrún wanted to get as much information about Elías as she could from Móna.

'What do you do?' she asked.

'I work for the local authority. But the doctor put me on maternity leave early. This hasn't been an easy pregnancy.'

She sighed.

'It must be difficult for you. But you must both be excited now it's getting closer.'

'Yes. We are,' Móna said, but her voice sounded heavy.

'You knew Elías well?'

'Hardly at all.' Móna gave a brisk shake of her head.

'Didn't he live here for a while?'

She hesitated. 'Upstairs, with Logi. He rented a room from him. Left at New Year. We didn't see much of him down here.'

'I suppose he must have been busy with all the charity work he did,' Ísrún said lightly, in order to maintain her subterfuge.

Móna snorted, making it clear that she had no faith in Elías's altruism. She sipped her milk and turned the page of the newspaper in front of her. It was obvious she had no intention of discussing Elías's affairs any further. In fact her mood was so dark that it was as if summer had not yet penetrated Móna's house. The view from the kitchen window was also overcast, hardly reminiscent of summer, and, although it was warm, anyone could have imagined that autumn was about to come early. A few conifers at the edge of the garden shivered, as if in a cool breeze.

'It must be difficult knowing a murder victim,' Ísrún suggested, determined not to leave right away.

'Yep,' Móna mumbled. 'A bit.'

'Unsettling,' Ísrún said.

Móna looked up. 'Yes, very much so,' she said and then relaxed. 'It has been very unsettling,' she agreed, almost as if speaking to herself.

'I'm sure I'd find it really uncomfortable,' Ísrún said. 'He lived here in the same house not so long ago. And now … now someone has found a reason to kill him. It's so hard to fathom. But maybe this isn't the best topic of conversation for someone who's pregnant,' she added, feeling a rare twinge of conscience.

'You get over it; try not to think about it,' Móna replied with a humourless smile. 'You push to the back of your mind the mental images that pop up when you hear about such a violent crime.'

'If the reports are to be believed, then it was a very brutal crime. I do have some faith in the news, at least the news my station carries,' Ísrún said.

Móna shuddered discreetly but did her best to hide it. Then she yawned, and this time failed to hide her gaping mouth.

'Sorry. I'm tired.'

'That kind of news must keep you awake, especially in your condition,' Ísrún said.

'It's kept me awake the last two nights. I was going to lie down today and see if I could get some sleep.'

Ísrún took the hint, and decided that she couldn't refuse a pregnant woman her rest.

'I'll be on my way, then. I'll drop by later.'

'It's all right, I didn't mean it like that. I'll call Logi.' She stood up with some difficulty and went into the other room, out of sight. Ísrún could hear the murmur of her voice.

'He's still at work. He says he'll be another hour. I hope that's not a problem for you?' Móna said when she came back into the kitchen.

'Not a problem. It'll work out. I'll drop back later.'

'What about your camera guy? Isn't he on the way?' she asked with a touch of suspicion in her voice.

This took Ísrún by surprise, and reminded her that lies need careful maintenance.

'Of course. I'll call him,' she said lightly on her way to the front door. 'Thanks for the chat.'

12

'What about Jói?' Ari Thór asked.

He and Tómas were sitting in the coffee corner. Hlynur would normally have joined them, but he seemed to be in a world of his own, with no interest in mixing with his colleagues.

Tómas had asked if Ari Thór had any concrete theory about the murder, anything they could contribute to that evening's meeting.

'Jói? Forget it, my boy. The man wouldn't hurt a fly,' Tómas said, apparently put out by Ari Thór's suggestion.

'I'm not so sure. I reckon there's a spark in him. He's definitely no pushover,' Ari Thór said to drive his point home.

Tómas looked doubtful. 'He and Elías hardly knew each other.'

'He told me they had an argument during the protest about the tunnel. You can never tell how far people can go.'

'I didn't know about that,' Tómas said, and his expression darkened. 'You're right, you can never tell, can you? You think you know someone, and then…'

Ari Thór decided to interrupt before Tómas brought the conversation around to his wife.

'I don't believe that any of Elías's work colleagues murdered him. To be honest, I don't imagine that any of them had any reason to. For me, the whole affair is most likely linked to some kind of dodgy business. And I doubt that Páll or Logi would have been involved in anything like that.'

'Good heavens, no,' Tómas said in a shocked tone. 'Páll used to be on the force and Logi is my cousin's brother-in-law. It's possible that Elías wasn't the intended victim, I suppose. Maybe the intention was to kill that doctor, Ríkhardur. He's the one who owns the land.'

Ari Thór took a deep breath. This was his own theory, and far-fetched as it was, he decided to squeeze out Tómas's agreement as far as he was able.

'That's what I was thinking. I was going to check this out before I mentioned it to you, but I looked up an old boy in Akureyri yesterday.' Ari Thór had to try hard to hide his excitement. 'Ríkhardur murdered his wife, or as good as murdered her.'

'Really? So you think some old chap in Akureyri attacked Elías?' Tómas smiled cheerfully. 'I find that hard to believe.'

'So do I. The old boy hates Ríkhardur with every fibre in his body, but I can't see him committing such a brutal killing.'

'Maybe it's not up to us to solve this one, my boy,' Tómas said, sounding paternal. 'But we have done our best so far, anyway. Perhaps something new will come up at tonight's conference.'

Ríkhardur Lindgren had received visitors twice in two days. That was taking things too far. First there had been that unpleasant reporter pretending to be from the police, and today some real police officers had called. He had let them in despite his strong reservations, being cautious after that woman's visit; and as they were in plain clothes, he had demanded to see their identification. In the end he had no option but allow them inside and try not to think of all the germs they were bringing in with them.

After their visit, he made an effort to carefully clean the chairs.

The television was switched off and for once he had no desire to read. Instead, he listened to a violin concerto by Shostakovich.

The police officers' questions had been endless; all this fuss over one man who had been murdered. He had hardly known him. One of the two police officers even suggested that Elías had been murdered by mistake, and that he, Ríkhardur, was the intended victim.

How facile. Someone might put on the wrong coat, but people don't go so far as to commit murder in error.

Rikhardur had noticed that the media had mentioned his name in relation to the case. And they had dug up their old news pieces, just when he had thought that was all behind him; hadn't he paid compensation – and in pretty generous amounts too?

Clearly, there was no possibility of being able to escape to the house in the north now.

He turned up the volume and tried to relax in his chair.

He would never get peace and quiet there, and the place would always be linked to that damned builder.

All things considered, maybe it would be best if he were to leave the country.

That way he could perhaps be left in peace.

13

There had been no preconceptions about Iceland in her mind; the only things about which she had been certain were that it would be cold, probably snowy, and it might be dark.

She had moved back to her place beside the wall. She wasn't sure when she had done that or why, but found suddenly that she could relax and rest her tired bones. That was good.

Her heart beat faster than she knew was natural. She was uncomfortably hot, something she had never expected to experience in Iceland.

Sometimes, when she closed her eyes, she had the feeling that she was back home.

She had done her best to break out of her prison. The door was the only possible escape route, but it was dishearteningly heavy and well made. It made no difference that there was a narrow gap at the bottom of the door. All it did was bring her a tiny slither of light and air.

Her head throbbed with pain and she was nauseous.

She thought of home, of her family, of the sunshine and the light.

She was so tired now; she would have to rest for a while.

It was time to let her mind wander homewards for a few moments.

It would soon be time to welcome death.

14

Svavar couldn't get her out of his head.

He was surprised by this. He thought he was stronger, more able to control his own mind.

He imagined her, locked in, waiting for Elías.

Everything would have been so much simpler if Elías had never mentioned her. That way she could have died quietly, shut away, and Svavar would never have been burdened with the knowledge that he could possibly have saved her life. Although he didn't know exactly where she had been imprisoned, he could at least have let the police know about her, provided them with a reason to search for her and given her a slight chance of survival.

He knew that chance was now fading fast; he would have to make a decision.

At first, being involved, if only as a silent partner, in this piece of work with Elías – bringing a young woman to Iceland for a life of slavery – hadn't troubled his conscience.

It's going to happen whether I like it or not, he had told himself. *If I don't do it, someone else will.*

But now, even though he had never seen her in person, in Svavar's imagination this young woman had become a very real, living person. She was someone who was waiting somewhere to die.

But his instinct for self-preservation was a powerful one. *You have to look after number one.* A spell in prison was too high a price to pay for saving her life. His dreams of living somewhere warmer would disappear in a puff of smoke.

He had tried to sleep, but without success. Now he sat by the window and stared into the sky.

He wasn't even sure what time it was. He had switched off his mobile and unplugged the landline. He hadn't spoken to anyone since the reporter had come to see him the previous evening.

The reporter – that was it.

He didn't know much about journalism, but he knew that a journalist never revealed a source, not ever. Why hadn't he thought of it before? It was such a simple solution, and so perfect.

He could regain his peace of mind by shifting the responsibility on to her. She wouldn't be able to finger him, but she'd be able to tell the police about the poor girl.

He felt better immediately and stood up from the wicker chair to search for his phone. Now he even felt hungry, and realised he hadn't eaten all day. He'd take a walk down to the dock later to see if anyone had any fish to sell, something he could cook simply and perfectly, just as his brainwave about the girl was perfect in its simplicity.

The phone was on the kitchen table. He located the scrap of paper with the journalist's number on it and switched the phone on.

It began buzzing straight away with endless messages. He quickly checked through them; most were from Páll and Hákon. He'd speak to them and tell them he felt ready to go back to work, but not until he had been in touch with this woman Ísrún, he decided, punching in her number.

Ísrún was on her way back to the guesthouse. She stood in the Town Hall Square and looked up towards the church. She was hungry, and was wondering whether or not to sit in one of the snack bars on the main street and order a quick pizza. But first she wanted to take a look at the church and gather her thoughts in peace and quiet.

She had never been religious, but over the last few months she'd found her feelings changing.

For some reason, now she wanted to believe, but wasn't sure how to find some kind of faith after all these years. Maybe going to church regularly might help?

Never being one for services, she instead enjoyed spending time in a church when nothing was happening, taking a seat on a pew and revelling in the tranquillity of the place.

Her feet felt heavy as she slowly ascended the steep steps to the church. She was still feeling the fatigue from what had been a long day and was sluggish after an unaccustomed daytime nap. Fortunately the church was open, and thankfully it appeared deserted.

Ísrún sighed as she sat on the nearest pew but one to the back, finally allowing herself to relax. She closed her eyes and tried to empty her thoughts, steering her mind away from those events of a year and a half before, which had led her to move south to Reykjavík and return to the newsroom. She also tried not to think of that visit to Katrín in Landeyjar a year ago.

What had happened in Akureyri eighteen months ago had been a shock, a body blow that she had managed to rise from through determination and denial.

The upset of what had taken place afterwards, in Landeyjar, though, had been little short of a knockout. She tried to seek shelter in the same denial that had worked in Akureyri, but she was painfully aware that that was only good as a short-term solution.

Straining to take her thoughts away from these two events, she still couldn't manage to empty her mind or relax properly. Instead she found herself thinking of the conversation with Móna, the sad and tired woman who had been so distant. It occurred to her that there was something in her account that didn't add up properly; some minor detail that nagged at her.

And then Ísrún realised just what that minor detail was. She was on her feet with such a start that she was relieved that there was nobody there to see her.

She ran down the church steps as fast as she dared, knowing she had to find Móna and get an answer, preferably before Logi or Jökull came home from work.

On the way, her phone rang. She stopped to peer at the screen. It was a number she didn't recognise. It could wait, she decided.

Only minutes later she was standing again on the steps in front of Móna's door. She knocked and didn't have to wait long before Móna let her in.

'I was half-expecting to see you again,' Móna said in a tone that seemed to combine apprehension with relief that her secret was finally shared. 'I let the cat out of the bag, didn't I?'

Ísrún nodded.

'Then you'd better hear the whole story,' said Móna, and it was as if a heavy load had been taken from her shoulders.

15

Oddrún thought of Gauti every day.

She worked for a software company in Reykjavík, where working days were long and standards were high. All the same, occasionally, and despite the demands her work made on her, thoughts of her brother and their mother would break through. Both of them had been snatched away from her far too early, each by their own hand.

Oddrún's and Gauti's father was dead. That had happened before Gauti's suicide. So it was always Oddrún that Gauti had come to when school had become too painful.

In fact, school had been painful from the very first day, as he never managed to fit in. Two years younger than her brother, Oddrún had done her best to support him, but she was just a child too. Of course, she should have gone to their parents, but Gauti wouldn't hear of it. And at that young age, she had failed to work out that he wasn't guilty of anything and was merely an innocent victim of bullying. She only realised this later as Gauti increasingly confided in her.

She knew precisely who his most vicious tormentor was; who was the one dispensing mental and physical cruelty. She remembered Hlynur clearly, although he would undoubtedly not remember her. She was repulsed by him, which was hardly surprising, as his brutality knew no limits. Gauti didn't tell his sister everything and sometimes she found out by roundabout routes what had happened to him. He had told her about the swimming pool incidents, though. Hlynur had held him under again and again, during almost every swimming lesson, always whispering the same words into his ear as he broke the surface, gasping for breath.

Next time I'll teach you how to die.

These words had stayed in her mind and given her nightmares, even though she had never witnessed this torture, let alone had to experience it as Gauti had.

Gauti had confessed to her that he had always expected the next swimming lesson to be the last one; that Hlynur would take things a step too far and hold him under until it was all over.

Gauti was a sensitive soul, a fragile character. But Hlynur hadn't broken him down with a single blow; rather, he had done so with a relentless barrage.

It was therefore no surprise that Gauti didn't finish college; he didn't even come close to it. He gave up after the first term and locked himself away. It had been his first opportunity to start afresh in a new school, with Hlynur nowhere to be seen, yet it had still been too much for him. The damage had already been done.

He never left home. Oddrún, however, had moved in with her boyfriend as soon as she started university. And it was then that Gauti's condition began to deteriorate rapidly, his grip on life becoming increasingly tenuous.

But the blame was Hlynur's, not hers. He might as well have appeared at the door that day and murdered Gauti on the spot.

Oddrún didn't take action right away; instead she allowed the hatred to build up inside her.

She knew that Gauti wasn't Hlynur's only victim, but he had been the one worst affected by that monster's brutality. Hlynur had systematically destroyed her brother's life and with it the lives of the entire family.

Gauti's suicide had affected their mother deeply and she had somehow convinced herself that she was to blame. Oddrún had tried her best to talk her out of feeling such guilt, but it was as if she was speaking to someone who couldn't hear her.

Finally her mother had given up on life as well. The source of her misery and the reason for Gauti's death were one in the same: Hlynur.

Over the years, Oddrún had done her best to smother the hatred inside her, trying to stop herself from descending to Hlynur's level. And she had been successful for a long time. That was until the middle of a normal working day,

It wasn't, in fact, a normal day. It was the anniversary of Gauti's suicide. And, as if in commemoration, Oddrún let the hatred take hold of her. With the decision she made that day came a deep feeling of relief.

Oddrún quickly found out where Hlynur was and what he had done in the intervening years. He had become a police officer in Siglufjörður, a long way from Reykjavík; too far for her to drive past his house and throw rocks through his windows. In any case, she had something more subtle planned for him.

Email gave her direct contact with him, both at work and at home. She set up an anonymous email account and did everything necessary to ensure that it couldn't be traced back to her. There was never any doubt about what the message would say.

After the first, she sent another message, with the same words. And then another. Hlynur didn't reply. She continued to send messages without any knowledge of whether or not they had any effect on Hlynur.

She still was not sure quite what she expected to achieve, other than the hope of some kind of justice. And then, perhaps, she would be free.

16

Tómas and Ari Thór were on their way to Akureyri. Hlynur had to remain on duty at the police station until the end of his shift later that evening.

But why? he wondered.

The town was at its quietest and there would hardly be a call-out tonight. Maybe he'd be expected to show his face if some revellers were making a nuisance of themselves, but that was it.

He wasn't trusted with anything more important any longer. It was no surprise to him.

He wondered now how he had ever imagined that he would be able to work as a police officer after the terrible things he had done in his younger days.

He stood up, read for the last time the latest email from the anonymous account and shut down the computer. Then he left the police station, locking the door behind him.

He had left his car at home. He made a habit of walking to work in summer – and in winter as well, if the weather allowed. So he set off on foot and was at his own door ten minutes later.

There was just one thought in his mind; the injustice of Gauti being dead while he was still living.

Now it was time to put that right.

17

They sat in Móna's kitchen, as if in a black-and-white dream – or, more accurately, a monochrome nightmare.

They remained silent until Ísrún took the initiative.

'Two nights.'

Móna nodded.

'You said the murder had kept you awake two nights in a row, but nobody knew about it until yesterday morning,' Ísrún said, her voice slow and serious. 'You accidentally gave the truth away there…'

'Yes…' Móna sighed. Tears had begun to creep down her cheeks. 'It's horrible.'

She buried her face in her hands for a moment, then looked back up.

'This secret has been dragging me down. I can't tell you what a relief it is to talk to someone about it. It's horrible,' she repeated. 'And it was all his fault.' Rising quickly to her feet she slapped the table. 'It was that man's fault!' she screeched.

Ísrún stood up and put an arm around Móna's shoulders.

'There … calm down. Take it easy. Sit down … please,' she said softly.

Obediently, Móna sat down again at the table.

'Are you talking about Elías?' Ísrún asked, as gently as she was able.

'Yes.' Móna was quiet now. 'Elías,' she said and then was silent.

'What did he do?' Ísrún asked, after waiting for her to continue.

Móna stayed silent, but the tears now flowed unchecked down her face.

Ísrún decided to try another tack.

'Did you kill him?' she asked. She was almost certain that the answer would be no. But the lesson journalism had taught her was that nothing could be ruled out. The truth could sometimes outstrip anything fiction could offer.

'No. They did it,' Móna muttered.

Ísrún pricked up her ears. 'They?'

'My husband and Logi,' she said and dissolved into sobs. 'They weren't going to kill him. They were going to give him a hiding … not … commit murder. That's what Jökull said when they came home. But there was a nail in the plank.'

Ísrún shuddered.

Móna sat in thought before she carried on. 'I … we had to lie to the police to give Logi an alibi. Of course he was a suspect, being one of the men who worked with Elías. Jökull didn't know Elías that well.'

'Why did they do it?' Ísrún asked.

Móna took a deep breath as she marshalled her courage.

'Elías came here the night before … the night before he died. Late. I let the bastard in. He was looking for Logi. Logi told my husband later what he said. Elías was working some scam. He said he could get paid for bringing foreign women to Europe so they could start a new life. A new life!' she echoed, contempt colouring her voice.

'Elías wanted Logi to be part of it. It was terrible having to see Elías that night. It was a long time since I had seen him. I went into the bedroom and howled. Jökull wanted to know what was the matter. I had promised myself after it happened that I wouldn't say anything to Jökull about it, but I couldn't keep it up. I don't know why, maybe the shock of seeing Elías that night was too much for me.'

Ísrún listened, stiff with shock. She said nothing and let Móna talk on.

'Finally I told Jökull everything,' she said after a pause. 'He freaked out. Jökull's the most even-tempered man you could hope to meet, but he went wild with rage.' She sighed and closed her eyes before continuing. 'He let Logi have it, as it was Logi who had brought the bastard to our house to begin with,' she snarled. 'When Logi understood what had happened, he was just as livid as Jökull was. *We're not letting him get away with it*, was what Logi said. Logi's more quick-tempered than Jökull. Before I knew it, they had gone, both of them, gone to Skagafjörður. God, how I regretted having told Jökull anything. Christ...'

Móna let out a howl of anguish. Ísrún hardly needed to ask the next question, so certain was she that she knew the answer.

'Elías raped you?' she said.

'How did you know?' Móna asked between sobs.

'You're not the first one he's done this to. When did it happen?'

Móna spoke in a low voice, with long and frequent pauses. 'Right after New Year. In the middle of the day. I'd forgotten my phone and had come home to get it. Elías was living upstairs in Logi's place. There's access between the two apartments. It's just one big house, really. Logi was on a shift and Jökull was at work. I couldn't do anything. I tried to scream and fight him off, but he was too strong for me. I could tell he'd done it before. He was just so calm and calculating.'

Ísrún felt another shudder run down her back. It was all she could do to stay seated, to stop herself running from the house.

'I was in shock,' Móna continued. 'I didn't say a word to anyone. I don't know why. I just couldn't talk about it. But he had the sense to move out right away.'

Ísrún hesitated before letting fly with the question that begged to be asked.

'Is that his child?'

Móna didn't answer right away.

'Yes. I'm pretty sure it is,' she finally mumbled through her tears. 'Jökull and I had tried for a baby for so long but without any luck. And now I'm carrying a rapist's child. I swear I was never going to say a word to Jökull, not ever! He was so pleased that it had happened at last, that I was finally pregnant. You can imagine why they both went wild.'

'I understand completely. The scum deserved everything he got. It couldn't have happened too soon,' Ísrún said, letting her own fury come to the surface.

'He was a complete bastard. But they didn't set out to kill him,' Móna said.

'Of course,' Ísrún replied, upset on Móna's behalf, but doing her best to remain calm.

'It was Logi who hit him,' Móna said at last. 'Jökull told me about it. Elías admitted what he had done and Logi asked him simply why the hell he had done it. It was when he heard the answer that he grabbed a length of wood and lashed out.'

Móna's words were practically indistinguishable from her sobs.

'What was the answer Elías gave him?' Ísrún asked, against her own better judgement, falling unconsciously back into the role of inquisitor yet again.

'Because I could.'

18

Because I could.

Ísrún shivered, just as she felt the sting of her conscience. Did she also bear a level of responsibility for what had happened?

She and Móna looked at each other in silence.

'What did you mean?' Móna asked with a suddenness that caught Ísrún off guard.

'What?'

'You said just now that I wasn't his first victim,' Móna said, her voice gaining strength, her eyes widening

'That's right. He raped me as well.'

Ísrún said it without thinking. If was as if her subconscious self wanted her to say the words out loud before giving her the opportunity to think them over and change her mind.

It was a strange feeling, hearing the sound of those words now that she had finally found the courage to tell someone after all the sleepless nights, all the nightmares. A year and a half had passed since then and she was still not sure if she would ever recover. She had not been in a relationship with a man since and the thought of it made her stomach churn with revulsion.

Móna was staring at her in amazement. Ísrún's statement had obviously come as a clear shock.

'He did it to you as well?' she asked, as if unable to believe her own ears. And then came the question Ísrún had been so frightened of. 'Then why was the man free?'

'I haven't told anyone about it. Not until now. I felt so bad,' she said, forcing herself to hold back the tears. Crying wasn't her style.

'I couldn't bring myself to go to the police and tell them about what had happened. That was the wrong thing to do. I see that now.'

'For fuck's sake!' Móna yelled, on her feet in an instant. 'You could have spared me the same thing!' She slumped back down into her seat, and Ísrún could see her quivering with emotion as she fought to regain control of her anger.

'I'm sorry. If anyone ought to understand how you feel, then it should be me,' Móna said, her voice shaking.

'It's a horrific experience that nobody would want to share. You'll have to decide for yourself whether or not you tell the police about what he did to you, and if you tell them about what Jökull and Logi did. It's not my affair and I won't say a word,' Ísrún said, to her own surprise.

She had fought for this assignment to find out more about Elías. She had been determined to revenge herself on him, to dig up some secret from his past and plaster it across the news. A tooth for a tooth. But she had no intention of telling anyone what she had been through.

'Thank you,' Móna said, although she sounded unconvinced.

'In return, can I trust you to keep to yourself what I have just told you?' Ísrún said hesitantly.

'When did it happen?'

'January last year. I was living in Akureyri and had a job there. I was out on the town one night and this man I'd never seen before wouldn't leave me alone. He followed me out of the bar and forced me into some fucking storeroom…' She sighed, unable to put what had happened into words. 'I did the same as you. Didn't say a word. Retreated into my shell. I couldn't stay in Akureyri after that. I moved back south as soon as I could and got a job at the TV station.'

'And then you get an assignment to do a report about him? That must have been a shock,' Móna said, her tears gone.

'It wasn't quite like that,' Ísrún said, and then fell silent. Should she tell the whole story? It wasn't as if Móna was likely to pass it on to Ívar or María. She decided she would. It was half told already.

'I didn't go to the police. I didn't even know the man's name and didn't try to find it out, either. I wanted to forget the whole thing as quickly as I could. But I couldn't forget what he looked like or what he did to me. I saw his face in my nightmares every single night. Yesterday we got a report that a man had been found dead in Skagafjörður. I was on shift. Normally I don't get to do much hard news.' She tried to put on a smile. 'But when his name came up, I typed it into a search engine, and there was his face looking back at me. That man. The man who raped me. You can imagine how I felt.'

Móna nodded and dried her tears.

'There was no doubt in my mind that this was my rapist,' Ísrún continued. 'Elías Freysson. I just sat and stared for a while, and felt myself getting angrier and angrier. Now I knew who he was I wanted desperately to get my own back on him. But the bastard was dead, so I couldn't kill him. What I could do was destroy what he had left: his reputation. After our encounter I had no doubt what sort of man he was and I was sure he had plenty of other things on his conscience. All I had to do was get the newsroom to let me dig into it, turn over a few stones and find what might be underneath.' She continued earnestly now: 'I told the desk editor that someone had called me to say that Elías had been involved in drug trafficking, and persuaded him to let me follow it up. In fact, I'm sure he was happy to let me disappear to the country for a few days. We don't get on, you see.'

'And what are you going to do now?' Móna asked quietly.

'Nothing. I've no intention of dragging your family into the media circus just because of my need for revenge. You'll have to decide for yourselves what you do.'

Móna leaned forward and stared into the distance. A new, stray tear found its way down her cheek and dropped onto the surface of the table, taking with it any vestiges of energy left in Móna's body.

19

It was a wonderful feeling to have finally told someone about the rape, at long last to have talked about what she had never intended to mention to anyone. This was a first step. Now Ísrún felt she might find the strength to seek out the specialist help that could help her put this terrible experience behind her.

It was only when she was back at the guesthouse that she remembered that someone had tried to call when she was on the way to Móna's. She sat weakly on the edge of the bed. She was tempted to turn her phone off, but at last decided to be a conscientious journalist and make the call anyway.

'Hello?' The voice on the other end was harsh. 'Is that Ísrún?'

'That's me. You tried to call me earlier? Who is this?'

'Hi. It's Svavar here, over in Dalvík.'

'Hi,' she replied in surprise, not expecting to hear from him again. What could the man want? For a moment it occurred to her to say she was busy and end the call right there. She was exhausted, physically and emotionally, and she had little or no interest in talking to Svavar. Her part in this story was over. The mystery was solved. She had established that Elías had raped at least one other woman apart from herself, and doubtless more. But she could never bring herself to use this material, even though this had been her original aim in pursuing the story: to expose the bastard. Now she had met Móna she was reluctant to drag her into this.

'What do you want?' she asked abruptly.

'I need to talk to you about something … in confidence,' he said and she heard him hesitate. 'You know, I'm a … a source.'

'Fair enough,' she replied, her interest still at a low ebb.

'Isn't it right that you never reveal a source's name?' he asked; his eagerness was unmistakeable now.

'That's right. Fire away. You can trust me,' she said, her curiosity sparking a little, despite everything.

'All right, but I'm not sure of the best way to put this.'

She could hear from his voice that he was nervous and short of breath. Maybe there could be a scoop in this after all? That would earn her a few brownie points with Ívar and María.

There was a long pause, during which all that Ísrún could make out was his erratic breathing.

'I think Elías locked a girl up somewhere before he died. I'm starting to get concerned about her.'

Ísrún was on her feet, hardly able to believe what she was hearing.

'What was that? He locked a girl up? Why? It's almost two days since he died!'

'Yeah. That's why I'm a bit stressed out,' Svavar mumbled.

'Stressed out!' she snapped. 'You weren't before?'

Svavar didn't reply.

'Are you going to help me or not?' he demanded at last.

'Yes, but why don't you just call the police?'

'I don't want to get mixed up in all this.'

'You're an arsehole,' she snarled. Then she collected herself, the thought of a young woman imprisoned somewhere slamming into her mind. 'I'm sorry,' she said quickly. 'You mean you want me to pass this on to the police?'

'Yes,' he answered.

'Who is this woman and where is she?'

'I don't know,' Svavar replied, and quickly told the tale of Elías's travels to Asia, how he had been paid by a group of men to fetch a girl from Nepal and bring her to Iceland. 'This was supposed to be a trial run. If he did a good job and brought in the goods undamaged, then there would be plenty more work for him.'

'Christ,' Ísrún swore. She rarely brought God into anything she said, but this phone call was something outside her experience. 'And you've no idea where she is?'

'I was hoping the cops could find that out.'

His voice betrayed how tired he was.

'All right. I'll pass the message on and I won't mention you, but I'll certainly cover this in a news report. Just so you're aware of that.'

'Do what you like. Just keep me out of it, please,' Svavar said, his voice desperate.

She was about to end the call when she remembered the apartment in Akureyri.

'What about the flat?' she asked, her heart beating faster.

'What flat?'

'The flat in Akureyri,' Ísrún snapped, her patience at an end. If Svavar was telling the truth, then minutes or even seconds could count. 'Could she be there?'

'The flat in Akureyri? That's Idunn's place, Elías's wife. I guess it's still hers.'

'No. Elías got it when they split up.'

'Really?' Svavar said, clearly taken by surprise. 'He never mentioned that.'

'He wasn't short of secrets.'

Ísrún ended the call and dialled the Akureyri stringer to get a number for Helga at CID in Akureyri.

As the call connected Ísrún rushed out of the guest house, determined not to lose a second.

Helga answered after a couple of rings and Ísrún breathlessly gave her name.

'How did you get this number? I'm in a meeting and I can't answer questions now,' Helga said quietly, the sharpness of her tone conveying her irritation at being disturbed.

'This is an emergency, life or death,' Ísrún said, making every effort to keep her satisfaction to herself.

'What? Wait a moment, I'll go outside.'

'You'll have to let my cameraman be there. Us and nobody else,' Ísrún said, ashamed of herself for wasting precious seconds.

'No promises,' Helga said. 'But I'll do my best.'

'I have a reliable source…' Ísrún said, wondering how to word what she wanted to say. 'This is someone who tells me that Elías was involved in people trafficking, and…' she began and then paused.

'Trafficking? Well, dammit. I was hoping we'd never see that here…' Helga said.

This is going to be a hell of a story, Ísrún thought to herself, her commentary already half written in her mind.

'It seems he brought a young woman to Iceland. Did you know?'

'Yes, there was a passenger who came to Iceland on the same flight as Elías from Denmark,' Helga said guardedly. 'The same person had accompanied him from Nepal to Denmark. A girl. They didn't have adjacent seats, so there was no direct connection, but we noticed it when we checked the flight lists. We haven't been able to trace her so far. We're only a small team who've been working on this, I'm afraid, but you keep that to yourself.'

'My source is convinced that Elías has locked her away somewhere. She was supposed to be held until some contact of his collected her – and paid for her,' Ísrún said.

'Locked away? Where?' Helga asked. 'And who's your source?' she demanded.

'You know I'm not going to give away a source. This person said that he didn't know where she is. But I suspect that she's in an apartment that Elías owned in Akureyri,' Ísrún continued carefully.

'He didn't have a place here. We'd have known about it,' Helga replied shortly.

'He didn't register the place in his *own* name. It's registered to a company owned by his former wife,' Ísrún said, and quickly spelled out the address.

'Thanks. We'll be right there. Anything else?'

'No, but let me know what happens. I'm on my way,' Ísrún said, but Helga had already ended the call.

Ísrún got into her car, and pulled away at speed, taking the road to Akureyri.

Ignoring any concerns for her own safety or rules about using phones while driving, she made a call to María.

'Yes. Hello, Ísrún,' María said. 'I was trying to get hold of you earlier.'

'I need a cameraman in Akureyri right now,' Ísrún told her, speaking fast and hoping that nothing would be lost. 'The police are on their way to rescue a girl Elías locked up in his apartment there. He brought her from Nepal a few days ago and was going to sell her on to a prostitution ring – here or somewhere in Europe.'

'What?' María yelped. 'You're sure?'

'I've informed the police and the source is reliable. We don't know exactly where she is, but they'll be starting the search at Elías's place in Akureyri any minute. We need to get our stringer there right away,' she said, her voice strained. 'OK to call him out?'

'Do it.'

'Thanks,' Ísrún said. 'Why were you trying to reach me?'

'Nothing special,' María assured her. 'Just get yourself there.'

Ísrún didn't need to be told twice and ignored every speed limit as she pushed the car as hard as she could.

Her next call was to Móna. Before she had left her they had exchanged numbers. Ísrún had told her to call whenever she needed any kind of support.

'I had a thought,' she said as soon as Móna picked up. 'There might be a way for Logi and Jökull to admit to the murder, if that's what it comes to, without bringing you or the baby into it. Elías was involved in people trafficking and he had brought a girl from Nepal to Iceland to sell her on. This is information that won't be made public right away. If Logi and Jökull talk to the cops tonight and say that this was the reason behind the murder – that they were trying to save the girl – then I reckon it would sound credible.'

Móna listened in silence.

'Thanks. That's interesting,' she said after a moment. 'I'll talk to the boys and see what they say. But you're right. It's probably the only way out.'

'You need to act quickly, though,' Ísrún said, thinking of the desperately sad woman with the baby growing inside her. 'I know it's hard, but you have to do it right away if it's going to work.'

'Yes, yes, I know… '

Móna sounded hesitant, so Ísrún decided to press her.

'You can tell them I told you. But, please, please my name can't be brought into this. And no one must know what Elías did to me.'

'Of course. I'll make sure they know. Thank you, Ísrún. I really mean it.'

Sometimes Ísrún's own flexible attitude to the truth was something that took her by surprise, but she decided that this time the end justified the means.

20

'I'm expecting a friend,' Kristín had said in her email. A friend? The message didn't say a male friend, but Ari Thór had a good idea what she meant.

He and Tómas were at the case review meeting in Akureyri. Helga from CID was taking charge in her usual efficient manner, but now she had gone out to answer a phone call.

Not much had come out of the meeting that was new. The police had interviewed Ríkhardur Lindgren, and the thinking was that, directly or indirectly, the case was unlikely to have anything to do with him.

Ari Thór's thoughts were entirely on Kristín, however. Knowing that she was so close by, in the same town, meeting some other man, was an agony for him.

Did this simply confirm that everything between them was over? Was this the painful reality he was going to have to face? Or was she just playing some kind of game with him – trying to make him jealous? Or perhaps she was waiting for him to take the initiative?

He didn't feel that was likely. What he really wanted to do was bang on her door, right now, this evening, interrupt whatever was going on and tell her that he wanted her back. He would apologise in person, face to face.

That way she'd have to choose one of them or the other.

He pushed his thoughts aside. Of course he would never do anything like that.

Helga came back into the meeting room. Her face was taut and serious. Something had clearly happened.

'There's an aspect to the case we have been exploring that I need to explain,' she said with an awkward expression on her face. 'We've been trying to track down a girl who travelled from Nepal to Iceland on the same flights as Elías. We haven't been able to trace her, but I've just had confirmation that she did accompany him to Iceland, in connection with a people-trafficking ring.'

She paused to let her words sink in.

'Elías was holding her when he died, probably in an apartment in Akureyri. She has more than likely been locked in there for forty-eight hours, if not longer.'

It would have been possible to hear a pin drop in the room.

Helga broke the silence. 'I've already dispatched an ambulance and a squad car in the area to the location. Now we need to be there right away.'

Ari Thór was on his feet in an instant. For now Kristín was forgotten.

⌖

For once, Ari Thór was in the driving seat before Tómas got to the car. He had no intention of being the last one on the scene, which would be a definite possibility if Tómas was behind the wheel.

'I doubt we'll be able to do much for the poor girl, my boy,' Tómas said as Ari Thór put his foot down. 'We don't need to rush.'

The house stood on its own on the edge of town. It was a gloomy, neglected building. The ground-floor windows had been boarded over and upstairs the curtains were drawn.

Ari Thór drew up outside and was out of the car in a flash. There was already an ambulance in front of the house, as well as several police cars and an old station wagon with a TV station's logo on the side. The flashing blue lights underscored the urgency of the situation. He noticed a cameraman filming without interference.

Helga was standing to one side, waiting.

'Do we have a warrant for this?' Ari Thór heard a police officer from Sauðárkrókur asking Helga.

'There's no time,' she said, her voice hard. 'I'll take responsibility.'

21

The little apartment Kristín had rented in Akureyri was on the ground floor of a charming old house in a quiet neighbourhood, not far from the college, the same college where her mother had studied many years before.

Kristín's mother had become an architect and her father had worked for a bank. Now her parents had moved to Norway, both having lost their jobs in the wake of the financial crash.

Kristín missed them, and she intended to visit them if she could get enough time off work. She had protested unconvincingly when they had told her of their plans, but she could hardly complain. She had moved out of Reykjavík herself and visited them all too rarely. There was no work for her mother in the capital, or for any other architect for that matter, and she had been offered a well-paid position in Oslo. Most jobs overseas now seemed to be well paid in comparison to the weak state of Iceland's currency.

Her father had found a position with another bank in Reykjavík, one that had risen from the ashes of the crash, but that was only a temporary post. And anyway, he was keen to make a change following the financial crisis. So now he was working for a small company in Norway that provided financial consultancy to the maritime sector, a field he had specialised in at the bank.

They had visited Kristín at Easter, bedding down on mattresses on the floor of her little living room.

'You'll have to find somewhere bigger,' her mother had said with her habitual forthrightness, which often bordered on the hurtful. 'This place is too small for a doctor and it's terribly bare.'

The last thing Kristín wanted was to fill the place with junk. She liked the place as it was. There was a single picture on the living room wall, a poster for *Casablanca*, her all-time favourite film, with Humphrey Bogart and Ingrid Bergman. The sofa and chairs set around a modest wooden table had come from a second-hand shop. She hadn't put up bookshelves and her books were stacked on the living room floor, her library consisting almost entirely of medical textbooks. The kitchen table had come with the flat and, like the rest of the fixtures and fittings, it was showing its age.

The kitchen was Spartan, demonstrating how little time the flat's occupant spent there. Kristín preferred to eat at work, where the canteen always offered decent midday and evening meals. Her shift rota meant that she could normally eat both lunch and dinner there. Apart from that, she relied on fast food, taking care to keep to the more healthy varieties.

Now Kristín sat at the kitchen table opposite the widower. They were perched on worn green stools and sipped red wine while the roast cooked itself to tenderness in the oven.

'I didn't time it right,' Kristín said in a voice that was both warm and apologetic. 'It's a long time since I've had time to cook like this. It's going to need another half an hour.'

The man smiled. His face was sharply chiselled and his hair shaded with a touch of grey.

In the short time she had known him, they had hardly mentioned previous relationships. It seemed to be a topic they were both anxious to avoid. She certainly had no wish to talk about Ari Thór, and he seemed reluctant to say anything about his late wife.

They clinked glasses for the third time that evening over the guttering tea lights on the table.

22

Helga was holding an impromptu conference outside Elías's apartment. Ari Thór and Tómas stood among the other police officers and listened.

The cameraman kept his camera running until Helga asked him to switch it off while she talked to her colleagues. He was reluctant to do so, but agreed to step back when she promised him that he would be the first to get an update on the situation.

'I'd have arrested that guy with the camera,' Ari Thór whispered to Tómas, who grinned in reply. It wasn't often that he saw a smile on Tómas's face these days.

The cameraman stopped recording and walked away, although Ari Thór was certain he was still close enough to hear most of the conversation.

'The girl isn't here,' Helga said, even though this hadn't escaped any of them. 'It could be that the reporter's source was leading us up the garden path, or maybe the unfortunate woman is locked away somewhere else. If that's the case, then we're on borrowed time, as you can well appreciate. We need to go over everything right away, and work out what other potential locations there might be. This means interrogating Elías's friends and colleagues again – by phone if there's no other option,' she said. 'Although we didn't find the girl,' she went on, 'we did find what look to be stolen goods in there.'

Helga began to assign specific tasks to the Akureyri officers. When she reached Ari Thór and Tómas, she said,

'You need to talk to your people – Elías's colleagues in Siglufjörður: Páll and Logi, and the foreman at the tunnel.'

'That's Hákon,' Tómas said. 'Hákon the Herring Lad.'

Helga stared at him, baffled.

'I'll call Hlynur,' Ari Thór said. 'He's on duty. He's not up to speed on this case, but we need to work fast.'

He dialled Hlynur's mobile and listened to the phone ring, doubting, however, that a contribution from Hlynur would be any kind of help. When Hlynur failed to answer, he called the police station's direct number. But there was no answer there either.

'That's weird,' Ari Thór muttered. 'I can't reach him.'

'What the hell?' Tómas's scowl showed both his anger and embarrassment.

Helga looked over. 'Did I just hear that you can't you reach anyone at Siglufjörður station?' Her tone made her disapproval clear. 'What kind of shambles is it over there? You two had better go straight back,' she said, without waiting for a reply. 'And when all this is over, I want a full explanation of exactly why there's no one on duty. This is not acceptable.'

'We're on our way,' Tómas said shamefacedly, walking hurriedly towards the car.

But Ari Thór stayed where he was. A sudden idea had rooted him to the spot.

Helga had left two key people out of the list of contacts she thought they should talk to in Siglufjörður: Jói the artist and Jónatan. Ari Thór hadn't yet told Tómas about his conversation with the strange, prematurely aged Jónatan, with his painfully bent back. Thinking about him now, in front of Elías's empty house, Ari Thór felt certain his instinct was right.

'I think I know where the girl is,' he said out loud.

'What? What do you mean?' Tómas boomed, almost running back from the car. 'Out with it,' he ordered, making Helga spin around.

'Elías spent his summers in the country when he was a boy, on a farm not far from here – in Skagafjörður. It's abandoned now. He must have known his way around there. Where better to hide someone than an abandoned farm nobody ever goes near?'

'Hell and damnation, why didn't you say so before?' Helga snapped, her eyes flaring with anger.

This wasn't quite the positive response Ari Thór had expected; no thanks or a pat on the back.

'You know where the farm is?' Tómas asked.

'No. But I know who does,' Ari Thór said, already looking up Jónatan's number.

⌖

Ísrún was speeding towards Akureyri, doing her best to keep the car on the right side of the road. She had no intention of slowing down, though; this kind of scoop didn't turn up every day, and she was determined not to miss it. She drove the same route that had brought her to Siglufjörður, the Low Heath road. The stretch she was on now was an unmade dirt road and more than once she was sure that she was about to lose control of the car.

Her phoned buzzed. She picked it up with one hand, struggling to keep hold of the wheel and control her spinning tyres with the other.

'Where are you?' the cameraman from Akureyri asked urgently.

'On the Low Heath road.'

'Then turn round,' he told her. 'The girl wasn't in the place in Akureyri. They reckon she's in some abandoned farmhouse in Skagafjörður. We're on our way there.'

She slammed the brakes on and was thrown forward in her seat. The cameraman was reading out instructions for where she needed to go. She repeated them back, using all her journalist's skill to quickly memorise the location.

'OK. I'm on my way,' she said, trying with difficulty to turn the car around one-handed in the middle of the narrow dirt road. 'Don't lose sight of them! This is going to be a hell of a story!' She was almost yelling into the phone.

She finally managed to complete her manoeuvre with a bad skid, and headed back the way she had come, putting her foot down so that a trail of dust rose up behind the car in the still summer air.

⌖

'You should have mentioned that before,' Tómas said in quiet voice, as Ari Thór took his place in the driving seat.

Ari Thór didn't reply. Why was he being criticised? Hadn't he just sorted the case out for them?

They were on the way out of town when he stamped hard on the brakes. As they always did when he was in Akureyri, his thoughts went to Kristín and a terrible thought occurred to him as he recalled what Natan had told him.

She met him playing golf. He's older and his wife died.

The thought came to him with sudden, sickening realisation. A year and a half earlier, he had been caught up in a serious dispute in Siglufjörður with a man who had been cleared of one murder but who had undoubtedly committed another one, although that could never be proved. The description matched perfectly. He was somewhat older than Kristín. His wife had died and he had moved to Akureyri, as far as Ari Thór knew. This was a man who had never had a problem with women, a character who blended charm with a lack of scruples – a dangerous mix. He certainly bore Ari Thór a grudge and had been forced to leave Siglufjörður after rumours about him appeared in the press – rumours that could be traced to Ari Thór.

Could he have decided to get his own back by starting a relationship with Kristín?

Ari Thór felt a cold sweat prick out on his forehead. Kristín could be in real danger; it was possible she could lose her life.

'What the hell are you playing at?' roared the usually equable Tómas.

'I have to get out here. I'll explain later.'

'Are you off your head? We're on duty, dammit,' Tómas yelled furiously.

'I have to go,' Ari Thór shouted back, the first time he had ever raised his voice to Tómas. He swung open the door and ran. He had never before seen Tómas so angry. But right now he didn't care. He had more important things to worry about.

23

As the evening drew on, the weather was clearing. It had been a cool, overcast summer day. Although there was no real darkness at this time of the year, the evening sun dipped behind the high mountains surrounding Siglufjörður so there was no chance of any of the late sunshine making its way into the town. All the same, Jónatan sat on a stool in his garden and enjoyed the warmth that the end of the day brought.

The cop, the young one, Ari Thór, had called and asked about the place in Skagafjörður where his parents had farmed. It had been a short conversation, with Ari Thór clearly in a hurry. Jónatan had answered every question conscientiously, and when he had been about to enquire courteously why the police needed to know about the farm, he found that Ari Thór had already hung up.

It had to be something to do with Elías's murder. But what? Had the police heard about what had gone on there, back in the old days? Now the whole story might come out: the horrific tale of what the boys had been forced to endure; Jónatan himself, Elías, and most of those who had been unfortunate enough to have been sent to spend a summer on the family's farm.

Jónatan had always been at a loss to understand what lay behind the brutality. What could have created such viciousness in someone, the need to make others suffer? He had never experienced any such urges himself. He hoped that it wasn't something that could be passed down from one generation to the next.

Maybe it was time to tell the whole story, after all.

Whatever the reasons for his murder, Elías was dead, so there was no help for him anymore. But it might be possible to do something for the others who had been made to suffer during their stay on the farm. Perhaps in some way Elías's death itself could be traced back to those black days.

Jónatan knew it would look bad for his whole family; his brothers and sisters would be unlikely to thank him for bringing it up again after all these years. He himself would be labelled a victim and the son of a monster, and there would be endless public sympathy and sensationalised interest.

The thought made him shudder. The last thing he wanted was to attract attention.

He just wanted to be left alone.

He heaved a deep sigh. Sometimes things had to change regardless of what the consequences might be.

He stood up and limped into the living room, without bothering to find his stick to help him. Sitting down heavily by the phone, he dialled the number Ari Thór had called from.

Ari Thór answered. He sounded breathless.

Jónatan paused, gulped and then forced himself to speak. 'I need to talk to you—'

But Ari Thór cut him off. 'I can't. Not right now. I … I'm busy. It's an emergency. You'll have to call Tómas instead.'

He rattled out a telephone number and hung up without waiting for a reply.

Jónatan waited a minute while he gathered the strength to dial again.

The reply he received was just as sharp and almost as breathless as Ari Thór's.

'Tómas!'

The background rumble told Jónatan that Tómas was driving. He was probably in a police car on the way to the farmhouse in Skagafjörður.

'Hello, Tómas,' Jónatan said uncertainly. 'This is Jónatan. Ari Thór called me earlier, asking about the old farm in Skagafjörður…'

But again Jónatan was interrupted. 'I'm in a hurry,' Tómas said, before he could get to the point.

But Jónatan knew it would have to be now or never. He had finally summoned up the courage to tell the truth, and he was determined to be heard.

'I need a few minutes of your time,' he said, making an effort to be clear and firm. 'It's important. Very important.'

'Talk. Talk then.'

Tómas's voice barely disguised the fact that he thought he had more important things to deal with at that moment.

'Why did you want to know where the farm is?' Jónatan asked, preferring to tread carefully at the outset.

For a while Jónatan could hear only the noise of the car, the hum of the engine.

'We're looking for someone, a woman,' Tómas replied gruffly. 'We think she could be there. Elías knows his way around the place. We think he could have taken her there.'

Jónatan felt a surge of nausea. The brightness of the evening seemed to darken suddenly and his heart beat faster. Had Elías murdered some poor woman and hidden her body at the farm? He could well believe it. His mind raced. He instantly knew where the most likely hiding place would be.

'It's … it's very possible,' Jónatan said, almost without intending to.

'What do you mean?' Tómas asked, his voice still distracted.

'A lot happened there that wouldn't bear the light of day,' Jónatan said, choosing his words with care. 'Elías had a hard time … and that doubtless affected him in later life.'

'A hard time?' Tómas asked in surprise.

'The boys there, myself included, didn't have a happy time of it,' Jónatan said. He spoke slowly, struggling to state the facts in direct terms.

'Hold on. Are you telling me that they were abused?'

Now it seemed to Jónatan that he had Tómas's attention.

'That's right.' He almost whispered the words.

'What the hell? What kind of abuse? Sexual abuse?' Tómas demanded in a sharp tone.

'What? No. Fortunately not,' Jónatan replied. He had been taken off-guard. 'But all kinds of other abuse – physical, mental, beatings, being locked up...'

'And why the hell haven't you said anything about this before?' Tómas asked.

'I ... I ...' Jónatan could feel the words drying up in his mouth. He had not shed tears since leaving childhood behind, but this conversation was more of a trial than he could have imagined. 'I couldn't say anything while my parents were alive. And when they died, I thought it was all in the past, that it would do no good to rake over cold ashes.'

'And you say Elías was badly treated?'

'He was. Very badly.' Jónatan sighed. He paused to gather the strength to continue. 'He came to us the second year that my parents were taking boys in over the summer. Summer camp, they called it.' Jónatan laughed, but his laughter was heavy with sorrow. 'It was plain hell. That first year, there were three or four boys and they were made to work from morning to night, beaten into obedience and locked in. There were all kinds of threats not to say a word. Some of them were told to come back the following summer, or else something bad would happen to their families down south. That's what happened to Elías. And he did as he was told – he came back the next summer.'

'Beaten and locked up?' Tómas said.

'Elías was a strong character,' Jónatan said, carrying on, drifting off into a world of his own, so that he almost forgot he was on the phone. 'He was plucky and strong right from the first day, even though he was only six or seven. That wasn't going to be tolerated. But he showed a weak point. He was frightened of the yard dog. I don't know why – she was such a lovely dog. Maybe he'd been bitten by one, I don't know. That first night he was allowed to sleep in a room on his own – my room – and I was made to use a sleeping bag in the garage with the other boys. But I was stubborn that night; I didn't want to go out there in the dark, so I sat in the hall for a while. That's how I saw what happened.'

Jónatan paused as the memories appeared before his eyes, like an old horror film he could barely watch. He had to force himself to look back. To tell what he had seen.

'Elías was locked in with the dog that night. He screamed with terror all night long. Nobody got a wink of sleep and the screams echoed through the house. The next morning Elías was completely different, broken and exhausted.

'That's what it was like there. Everyone had to follow all the rules. But they weren't written down anywhere. So there was no way we could avoid stepping out of line. It was like a trap that was set for us. It was hell! Pure hell!' Jónatan said, his voice rising to a near scream.

'And what happened if the rules were broken? Beatings until you behaved?' Tómas asked.

'Sometimes, but the worst was being locked up in the potato store. I spent many nights in there. There was a heavy door so there was no hope of breaking out. It was so tight to the floor that there was hardly a breath of fresh air. There was just a tiny strip of light when it was bright in summer, but otherwise it was pitch black. I've never been able to stand the bright nights since then – too many bad memories. Nobody was ever locked up in winter, that would have been going too far and the cold would have killed them. It only happened in summer, when we had visitors from down south.'

Jónatan sighed.

'That's appalling,' Tómas said, his voice heavy. 'Absolutely appalling. Why on earth didn't your mother do anything to stop all this? God knows how much damage your father must have done.'

Jónatan gasped.

'Listen … you're getting the wrong end of the stick. I'm sorry. I didn't make myself clear. It wasn't the old man who did all this. It was her. It was Mother.'

24

Ari Thór knew precisely where Kristín lived. He had made a point of looking the place up when he had been in Akureyri one day. It was easy to reach on foot.

He hoped he wouldn't be too late. He couldn't get rid of the feeling that Kristín was in grave danger.

Elías's murder was behind him now.

And he wasn't interested in the fate of the unknown woman who might be locked away somewhere, closer to death than life.

Now he was convinced he had an opportunity to save Kristín and win her back. That was all that mattered to him.

It took Tómas a while to appreciate everything Jónatan had told him. From the moment Jónatan had started with his revelations, he had assumed that it was Jónatan's father who had been responsible for the abuse handed out to the boys.

'Let me get this right. It was your mother who locked the boys in the potato store?' he asked in amazement.

It had clearly been a struggle for Jónatan to relate the events of long ago. His voice was small and flat now.

'That's it. She ruled the roost. Smacked us boys until we did as we were told. Most of us only needed one night in the spud store. It was so dark. Completely black.'

Tómas shuddered at the thought.

'And what did your father have to say about all this?'

'Not much,' Jónatan sighed. 'He couldn't handle the old woman. He'd help her if anyone showed a bit of resistance, not because he was a bad man but because he was as frightened of her as we boys were.'

'And you were on your own? No brothers and sisters?' Tómas asked, trying to do his best to concentrate on the road at the same time, and thankful for the hands-free phone. He needed to be quick, as the other vehicles in front of him were travelling fast.

'Yes, but they were a good bit older. They'd left home by the time my parents started running these summer camps.'

'You'll have to come to the station and make a statement tomorrow,' Tómas told him, trying to make his words as gentle as he could, and regretting his earlier abruptness. He couldn't help but feel a deep sympathy for this man who had finally been able to recount a childhood ruined by his parents. 'Why don't you drop by in the morning? Any time.'

'I'll do that,' Jónatan said, and Tómas could sense the exhaustion and relief in his voice.

'And Jónatan,' Tómas said, gently. 'Thank you for telling me.'

Tómas ended the call. He felt he need a few moments to recover himself, but he didn't have them. He dialled Helga straightaway. She was upfront in the vehicle leading the convoy. Tómas briefly recounted what Jónatan had told him.

'So the first thing should be to check the potato store,' he said. 'Our man says it has a heavy door. No windows.'

'I've already requested the Sauðárkrókur police to go the location,' Helga replied. 'They'll be there before us. I'll let them know about the store. Thanks for that. The Siglufjörður team have been a great help,' she added, perhaps a little grudgingly, and then hung up before Tómas could acknowledge the compliment.

Tómas glowed a little at her words.

25

Ari Thór stood in front of the house.

There was a light in the big ground-floor window, but the curtains were drawn tight so there was no opportunity to see inside. She was definitely at home, and *he* was undoubtedly her visitor. *The bastard.*

The light of the low sun cast a mellow glow over the houses in the street. The whole neighbourhood was basking peacefully in the evening warmth.

Ari Thór stood still for a moment, pretending to himself that he was thinking over what to do, even though he had already made his decision. Every step of the way had made him more certain of his hunch. Kristín had almost certainly invited a highly dangerous character into her home and Ari Thór was the only one who would be able to help her.

He walked up to the door and put a finger on the doorbell. But before he pressed it, another thought came to him. He had to take a different approach.

He banged on the door, hard, and with authority.

As he waited, his heart hammered. It was as if a fire burned inside him.

A second later she stood in the doorway in front of him, so perfectly beautiful.

This was the woman he was supposed to spend his life with. He knew it so clearly now. Why had he let her go?

'Ari Thór?'

There was no hiding her astonishment; it was clear from her wide eyes, raised brows and her startled voice.

'What are you doing here? Didn't you get my email? I said I'm busy this evening.'

Despite her chiding tone, Ari Thór felt there was a warmth in her voice; she didn't seem angry at all.

He fumbled for the right words. He told himself to relax and took a deep breath, but could still feel his heart beating fast.

'Is he here?' was the first thing he was able to say. It was too sharp; Kristín blanched.

'He? What's this about, Ari Thór?' Now she did seem angry.

'I knew him in Siglufjörður … he's only … he's only seeing you to get back at me,' he said, the words tripping over themselves in his haste.

By now he was inside, standing on a worn mat with a 'welcome' message that wasn't meant for him.

'Don't be ridiculous,' Kristín said, trying to keep her voice low, but needing to show her exasperation. 'We can talk later. I'm busy now.'

'Everything all right?' a voice called from inside the apartment.

Ari Thór followed the sound and, despite Kristín's efforts to stop him, was in the kitchen before he knew it, face to face with a man who sat at the kitchen table with a fork in one hand and a knife in the other, potatoes, greens and a slice of meat on the plate in front of him, red wine in his glass.

Hell.

Ari Thór had never seen this man in his life.

Hell!

He blinked, trying and failing to regain control over himself. A dense darkness had fallen in front of his eyes and he was suddenly back at a class party in Hafnarfjörður, all those years ago.

The jealousy flooded through him like a fast poison. What the hell was this stranger doing in Kristín's apartment? How dare he?

He took a step forward. Deep down he knew it was a mistake, but he was unable to control the wave of temper that crashed over him. He took two steps so that he stood over the stranger, who seemed to be struck dumb with astonishment, blinking and not saying a word.

Ari Thór grabbed the collar of the man's cheap checked shirt and hauled him bodily off the stool. At the same time he noticed that the man had dropped his fork; nobody takes a fork into a fight. But the steak knife was still in his right hand.

Ari Thór was back again at that class party; his fist was raised and ready to strike. He was ready to relive the past.

The man dodged his punch, but then found himself backed into a corner against the fridge. Ari Thór had him trapped. He rushed towards him.

The last thing he heard before the stinging pain was Kristín's repeated 'No … no … no!'

26

Tómas drove up the track towards the old farmhouse. The convoy had left him behind, and in any case, the Sauðárkrókur police would have been there well ahead of them all.

Pulling up, he got out and hurried from the car. The police team was grouped around an ambulance in the middle of the yard. But the ambulance crew showed no sign of being in a hurry to get away to the hospital.

Was the girl already dead?

He pushed his way through the crowd and peered in through the ambulance's open rear doors. The girl lay on a stretcher. He couldn't see her face, just the cluster of tubes that had been attached to her. That told him that she had to be alive. He could see that she was slightly built, with very long, coal-black hair.

He turned to the paramedic at his side.

'Is she alive?'

'She is, but she's in a bad way. Unconscious and badly dehydrated. The helicopter's on its way. She needs to get to a hospital immediately.'

His tone was flat, an emotionless list of facts.

'Where was she?'

'Some old storeroom that had been dug out just by here. It's an old potato store, or so I'm told,' the paramedic said, his expression finally changing. 'Horrific, absolutely horrific. I'm no psychologist, but that kind of treatment is bound to leave lifelong scars,' he added, shaking his head in disgust as he climbed into the ambulance.

You hit the nail on the head there, Tómas thought, looking at the unfortunate girl and wondering how the responsibility for this foul treatment could be divided between Elías and Jónatan's mother. That task could be left to higher powers, he thought. He was relieved. He didn't know if he would ever be able to make such a judgement.

27

Every one of Ísrún's problems – the rape and the dreadful news she had received after the visit to the Landeyjar a year before – had retreated to the back of her mind. Now there was only one thing to focus on, the news story of the year. She was in the right place just as it was all happening. She could already see an award taking pride of place on her shelf.

The helicopter had been and gone. Fortunately for the girl, she was still alive. And fortunately for Ísrún, there had been no other journalist on the spot. The Akureyri stringer had been able to get some great footage. The news desk editor on duty had taken an interview with Ísrún for the next radio news broadcast, and she had stood in front of the helicopter and recounted what was happening for the camera. This was going to be one of the year's best exclusives.

María had suggested she stay in the north that night and travel south in the morning so that she would be there the next day to edit the news feature for the evening bulletin. Ísrún was relieved. She wanted to be working on the story, but she badly wanted rest. Her doctor had told her she needed it.

Her things were still in Siglufjörður so she decided to spend the night there. She made her way back there at a much more sedate and careful pace than she had left it.

28

Tómas was on his way to Siglufjörður, back to the overwhelming emptiness of home. It was late, but it could be worth stopping off at the station. He liked it there better than at home. Sometimes he even slept there. He'd have to find out what had become of Hlynur and why he hadn't answered the phone. Had he gone off somewhere when he knew he should have been on duty? Tómas scowled. He had had enough of Hlynur's poor behaviour; it had gone on for far too long.

But as he drove, he admitted to himself what he really wanted to do: turn around and drive south to Reykjavík to see his wife and lose himself in her warmth. His wonderful hometown, Siglufjörður, could be warm, but it never wrapped its arms around him.

He was startled out of these thoughts by his phone ringing.

'Hello, cousin,' a low, nervous voice greeted him. 'It's Móna.'

'Móna? Everything all right? Why are you calling so late?' he asked in surprise, a deep feeling of discomfort at what this call might hold welling up inside him.

'He...' she began and hesitated. 'He ... Logi, my brother-in-law, asked me to call you. He needs to meet you, as soon as possible.'

There was no mistaking the tension in her voice.

'This evening?'

'Preferably,' she replied quietly.

'What the hell's going on?' Tómas's patience was already at full stretch. He had to make a major effort to keep his temper.

'It's best if you two talk things over. But...' She hesitated again and Tómas could sense that she was close to tears. 'But he's going to confess.'

'Confess?' he demanded, astonished.

'Yes. Confess to the murder.'

'He killed Elías?'

'Yes.' There was a long pause. 'In self-defence. They argued over some people-trafficking business that Elías was involved with. There was some girl from Nepal Elías had brought here and Logi was trying to get her away from him.'

'*What the hell?*' Tómas burst out unintentionally, letting the unprofessional words echo round the car.

He thought silently for a moment.

'What the hell…?' he repeated, this time muttering the words to himself.

29

Móna was in turmoil as she put down the phone.

Logi had been adamant that he would take the blame to shield his brother and his family – Móna and the unborn child. Jökull and Móna had protested, but Logi's mind was made up.

'Nobody needs to know that Jökull was with me, and I was the one who let Elías have it,' he said. 'Bad luck that bit of wood had a nail in it,' he added in a low voice.

Logi had accepted Móna's suggestion – Ísrún's suggestion – that he should lie about the reason for the killing. Móna had told them about the journalist's visit. But she made them promise they wouldn't betray Ísrún's confidence.

'I'll look after myself,' Logi said, hiding his trepidation. 'You just keep your minds on the baby. The secret of whose child it really is goes with me to the grave.'

30

Tómas was sitting opposite Logi in the otherwise empty police station in Siglufjörður. A formal arrest had been made, and Logi had showed every sign of wanting to co-operate with the police. He had confessed to the killing without reservation, while claiming self-defence, but had refused the presence of a lawyer.

'Tell me what happened,' Tómas said as calmly as he could. He was very annoyed at the absence of his two deputies. Ari Thor had disappeared in Akureyri and as to Hlynur, well, it was anybody's guess where he might be.

'It was the girl,' Logi said. 'A girl he had brought from Asia. It was basically human trafficking and I never signed up for that. We may not have done everything by the book, but this was a step too far. I asked him to tell me where she was, told him we needed to send her back home before something happened, before the police found out…'

Something about the story didn't quite ring true, it felt rehearsed in some way. Yet Tómas had no real reason to doubt it. And, truth be told, it was a much-needed victory, a neat solution to the case – and indeed a full confession.

'I went to meet him that night. We fought, it got violent and I actually feared for my life. Elías had gone beyond the point of no return – I thought he might kill me because I was threatening to go to the police. The piece of wood was just lying there, I grabbed it and fought back. This bloody nail … you know … I had no intention of killing him. It wasn't murder, you know … I won't be convicted for *murder*, will I?'

'I can't be the judge of that, Logi. I'll need to ask you to stay here, in the holding cell we have here at the back, just for tonight. I'll take you to Akureyri tomorrow. We'll have to request that you'll be kept in custody there. I'm sure you understand.'

Logi nodded, without giving away any sort of emotion.

The cell was small but not too bad. Logi hadn't actually ever been inside a prison cell before, but he had never been claustrophobic, so he knew he could deal with it. The moment when Tómas locked the door was slightly unnerving, but he knew he'd have to get used to it.

It wasn't as dark as he thought it would be. Above the small bed was a skylight. 'In case you're wondering, no one has been able to break the glass in that one,' Tómas had said, 'and not for lack of trying.'

Logi had no intention of trying. He lay down on the bed and closed his eyes. He had to stick to his story. For his brother's sake.

Logi had been the one who had actually killed Elías – that was no lie. He had grabbed the piece of wood and hit him. Also, he had told the truth about the nail, he hadn't known it was there. He hadn't meant to kill him.

There were only two lies: Jökull had been with him, and they had gone to Elías to beat him up after they had found out about him having raped Móna. Well, he hadn't only raped her, but actually made her pregnant – there was no doubt about that, Móna and Jökull having tried so long and without success to have a child. There was no reason for anyone, except himself, Móna and Jökull, to know that the unborn child had been fathered by a rapist. No, it would be brought up as Jökull's and Móna's child, and in a matter of few years Logi would be able to visit his niece or nephew. He wasn't sure that he would convince anyone with the story of self-defence, so he might be looking at sixteen years in jail, out on parole in eight … He was sure he could handle it. He just had to be strong.

⌖

The phone at the police station rang as Tómas was heading out. He needed to get home for a quick nap, although he knew he shouldn't leave the prisoner alone. Where the hell were Hlynur and Ari Thór? Neither of them were picking up, he had tried their mobile numbers again and again.

'Hello, hello?' It was a female voice. 'Is this the police station in Siglufjörður?' The lady was obviously in a state of anxiety. 'I've been trying to contact someone for a couple of hours. It's about this guy, Hlynur…'

'Hlynur? Yes? Who is this?'

'Doesn't really matter. I just knew him in the past, he went to school with my late brother, you see. He called me earlier tonight, said he had found out that I was Gauti's, my brother's, closest relative. It was a very, very strange call. He … well, I have always blamed him for my brother's suicide … it's a complex story … but tonight, he called to say he was sorry, that he was *very* sorry … And there was something about his tone that was very disturbing, you know…'

Tómas had the feeling that the woman on the line was on the verge of crying. She was breathing heavily and sounded genuinely worried.

'Disturbing in what way?'

'Well, I sort of had the feeling that he might be contemplating … well…' After a short pause she added, almost whispering: '… suicide.'

Bloody hell!

Tómas hung up the phone without saying goodbye and hurried to the car.

Bloody hell!

He just hoped he wasn't too late.

31

Tómas had to admit that he had never visited Hlynur's apartment. Yet he knew where he lived – he knew more or less every house in the town, in fact. It was one of the very few apartment blocks in Siglufjörður, only four apartments per house though, nothing like the tall blocks of Reykjavík. Each apartment had its own entrance. At first glance there was little sign of life in Hlynur's place, the curtains drawn in all the windows which were visible to Tómas. That was slightly strange of course, but not necessarily without explanation. The nights were so bright this time of year, especially in the far north, that people went to extreme measures to create darkness indoors.

Tómas knocked quite forcefully. There was no answer.

He felt his heart beating very rapidly, and he almost felt sick. He knew, he just knew, that something had happened, and that he was to blame, at least partly. He had treated Hlynur very badly. He'd been impatient and brusque instead of simply sitting down with him to try to get to the bottom of the problem.

He tried the doorbell, and then knocked again. He waited impatiently for a few moments and then took a few steps back and ran into the door with all his power. The door shifted, but didn't open. On the second attempt he broke through.

He hurried into the living room; no one was there. He called out at the top of his voice: 'Hlynur? Hlynur?'

The apartment was slightly bigger than he had anticipated and there were a few more rooms to check. By instinct he headed towards what he guessed was the bedroom.

There he saw what he had feared: Hlynur lying motionless on the bed. Next to the body, an empty bottle of pills. Tómas checked for a pulse, but without any success.

He pulled out his phone and mechanically called an ambulance, but he knew it was too late. He knew that he would have to live with the guilt of failing this young man at such a critical time, with such horrendous consequences.

32

For Kristín, the shock of seeing Ari Thór being stabbed had been severe. For a moment she was certain that it might be fatal, the steak knife was razor sharp and only by chance had it missed his vital organs. The wound had looked bad, though, quite a lot of blood. But she had kept calm and stopped the bleeding while waiting for the ambulance. The stabbing had obviously been accidental, but her new friend had literally collapsed on the kitchen floor when he saw what had happened.

'When the police get here,' she had said, 'tell them it was an accident. OK?'

Her friend had nodded.

She repeated the request. 'Just an accident. Don't mention any fight, do you understand me?'

Her voice had been firm. For some reason she felt it of utmost importance to look out for Ari Thór. He had indeed started the fight, but if that fact came out it might seriously jeopardize his police career.

And now she sat next to him in the hospital. He was sleeping, so she just held his hand and reflected on how close she had come to losing him. And how horrible that thought had been. He was really quite impossible, jealous by nature and always making these stupid decisions. But despite all that, she was still in love with him.

33

One year earlier

I'd never made a habit of fainting in other people's homes, but something came over me that day and I suddenly found myself as weak as water.

At first I thought it was the overwhelming heat inside the house; it certainly couldn't have helped.

'Are you all right, dear? You're as pale as a death! Wouldn't you prefer to lie down?'

The old lady pointed at a short, shabby sofa.

I stumbled over to it and lay back for a while. I had to regain some strength.

I hadn't been at my best for a while and had been unusually off-colour. I'd convinced myself that I had simply been overdoing it at work.

As I lay there, trying to relax, collect myself and lose the weakness that weighed down my limbs, she told me.

Sometimes I wish she had just kept quiet. That way I could have fooled myself for longer that everything was just fine.

'That's how your grandmother's illness began,' the old lady said absently, without even looking at me. 'That damn smoking.'

'What do you mean?' I asked as I lay on the sofa trying to summon energy from somewhere in my body.

'She just fainted away, all of a sudden. Then she went to the doctor and that's when she found out about the sickness.'

I tried to sit up and felt my heart hammering with the effort. This was something I didn't want to talk about. Could I be sick, just as my grandmother had been? I couldn't help shuddering at the thought. I wanted to push it from my mind. But I couldn't help asking more about her illness. Maybe I did it to convince myself that this faintness, this fatigue and weakness had nothing in common with what had killed my late grandmother.

'What were her symptoms?'

'Well … I'm no doctor, my dear. Far from it. I remember how she had no appetite and she had endless aches and pains. She slept badly and was always exhausted.'

Now I felt I was about to faint again. Aches, fatigue – that all fitted.

'Nausea?' I said, almost too frightened to ask.

'Yes … poor girl.'

Katrín seemed to have realised where my questions were leading.

'But those symptoms can have all kinds of explanations,' she said, smiling, trying to cheer me up. 'I'm sure you're perfectly fine. I remember she once had a swelling in her throat. You haven't had anything like that, have you?'

I lay back, terrified. I had certainly had had a sore throat that could be described as an inflammation or even a swelling. I hadn't worried about it, as I'd just assumed I'd been a little out of sorts and it was just an infection.

I couldn't hold the tears back then, unable to believe that I could be seriously ill.

My heart continued its rapid drumming, and I couldn't think of anything else other than that I was horribly sick.

It was smoking that had killed my grandmother. It was as simple as that – or was it?

The old lady put a hand on my forehead.

'You'll be fine, my dear.'

I closed my eyes and listened to her gentle voice.

'You'll be fine,' Katrín repeated.

34

Not having to drive through the night back south to Reykjavík was a relief. Ísrún was in no hurry to get back to darknes, the ash-poisoned air, and the bustle of city life, not right away.

She had lain awake at the guest house in Siglufjörður, far from sleep after the day's excitement. Normally when this happened, experience told her that a long walk was the best remedy.

It was past midnight when she left the guesthouse and drove along the fjord road towards the new Héðinsfjörður tunnel. She parked near the new churchyard at the town's furthest extremity, with the intention of walking towards the point at Siglunes on the far side of the fjord, opposite the town.

Out here nature remained unspoiled, unlike the spit of land jutting into the water on which Siglufjörður had been built. The town had risen on the other side of the fjord for a reason, that's where the best conditions were for houses, enough flat land. She set off, aiming to spend an hour walking out to the point along the shore of the uninhabited eastern side of the fjord.

The path turned out to be less easy than she had expected. There was deep grass to negotiate and and streams to cross. In some places old wooden beams served as makeshift bridges, while in others there was nothing for it but to jump from one bank to the other. A few birds scattered away from her as she approached their nests, crying their alarm into the night.

She stopped at one of the streams and drank icy water from her cupped hands. Bright-green moss clung to the banks by the water, but elsewhere the coarse, stunted grass this far north showed no sign that it was summer, regardless of whatever the calendar might say.

She walked slowly. She was in no hurry, and was anxious to avoid stepping on the any nests that might be hidden in the grass. Always tired, she had to admit to herself that her body was asking her to take it easy.

She stopped by the ruins of a house where, according to the information notice, an avalanche ninety years before had buried a herring factory and a farm.

Finally reaching the shore, she gazed for a long time over the fjord at the town opposite, peaceful and innocent at this distance. Apart from the birdsong, there was silence; the air was still and the water mirror calm.

After the visit to Katrín in Landeyjar the summer before, Ísrún had gone directly to her doctor, certain that she was at death's door. A few visits to specialists later and she had confirmation, or at least a strong likelihood, that she was suffering from a rare inherited condition. This could lead to the growth of tumours, which, while generally benign, could result in a variety of physical symptoms. There was also the possibility of something worse to come.

She had flatly refused to stop working. Instead she had used every sick day she was entitled to and swapped shifts with colleagues when she needed to.

She told nobody about her disease. The doctors were not in agreement about the next step, but there was every indication that the tumours were indeed benign. There were differences of opinion over whether or not surgery was the right option. She was sure that the doctors were still swapping emails about her case. All Ísrún could do was remain as calm as she could in the midst of all this.

It was more than likely that her grandmother had been wrongly diagnosed; she had probably suffered from the same condition and it had killed her. Was it now Ísrún's turn?

She felt she was living in a vacuum, unwilling to discuss it with anyone other than the doctors. She had lived through a winter of fear, but, as the sun rose in the sky, things seemed brighter. Yet she had no idea what might happen next.

It would be difficult, but she was determined to beat the fear.

She gazed out over the placid sea, bright under the night-time sun. She thought of her grandmother's phrase for sudden darkness: blackout. For the past year, since the diagnosis, she had been living under a dark cloud. But now she suddenly felt as if daylight had conquered the blackout, at least for the time being.

Acknowledgements

Blackout is dedicated to my parents, Jónas Ragnarsson and Katrín Guðjónsdóttir, who have encouraged me to write from a very early age. They have read and reviewed the drafts of my stories and books, providing invaluable support, from the short detective stories I wrote as a young boy for friends and family, to the full-length novels I have since gone on to write, including the Dark Iceland series. Thanks, Mum and Dad.

I would also like to acknowledge my late grandparents, as the book's locations are inspired by them. Guðjón Helgason and Magnþóra Magnúsdóttir were from the Landeyjar area in Iceland, where a part of *Blackout* is set, and Þ. Ragnar Jónasson and Guðrún Reykdal, lived in Siglufjörður.

There is a great team behind the publication of the Dark Iceland series, all of whom deserve my gratitude: My amazing US publishing team at St. Martin's Press; my English-language translator, crime writer Quentin Bates; my agents, Monica Gram at Copenhagen Literary Agency, and David Headley at DHH Literary Agency; my Icelandic publisher, Pétur Már Ólafsson, and my Icelandic editor, Bjarni Þorsteinsson.

I would also especially like to thank all the wonderful readers of the Dark Iceland series in the US. The reception of the series, starting with *Snowblind* and *Nightblind*, in the US has been beyond belief and this support has certainly provided me with encouragement to continue to write about Ari Thór.

And as always, I owe the biggest debt of gratitude to my family, my wife María, and my daughters, Kira and Natalía, for their unlimited support.

An exclusive extract from Ragnar Jónasson's *Rupture*, translated by Quentin Bates and published in Winter 2019 by Minotaur Books

1

It had been an evening like any other, spent stretched out on the sofa.

They lived in a little apartment on the ground floor of an old house in the western end of Reykjavík, just off Ljósvallagata – one of three joined together. It was positioned in the middle of an old fashioned terrace, built back in the 1930s. Róbert sat up, rubbed his eyes and looked out of the window at the little front garden. It was getting dark. It was March, when weather of any description could be expected, but right now it was raining. There was something comforting in the patter of raindrops against the window while he was safely ensconced indoors.

His studies weren't going badly. A mature student at twenty-eight, he was in the first year of an engineering degree. Numbers had always been one of his pleasures. His parents were accountants, living uptown in Árbær, and while his relationship with them had been difficult, it was now almost non-existent, as his lifestyle had no place in their formula for success. They had done what they could to steer him towards bookkeeping, and that was fair enough.

But now he was at university, at last, and he hadn't even bothered to let the old folks know. Instead, he attempted to focus on his studies, although these days his mind tended to wander to the Westfjords. He owned a small boat there, along with a couple of friends, and he was already looking forward to summer; it was so easy to forget everything – good and bad – when he was out at sea. The rocking of the boat was a tonic for any stress and his spirit soared when he was enveloped by the complete peace he found there. At the end of March he'd be heading west to get the boat ready. For his friends, the trip to the fjords was to some extent an excuse to go on a drinking binge. But not Róbert. He had been dry now for two years – a necessity after the serious drinking that began with the events that unfolded on that fateful day eight years earlier.

It was a beautiful day. There was scarcely a breath of wind on the pitch, it was warm under the summer sun and there was a respectable crowd. They were on their way to a convincing win against an unconvincing opposition. Ahead of him lay training with the national youth team, and later that summer the possibility of a trial with a top Norwegian team. His agent had even mentioned interest from some of the teams lower down in the English league. The old man was as proud as hell of him. He had been a decent player himself, but never had the chance to play professionally. Now times had changed; there were more opportunities out there.

Five minutes remained when Róbert was passed the ball. He pushed past the defenders, and saw the mouth of the goal and the fear on the goalkeeper's face. This was becoming a familiar experience, as a five-nil victory loomed. He didn't see the tackle coming in, just heard the crack as his leg broke in three places and felt the shattering pain. He looked down, paralysed by the searing agony, and saw the open fracture.

It was a sight that was etched onto his memory. The days spent in hospital passed in a fog, although he wouldn't forget the doctor telling him that his chances of playing football again were slim, at a professional level, at any rate. He gave up, and after that sought solace in the bottle; each drink quickly followed by another. The worst part was that he made a better recovery than expected, but by then it was too late to turn the clock back.

Now things were better. He had Sunna, and little Kjartan had a place in his heart as well.

It was well into the evening when Sunna came home, tapping at the window to let him know that she had forgotten her keys. She was as beautiful as ever, in black jeans and a grey roll-neck sweater. Raven hair, long and glossy, framed a strong face. To begin with, it had been her eyes that had enchanted him, closely followed by her magnificent figure. She was a dancer and sometimes it was as if she danced rather than walked around their little apartment, with a confident grace imbued in every movement.

He knew he had been lucky with this one. He had first chatted to her at a friend's birthday party, and they'd clicked instantly. They'd been together for six months now, and three months ago they had moved in together.

Sunna turned up the heating as she came in; she felt the cold more than he did.

'Cold outside,' she said, and the chill crept into the room. The big living-room window wasn't as airtight as it could have been and it was difficult to get used to the constant draughts.

Life wasn't easy for them, even though their relationship was becoming stronger. She had a child, little Kjartan, from a previous relationship and was engaged in a bitter custody battle with Breki, the boy's father. To begin with, Breki and Sunna had agreed on joint custody and at the moment Kjartan was with his father.

Now, though, Sunna had engaged a lawyer and was pressing for full custody. She was also exploring the possibility of continuing her studies in Britain, but this was not something that she and Róbert had discussed in depth. It was a piece of news that Breki wasn't going to accept without a fight, so it looked as if the dispute would end up in court, where Sunna believed her strong case would see Kjartan returned to her.

'Sit down, sweetheart,' Róbert said. 'There's pasta.'

'Mmm. Great,' she said and curled up on the sofa.

Róbert fetched the food from the kitchen, bringing plates and glasses and filling a jug with water.

'I hope there's some flavour in this,' he said. 'I'm still finding my way.'

'I'm so hungry it won't matter what it tastes like.'

He put on some relaxing music and sat down next to her.

She told him about her day, the rehearsals and the pressure she was under. Sunna was set on perfection, and hated to get anything wrong.

Róbert was satisfied that his pasta had been a success; nothing outstanding, but good enough.

Sunna got to her feet and took his hand.

'Stand up, my love. Time to dance.'

He stood up and wrapped his arms around her as they moved in time to a languid South American ballad. He slid a hand under her sweater and his fingertips stroked her back, unclipping her bra strap in one seamless movement. This was where he wanted to be.

'Hey, young man,' she said with mock sharpness, her eyes warm. 'What do you think you're up to?'

'Making the most of Kjartan being with his dad,' Róbert answered, and they moved into a long, deep kiss. The temperature between them was rising, as was that of the room, and before long they had made their way to the bedroom.

Out of habit, Róbert pushed the door to and drew the curtains across the bedroom window overlooking the garden, but none of these precautions stopped the sounds of their lovemaking carrying across to the apartment next door.

Spent and relaxed, he heard the indistinct slamming of a door, muffled by the hammering rain. His first thought was that it was the back door to the porch behind the old house.

Sunna looked up in alarm and glanced at him, disquiet in her eyes. He tried to stifle his own fear behind a show of bravado and, getting to his feet, ventured naked into the living room. It was empty.

But the back door was open, banging to and fro in the wind. He glanced quickly into the porch, just long enough to be able to say that he had taken a look, and hurriedly pulled it closed. A whole regiment of men could have been out there for all he knew, but he could make out nothing in the darkness.

He went from one room to another, his heart beating harder and faster, but there was no unwelcome guest to be seen. It was just as well that Kjartan was not at home.

And then he noticed something that would keep him awake for the rest of the night.

He hurried through the living room, frightened for Sunna, terrified that something had happened to her. Holding his breath, he made his way to the bedroom to find her seated on the edge of the bed, pulling on a shirt. She smiled weakly, unable to hide her concern.

'It was nothing, sweetheart,' he said, a tremor in his voice that he hoped she would not notice. 'I forgot to lock the door after I took the rubbish out; didn't shut it properly behind me. You know what tricks the wind plays out back. Stay there and I'll get you a drink.'

He stepped quickly out of the bedroom and rapidly cleared away what he had seen.

He hoped it had been the right thing to do, not to tell Sunna about the water on the floor, the wet footprints left by the uninvited guest who had come in out of the rain. The worst part was that they hadn't been stopped there, inside the back door. The trail had gone all the way to the bedroom door.